THE GIRL WHO WALKED

OFF THE MOON

By Carlo Ortu

For Marie, Matteo and Amelia.

'We cannot learn without pain.'

- Aristotle

PART ONE

I see a man on a stage. He's wearing white. It's like a suit. Flared trousers I think. The suit is decorated with what look like... diamonds. The suit is open at the top and I can see his chest. He's wearing a medallion and holding a microphone. He's singing and doing... what is that? It's like karate moves. Hang on, it's Elvis Presley. It's Elvis Presley singing on a stage. But he looks fat. Not like the Elvis we know. His hair is still black and he has his thick sideburns but he's overweight. He doesn't look healthy. Now we've changed scenes. He's sat down and looks so unwell. He's on the toilet. Oh my, why am I looking at Elvis on the toilet? He's fallen off. He's having a heart attack or something. Jesus, he's stopped moving. I think he's dead. No, please, no. Elvis is dead... The King is Dead!

CHAPTER ONE

1975

RHONA

Rhona sat in her car and stared through the rain as it beat down on her windscreen. In front of her all she could see were angry waves and dark skies as the sea and sky became one in the distance. She had stopped her car overlooking the cliff. And now she was truly alone. The car felt cold. Unwanted.

She had come as far as she wanted to come. It felt like the end of the earth. She felt washed up. Low.

She was in one of her funks. That was her name for it.

The problem this time was she could no longer write. Write anything good or worthwhile. The rejection letter which had arrived that morning and now sat at home confirmed that. Set her off and now there was no turning back.

The issue had suddenly overwhelmed her. Sent her spinning. Sent her here.

Her talent had deserted her. She was devoid of ideas. That's what it felt like.

She had no talent. That was the truth.

She saw that now.

A truth that stared her in the face each morning as she looked in her mirror and saw her ugly face in her ugly flat in that ugly city. She was worn out by it all. And she was only twenty-six.

Now all she kept thinking was, should she drive over the cliff that was in front of her and die, thereby just getting this whole farce over with, or live the rest of her life knowing she would never succeed in doing the only thing she cared about? She thought about other people who had died young. Jim Morrison. Janis Joplin. Brian Jones. Perhaps she would join their ranks now. Although they had all been twenty-seven. Perhaps, Rhona thought, she should give it another year before making a final decision. A cloud shifted. The drive had worn her down. Seen the worst of it off. Beaten the darkness.

She sat and thought of nothing, letting her eyes drift across the sea and her mind wander, slowly feeling the final grip of her funk gently loosen its grip.

Rhona drove to a café instead of killing herself. She decided not to drive over the cliff after all. It was just a bit melodramatic and ill thought out. As usual. She had experienced one of her black moods again. She hadn't written a note anyway. A suicide note would have alerted and reminded the world of her literary talent and kick-started a retrospective that would see her only appreciated after her death. Like Van Gogh but with less work and a lot less talent to show for it.

She hadn't written a note because she didn't know what to say. She had appreciated this irony. She was also concerned driving over the cliff might not actually kill her but leave her incapacitated for the rest of her life. And she didn't want that. Lying in a bed with nurses all around her shaking their heads and telling her she has made a silly mistake. And she'd be nothing more than a vegetable with no avenue to escape and try again. She didn't want that.

What if she landed on someone and killed them? Then what would happen? Some poor sod walking his or her dog gets a car landing on them. And the dog might die too. The English loved their dogs. Not like her father back in Ireland who had shot their dog when he had become too old. But she didn't want to dwell on that. And she might live and they die and then she'd end up in prison. For life. As a vegetable. Perhaps that might inspire her to write something good but she didn't want to take that chance.

And last of all she hadn't driven over the cliff because she just didn't want to die.

So instead she drove to a café and ordered a coffee. But the coffee was terrible. She had grown used to what she got in the

Italian coffee bars in Soho she liked to frequent. Here they would rather serve you tea. Or bad coffee like she had now.

She lit a cigarette and inhaled deeply, shook up after her near-death experience. She needed to get a grip. Stop thinking these dark thoughts. Good ideas might return. Would return. Success was still within her grasp. She just needed a spark.

She looked around the café and surveyed the other customers through the thick fog of cigarette smoke and watched them sipping their teas, reading their papers, talking about this and that. She felt alone. She was alone and had always been alone, especially since she left Ireland for England six years before.

That was back in 1969. London was still swinging then, and she'd arrived just in time to attend the free Rolling Stones concert in Hyde Park. She remembered that hot day. Mick Jagger was in some kind of white dress and released lots of butterflies and eventually sang "Sympathy with the Devil". From where she stood she could hardly see a thing. But she also remembered being alone at the concert. Even in Ireland she felt isolated from events, from people. From love.

A man across the café was watching her. He was sat hunched over a cup of tea, playing with a Zippo lighter. He was about her age, clean shaven with a dark coat wrapped around him. The steam from his tea rose and evaporated in front of his face. She looked away, self-conscious now. The man smiled, got up and put his lighter away. He picked up his tea then came over to her table. He sat down heavily and stared at her a moment before speaking.

'Are you as bored as I am?' he asked. He had a deep, confident voice.

Rhona took a drag on her cigarette and tapped ash into the ashtray for effect like she'd seen in a film, making sure not to have eye contact but to instead concentrate on the filthy ashtray, like she was thinking and mulling over his insightful question and she was verging on a witty response. He was like the young men back in her village who had never set foot anywhere else. Cocky and ignorant.

'I don't know. How bored are you?' she responded, hopefully revealing her innate sophistication and confidence.

The man smiled and took a sip of his tea. Also possibly for effect. She liked to think she could read his mind and see how he thought that they were engaged in some clever and classy verbal dance that would end with him seducing her. She would humour him for a bit, the poor boy. But then he said this.

'London not treating you right?'

Rhona shuddered slightly. Not enough for him to notice, but enough to remind her of what her Grandma had told her about shuddering. It meant someone was walking across your grave. Which, thinking about it now, was a strange thing to tell a young, impressionable girl who was very much alive. She felt embarrassed for showing the emotion and tried to regain a sense of control and composure.

'How…' she started. But he jumped in, interrupting her.

'But you would never go back to Ireland. I get that. Good ideas will return though.'

Now she was confused. Rhona looked around the café. She felt hot and nervous all of a sudden. She wanted to know how he knew these things. Recognising her Irish accent wasn't too hard but the London and the 'ideas will return' comments were just downright strange. Perhaps they had met before. At a party or at work. And perhaps she had opened up to him about her failings and desires and concerns.

But that wouldn't have happened. She would surely have remembered him for starters and she was sure she had never met this man before. Furthermore, she never opened up like that to strangers. Not to anyone in fact.

'You want to know how I know these things?' he asked casually, sitting back in a relaxed pose, watching her squirm like he was the one reading her mind now.

'Do I know you?' asked Rhona icily.

'No,' he said emphatically. 'But I know you and that is why I am here.'

Rhona stood up. She wanted to go. The urge to run was almost overwhelming. Get out of that damn café and away from its lard smelling, shoddy coffee and odd men in dark coats who could read minds. He held his hand up for her to stop.

'Wait. Sit down. Please. I want to talk to you, Rhona O'Shea. About your visions.'

Rhona sat down. Like she was in a trance. As though she had been hypnotised. Later she realised if she hadn't had sat she might not have made it to the door to escape without fainting. Knowing her name was one thing but how did he know about them? The visions. How did he know about the visions?

'How do you know these things?' she managed to utter. It came out as a plea.

'You like to write. Or you did before the rejections got you down and you stopped having confidence in yourself.'

He said these things as statements. Not questions.

'But let me ask you. When you did write, were you writing what you wanted to write or were you writing what you thought others would like?'

Rhona stared at him. Into his dark brown eyes, searching for the truth, but finding nothing to grasp. She was lost in a fog of confusion. Helpless.

'We both know the answer to that don't we? Deep down. So I'm here to tell you to write about the visions,' said the man.

Rhona swallowed. Her mouth was dry, but she refrained from taking a sip of the awful coffee as he would see her hand shaking.

'Obviously you need to dress them up a bit. Not make it so obvious what they really are. Any plot. Genre. Your choosing.'

'Why?'

'Because then you will have the success you crave.'

Rhona drove back to London. On the motorway she kept in the slow lane. On autopilot now, she went over and over the scene in the café again and again. How he had offered no other information about his knowledge of her visions after telling her to write about them in any way she chose. And Rhona had just sat and listened, too dumbstruck to ask any of the questions screaming at her now.

He merely said she should write about them and then he got up, said goodbye and left. Just like that. The door had closed in the café before she had even properly absorbed what he had said. She had then sat alone looking at the empty chair where he had been, debating whether she had in fact just imagined the whole thing.

She had glanced around the café but no one was looking at her or giving her any attention. It was almost as though she wasn't there.

His tea cup sat on the table. She touched it. It was stone cold.

CHAPTER TWO

2019

JOE

Joe stirred the sugar into his macchiato as he stood behind the bar. It was ten o'clock in the morning and they'd only had four customers so far today and all of them had been before nine-thirty, all wanting take-away coffee. Trade was slow and Joe was bored.

That was the problem with opening Porto, which was essentially a Portuguese themed bar, at eight-thirty in the morning in an area like Charminster. The high street was full of bars and restaurants that only opened later in the day. The cafes that did exist mainly catered to the large North African and Arabic community and were mainly owned by North Africans or Arabs. Porto was not one of those places. So with few offices, parks or any kind of amusements, there just weren't that many people hanging around the neighbourhood at that time.

Bournemouth, which Charminster was a suburb of, was also the kind of town where, if you were inclined to drink alcohol so early, you would probably head to a Weatherspoons for the cheap beer rather than sip the expensive, imported lager they sold at Porto. He agreed with the principal of attracting the morning coffee drinkers as well as the infrequent alcohol imbibers but the footfall before ten am, or lack of it, made Joe question if Sergio, the bar's owner, would change his mind, admit defeat, and open just that little bit later. Porto, like a lot of Charminster, was a place that only really got going in the evening.

At least the sun was shining thought Joe. He was on the day shift until four which suited him. Earlier he'd sat out front on the small veranda they had with only three tables and watched the world go by. Charminster, with its shisha bars and various restaurants with Arabic menus, reminded Joe a little of London where he had lived for a number of years before returning to the seaside town. The many thousands of foreign students who came to Bournemouth each year to study English also found the area favourable and friendly. The atmosphere was far more cosmopolitan than Winton or Boscombe, other areas of the town.

Joe took a sip of the coffee and caught himself in the mirror. He saw his dark hair flecked with white and a face that matched his forty-four years. He turned away and was just about to move around the bar when a woman walked in. She was about forty, English he guessed, and dressed in smart clothing and jacket as though she has just nipped out of an office to grab a hot drink. She paused in the doorway holding her handbag in front of her, taking in the empty bar before approaching Joe.

'Morning,' said Joe.

'Hi, I'm looking for Joe Zucco.'

'Joe Zuccu you mean? I'm Joe Zuccu.'

'Oh, I'm sorry. I thought it ended with an O.'

'That's okay. Everyone thinks that. How can I help you?'

'My name is Samantha Melis. You know my brother, Lee Melis, I believe?'

'Do I? Lee Melis?'

She hesitated. She stared at Joe as though she were trying to work something out and almost, for some reason, looked like she was irritated by his reply. She reached into her bag, pulled out a photo and put it on the bar in front of Joe.

Joe peered at the photo. Lee Melis, or at least Joe presumed it was Lee Melis, was possibly about Joe's age but with an unkempt beard and straggly brown hair. He was smiling but his face was creased and worn either from outdoor work or, Joe guessed, from partying too hard. Joe picked up the photo to get a better look and some dim recognition sparked.

'You knew him better years ago probably. He used to go to Madisons.'

'Okay. Yeah. I do remember him.'

Madisons was a nightclub he went to back in the early nineties. It had taken on a near mythical status now in Bournemouth because it has been the first club that had really embraced dance music or 'rave' as it was known back then.

Joe looked at the photo some more. He did remember Lee, but not very well. Madisons closed down around the mid-nineties. He looked up at Samantha.

'So...?'

'Lee went missing about three weeks ago.'

'Well I haven't seen him if that's what you're wondering? In fact, I haven't seen him in years.'

'Lee told me that if anything ever happened to him that I should find you. And you'd help.'

Joe slowly finished his coffee, not wanting to appear as confused as he felt, and unsure how to navigate this unfolding conversation. 'You want *me* to help find him? Is that what you're asking? I'm sorry, I don't get it.'

'Lee said if anything ever happened to him that you'd help.'

'But... When did he say this?'

'About a month or so ago.'

Joe stared back at the photo, all the time feeling Samantha's eyes on him.

'Have you spoken to the police? Or his friends?'

'Lee hasn't got many friends and the police don't seem interested. Lee has a bit of a history. They know him so they don't think it's anything out of the ordinary for him to just disappear.'

'Has he ever disappeared before?'

'He's gone off but he's always texted me or someone. This time there's been nothing. His phone's off and he's been missing for three weeks.'

'So you think something bad may have happened?'

'A week before he disappeared he got beaten up. I don't know who by, but I think it may be connected.'

'Look, I really don't think I'm the best person to help find him to be honest. I haven't seen Lee in years. I work in a bar. I'm not... I don't find people.'

'So why did he say that I should ask you to help?'

'I honestly don't know.' He considered that it may be another Joe Zuccu but knew with a name like his that would be very unlikely.

Samantha stared at the bar, thinking.

'I can pay you.'

'It would be a waste of money. Maybe go to a private investigator.'

'You used to be friends though, right?'

'Years ago.'

'You stayed over our house once. I remember you. You used to have long, curly hair. You and Lee stayed up late smoking weed on the garage roof.'

Joe smiled but didn't know what to say. The memory of that night lay submerged, not yet extracted and dusted off for another viewing.

Samantha put a card down onto the bar. 'Here's my contact details. Will you at least think about it and if you change your mind call me? If I don't hear from you by tomorrow night then I'll leave it at that.'

'Okay.'

Samantha smiled and left quickly. She seemed like someone on the emotional edge. Like she wanted to cry. Joe picked up the card and the photo of Lee that she had also left. He felt guilty but wasn't quite sure why.

The morning had suddenly taken an unexpected turn and he felt uncomfortable. He didn't know this woman and knew her brother from over twenty years ago. Now she turns up asking him to track him down like he does this sort of thing all the time.

Joe had trouble finding his socks sometimes let alone some bloke he hardly knew.

He looked at his empty cup and wanted another coffee.

CHAPTER THREE

2001

AMY

To: Andrew Hunter

From: Amy Greene

Date: September 28th 2001

Subject: Rhona O'Shea

Dear Mr Hunter,

I am writing in the hope that you may agree to a short interview to aid an article I am writing for the *Observer Magazine* on the writer, Rhona O'Shea. The article's subject is regarding 'books that predicted the future'. As someone who knew O'Shea well, I would very much like your input on her work, influences and inspirations.

I am also covering the work of H.G. Wells, Kurt Vonnegut and Arthur C. Clarke as a matter of course but I have so far interviewed John Harrison regarding the work of Gerald Sebastian, especially his 1981 novella *The Day We Will See*, and I also plan on interviewing Janet Quinn on her collection of sci-fi novels that have become international best sellers.

My aim is to present a contemporary retrospective of significant and influential authors who, through their work, have predicted many of the political and technological events we have experienced and, in many ways, that have presented clever metaphors on contemporary life and living.

Just so you know I have been a journalist for a number of years and have written extensively for *The Observer* and *Guardian* as well as *The Telegraph*, *Times* and on occasion, *The Daily Mirror*.

My contact details are below and I am happy to come and meet you at your convenience. I look forward to hearing from you.

Kind Regards,
Amy Greene

CHAPTER FOUR

1975

RHONA

Rhona arrived home to her flat in Shephard's Bush still unsettled from her encounter with the man in the café. Part of her wished she now flat shared so she could talk to someone, but she was alone. She lit the fire and looked through the kitchen cupboards for food but all she could find was some bread and some butter in the fridge.

Still sat on the small round dining table was her latest rejection letter for her latest novel from probably the last literary agent in the country. It had arrived in the post that morning. It had set her off. The catalyst to a long simmering depressive state she had been slowly sinking into over the last few months that ended on a clifftop in Sussex.

The flat depressed her. Her life depressed her. She was tired of trying and then being told she wasn't good enough. The rejection letter was for her latest novel she had written over the last six months. Six months of hard work. A novel that she had worked on almost every evening when she got home from work, and every weekend, where she sat alone in her depressing flat hunched over her second-hand Olivetti as her ashtray collected her dog ends.

She told herself she would soldier on and just write another novel. A novel that would be welcomed, fawned over and celebrated. But that was when she found the space she usually reserved in her mind for creativity was empty.

And being a failed novelist who couldn't write seemed like the last straw, far worse surely than a successful novelist who couldn't write.

Rhona attempted to spread the butter on some bread but the butter was too hard. She gave up and, clutching a slice of bread, she sat down and stared at the rejection letter. She had kept all her rejection letters for the four novels she had written which had all gone unpublished. At the time, she had decided to keep them so she could whip them out when she was famous, and while being interviewed, say, 'Look what they said about my work. And now look. Who's laughing now, eh?'

And now who's laughing indeed as Rhona sat back and chewed the bread realising now how hungry she was. Her mind went back to the four books she had written as she brooded over why it had come to this.

The first novel was set in the American deep south concerning a negro man wrongly accused of rape who finds an unlikely ally in the form of a young, white, new pastor, just arrived from Chicago, and keen to make a good impression.

She had enjoyed the process, so sure of success and her own talent. Thinking about it now, and echoing some of the sentiments in the rejection letters she received at the time, it did have certain similarities to *To Kill a Mockingbird,* her favourite book when she was growing up. Rhona did have to admit she knew little of coloured people in American or of the deep south.

Her second novel was set in Spain. It was about an art school graduate who goes to the country and falls in love with a gypsy girl against the backdrop of a fascist dictatorship. Again reflecting on the rejection letters she had received, she had to admit she knew nothing beyond what she had read in the newspapers regarding Franco's Spain and had never been there. She also knew nothing of the gypsies who lived in Spain either, or if there were in fact, any gypsies there at all.

At the time she had argued, only to herself it should be said, that the point of a novelist was to 'make stuff up'. Self-delusion had masked her insecurities and only now could she see that, to grip the reader and take them on that literary journey with you, a certain amount of believability was required.

Her third novel, written only the year before in this very flat, had been about an American Vietnam veteran who comes to London and falls in love with a rich hippy who has become embroiled in a Manson-like cult. Once again, she had scarce knowledge of the struggles of war veterans returning home, especially American ones, or about hippies, who she found rather tiresome, old hat and self-centred. She knew little about the Manson family besides what she'd seen on television and read in the papers and she also knew nothing about rich people having been poor all her life.

Rhona closed her eyes, recognising a trend emerging that she had failed to recognise until now. Until it was too late.

Her last novel and the one she had received the latest rejection letter for, which was still sat in front of her on her dining table, was about a girl who goes to Chile to search for her Marxist Chilean boyfriend who we later discover has sadly been killed in the recent military coup. She had thought it to be 'in the moment' but could now appreciate and admit she knew nothing about Chile, Marxism or the recent coup. She was also embarrassed to admit she knew nothing about love.

The rejection letter had been polite but generic, thanking her for sending in her work but that the agency just didn't feel like she was the right author for them to represent at this time but that she should keep writing.

It was considerably more polite than some of the rejection letters she had received. Many had said she wrote 'without a heart' and her main characters 'lacked authenticity', which she now, on reflection, understood. Many just said they didn't like her novel which, whilst honest, had stung.

Her ignorance depressed her. All her endeavours had been poorly planned and even more poorly executed. She had wasted all that time chasing the dream of literary success and financial security. She had fantasised of being loved but instead suffered constant rejection which felt like hate. This growing feeling of inadequacy, creative inactivity and the letter arriving earlier had been the last straw.

She had sat in a dark funk that very morning and it felt like the walls were closing in. A black cloud of utter futility consumed her, which made her feel weak and helpless. The next thing she knew was that she was driving her car.

She didn't know where or how long she had been driving for, which should have alarmed her. She rarely even took long drives in her car which was a second hand 2CV she had unwisely bought from someone at work. Following the trend of her literary endeavours she knew nothing about cars but bought it as she was going through a period of loving all things French, which mainly included watching any film made by Truffaut or Godard, smoking Gauloises cigarettes and reading novels like

L'Etranger by Camus which she had read self-consciously and very obviously in the Soho coffee shops whilst sipping good coffee and smoking the Gauloises.

Admittedly she had been late for the French obsession, it having arrived in the UK a decade before, but having come from Ireland, she was having to play cultural catch up. Whilst everyone else was suffering a hangover from the previous decade and wearing flares, Rhona was still following the fashion set by Jean Seberg in *Breathless*.

So, sat behind the wheel of her 2CV, she drove out of London and soon found herself on tree lined roads with fields on each side. Still gripped by the feeling of pointlessness she drove on until she saw seagulls and the coast. And then she saw the sea with its expansive horizon, crashing waves and murky depths.

She'd had these funks before. The black moods that made normal life impossible at times. She'd even had to call work and say she was sick on occasion. And she was sick in some ways. Americans would no doubt have gone to their 'shrinks' at this point but lapsed Catholic women from rural Ireland didn't do such things. They just lived with it. Some no doubt thought about suicide and some actually committed suicide.

Her mother had these moods as well. She used to say it was headaches but Rhona knew that wasn't the case. Her mother used to retreat to her bedroom when the moods struck where she closed the curtains, closed the door, and stayed there for days. Rhona would have to help her father cook and he would take her in food which she rarely ate. Rhona would hear her mother sobbing from within during the days and nights as her father attempted to go about normal life which usually ended with Rhona being sent to her Grandmother until the 'headaches' lifted.

She remembered her father always had a lost look in his eyes when her mother got like this as he struggled to comprehend what was happening to the woman he loved. One time, when Rhona was about nine years old, her mother had one of her moods and had gone to her bedroom when she heard her screaming. Her father, who had just gotten home, ran in and found her mother in bed with blood-soaked sheets around her.

Rhona remembers coming to the doorway and seeing her mother lying there, her arms and wrists all cut with blood everywhere. Her father screamed at Rhona to fetch the doctor and she had to run down to the village as they had no telephone then.

Rhona's mother was taken away for what felt like a long time for her to recover. Her father had explained she had tried to get out of bed when she fell over and cut herself somehow but Rhona had seen the kitchen knife on the floor when she had stood in the doorway and knew otherwise. It was shortly after that that Rhona's father had paid for a telephone to be installed in the house.

And so, all these years later, Rhona sat in her car overlooking a cliff, asking herself if she should end it. But instead she ended up in a café and then met the man who told her to write about her visions.

The visions. A name given to her dreams, by a priest of all people, to explain what had, in many ways, plagued her all her life.

CHAPTER FIVE

2019

JOE

Joe woke early the next day. Mike, his housemate he'd known since school, was already at his gym so Joe had the place to himself. He lived in a three-bedroom house near West Way.

Mike was currently going through a long, drawn-out divorce and this had coincided with Joe's return to Bournemouth from London about six months ago. With both needing a place to live they had teamed up. Mike paid the extra for the third bedroom, so his children could stay over at weekends and it had worked out fine. Mike had been a professional boxer for eleven years with a record of five wins and four losses and now had his own boxing club where he ran early morning and evening classes with private tuition throughout the day. Joe sometimes trained at the gym himself. Mike was the perfect flatmate. He was clean, tidy and not in much.

Joe put the kettle on to make a Rooibos tea and turned his iPad on to check up on *The Guardian* website for the news. He was a little slow this morning. After his shift had finished he stayed around to have an early dinner and a couple of drinks to keep Catalina, the barwoman who had taken over the bar from him, company. She was a long-legged Spanish woman who liked to flirt with him. Being a single guy Joe liked to flirt back although he made sure never to take the next step. And nor did she and that's how it was.

He'd enjoyed his tapas and beers before heading home at about ten to doze in front of *Newsnight* before going to bed. After cereal he stood up to put an espresso on and his phone rang. It was Melanie, an old friend.

'I heard you saw Samantha yesterday?'

'Samantha Melis? You know her?'

'Yeah. She was asking if I know you and how to find you.'

'Did you say I'd help find her brother?'

'No. She said Lee told her you'd help if anything ever happened to him.'

'But I don't even know Lee. Not anymore.'

'Sam is really sound, Joe. She's lovely.'

Joe sat down.

'Mel, don't you think this is odd?'

'She just needs someone to ask around about him. You know a few old faces.'

'So do you. And I've been away a long time.'

'I'll give you a hand if you want but Sam's worried he's in trouble somehow.'

'Then why would I want to get involved?'

'You handled my next-door neighbour okay.'

Joe sighed. He'd known Melanie since college. And it was true, Joe had helped her one time with her next-door neighbour, but it wasn't anything to do with finding anyone. She had moved into a new flat and the next-door neighbour soon proved to be a bit of a nightmare. Music at all hours, parties, rubbish left out. Melanie had tried to talk to him but that didn't work out and he had become abusive. The council got involved but that just seemed to wind the neighbour up further. That's when Melanie called Joe. Joe wasn't sure why. *Would he just have a word?*

Joe reluctantly agreed and visited the guy next door. The neighbour was a smallish, weedy guy in his late thirties with tattoos everywhere and a face that said substance abuse. Joe politely asked him to be more considerate and how nice it would be if everyone just got on. Joe thought it was going well. The neighbour nodded thoughtfully but then walked away from the door and came back with a hammer. That's when Joe took charge of the situation by barging into the guy's flat.

He simultaneously grabbed the guy's wrist that was holding the hammer with his left hand and punched the guy in the throat with his right hand. It was a common self-defence move which came from the theory that if you find yourself in these situations, don't let the other guy hit you first, especially if the other guy has a hammer.

It was also extremely effective. As the guy dropped the offending tool and dropped to the floor himself, clutching his throat and struggling to breathe, Joe stood over him and told him to be nicer from now on otherwise he'd be back.

Joe walked away, adrenaline surging through him and half expected the police to turn up any second as he tried to calm his breathing. But no police did turn up, and to Joe's surprise, that had been the end of it. The guy kept his music down and was polite, Melanie was pleased, and Joe questioned why he had ever agreed to get involved.

Joe realised he still had the phone to his ear.

'Yes, but I was lucky. He was small and I had a chance to stop him before he managed to hit me. I generally try and steer away from trouble and not go and find it.'

'She just needs some help.'

Joe stood up and walked over to the window. 'Hasn't Lee got his own mates to help?'

'Lee is a bit troubled. Sam will explain.'

'I'm not doing this.'

'You were his mate once. I remember.'

'That was years ago.'

'So? Can't you still be friends with someone over time?'

'I'm not sure.'

'Lee would have done the same for you.'

'Bullshit. How can you say that? You're just saying that.'

'I'm just trying to help Sam. Think about it. Just say you'll think about it.'

'I'll think about it.'

'Great. I'd better go. Speak laters.'

'Laters.'

He hung up. He felt sluggish but didn't feel like working out or going for a jog. This business with Lee Melis was bothering him. He wanted to say no and walk away guilt-free but the issue was niggling away at him. He went into the kitchen and prepared an espresso with his Bialetti espresso maker and Lavazza coffee. He turned on the gas and stood back, waiting for the water to boil with the lid up because one of his Italian cousins had sworn it tasted better this way. Joe wasn't convinced but had continued with the ritual out of habit. As he waited he forced himself to think of Lee and what he remembered about him.

Lee was one of the teenage crowd that had hung around McDonalds in Bournemouth town centre back in the late eighties and early nineties. The group, which could often reach over fifty strong and was made up of teenagers from all over town, would meet most weekends to stand or sit and chat until the last buses left for the suburbs.

Joe also remembered Lee from Galaxy, an old under-eighteens nightclub on Hinton Road that Joe went to when he was around the same age. He had vague memories of Lee being a pretty good graffiti artist and breakdancer, although he never reached the heights of the Second to None Crew – the local breakdance team known worldwide for their longevity and award-winning skills on the mats.

And then Joe remembered Lee from Madisons, everyone's favourite club. He had snapshots of Lee smiling on the edge of the dance floor and gurning from the effects of a particularly strong ecstasy tablet. Joe recalled they had become friendlier around this period. He wasn't sure why but he guessed Lee may have known one of Joe's friends.

The water boiled in the espresso maker and broke Joe's reverie. As the strong aroma of freshly brewed coffee filled the kitchen, the little machine spat out the last of its black liquid and started making its familiar gurgling sound. Joe turned off the gas and poured a double shot into one of his white espresso cups and added sugar. As he stirred the spoon another memory came back to him. It had been Lee that had helped him that night at Bump N Hustle.

Bump N Hustle, a club night that was still going, had started in Bournemouth back in the early nineties and was known for its house tunes. Joe had gone to one of its first nights and someone had spiked his drink with two ecstasy tablets. It had been done by someone Joe knew. Back then it was something people did without thinking about the consequences. They thought it was funny.

When Joe found out he didn't get angry as that could only make things worse, and at first, he thought he'd be able to ride out the effects or even enjoy it. He had been a keen clubber during that hedonistic period and was in no way anti-drugs. In fact, Joe had already necked half a pill that night before he discovered he'd been spiked.

Soon though, as the drugs worked their way through Joe's system, he began to feel overwhelmed and panicky as his heart rate went into overdrive. Reaching hyperventilating anxiety levels, Joe retreated outside to sit and calm himself down. Lee had come out and stayed with him as they both sat on the beach facing the dark waves crashing into the shore. He'd kept Joe calm and feeling safe and seen him through the worst of it. Still too high to go home, Joe had crashed at Lee's that night. They'd bumped into Samantha, only a young girl then, in the kitchen. Joe remembered her now.

They had climbed out of Lee's bedroom window onto the garage roof and smoked pot. And Lee had chatted for what seemed like hours. Joe could only remember Lee going off on one about something but he couldn't remember what about. But whatever it was had been deep in some way.

Joe sipped his coffee and threw the rest down his throat. It had been horrible that night and he'd been scared. At one point, he thought he might die. And Lee would have been the last person he might have seen.

Joe picked up his phone and fished out the card Samantha had given him. He dialled her number and waited. She answered.

'I'll see what I can find out. I don't want to be paid though. I'll ask around for a couple of weeks, but only a couple of weeks.'

'That's great. Thank you.'

Joe could sense her smile as she spoke. Relief flooded down the line.

'I can't promise anything, Samantha. I still think you're better off going back to the police or hiring a private detective.'

'I want you though. I feel better knowing that someone who knows Lee is looking for him.'

'Okay.'

'Where do you think you'll start?'

'I don't know.'

'How about his girlfriend?'

'Lee has a girlfriend?'

'She's his ex but yeah, I think they were engaged. You didn't know?'

'No. I don't know anything.'

CHAPTER SIX

1975

RHONA

Rhona had her first vision when she was just a young girl. It was after Christmas in 1958 and Rhona remembered it well.

That night she had dreamt a vivid dream and excitedly recounted it to her mother the next morning. She said she had seen a plane crash on what seemed like a runaway. It was snowing. The people inside were mainly smart young men and for some reason she knew they were English sportsmen. That had been it. She remembered her mother smiling at her, amused by the oddness but also the specific details of a dream of a seven-year-old girl.

And then, two days later, that smile disappeared as the reports came through of a plane crash in Munich where eight members of the Manchester United football team, nicknamed the Busby Babes, were killed.

It was all over the newspapers and radio. She could still see her mother reading the report in the paper and looking up to stare at Rhona who, although she had grasped the basic facts of what had happened, had still yet to appreciate the implications of what she had dreamt. Her mother stayed silent on the matter. Perhaps she had put it down to a bizarre but possible coincidence. And nothing was ever said about it again. But then, almost exactly a year later, Rhona had another dream and she told her mother about this one as well.

It had again been about a plane crash but this one involved a kind looking young man in glasses who liked to sing. The song Rhona heard as she dreamed was the one she had heard on the radio about a woman called Peggy Sue. Her mother nodded but didn't smile this time. There was a look of concern on her face which, a few days later, turned to a mixture of fear and horror when it was announced the famous singer, Buddy Holly, had died in a plane crash in a place called Iowa, America.

As far as she could remember her father had only been told of her dreams at this point as he had sat her down and quizzed her carefully about her dreams after Buddy Holly's death. He asked her what she had seen and whether she'd had any more. But she'd only had two so far.

After much hushed discussion in their bedroom between her parents, the next day Rhona's mother had taken Rhona to see the local priest. Father Hurley was a fat man with grey hair sticking out of his ears and nose. He had small eyes that never seemed to look at you directly but would look off to the side as though, when he was talking to you, would always feel like he was talking to someone else.

Rhona's mother told Father Hurley about the dreams and he listened in silence and nodded in a well-practised manner. Finally, Rhona's mother stopped talking and was silent. Father Hurley realised she was waiting for answers.

Father Hurley turned and looked at Rhona. or more precisely, he looked off to Rhona's right as though looking to the wall behind her. After a moment he then turned his gaze to the top of his scratched desk whilst Rhona continued to wait nervously. He seemed to be thinking. They sat in his small office with the ticking clock on the mantelpiece which added an ominous tempo to the occasion.

'Do you pray?' he asked.

'I do, Father,' answered Rhona. 'Every night.' This was a lie.

'Good. Good. That's good. Perhaps you should pray a bit more.'

Rhona's mother shifted in her seat as though she were becoming impatient.

'Does she perhaps have a gift, Father? From God?' asked Rhona's mother.

'Like Jesus?' asked Rhona.

Father Hurley chuckled. 'Jesus was a man and you're just a little girl, so I don't think you need worry about gifts from the Lord.'

'I thought Jesus was the Son of God?' asked Rhona.

'Yes. Yes of course. And that too obviously,' added Father Hurley quickly, throwing a nervous glance at Rhona's mother.

'So what do you think it is then, Father?' asked Rhona's mother.

Father Hurley drummed his fingers on his desk and stood up. 'I think... I think it's nothing to worry about. Probably just an active imagination and a strange coincidence that occurs from time to time. Don't be alarmed Mrs O'Shea,' he had said encouragingly. 'It is nothing to worry about. These.... Visions, or whatever you want to call it, will blow over.'

He said it as though Rhona had a cold and it would soon go away. Rhona's mother clenched her jaw, stood up and thanked him and attempted a humble smile.

And that was that. They went home with Father Hurley patting Rhona on her head as she left. After that Rhona called these dreams her visions. They sounded more important. More grand. More holy.

From then on Rhona's mother stood over her whilst she knelt and prayed by her bed every night, and although Father Hurley had offered his kindly advice, Rhona's mother never visited him again.

And so, she just went on living in Kilbaha, the small fishing village in County Clare, the only child of Maureen and David O'Shea. For a time, she thought she might only have visions of plane crashes and was unsure if she had some kind of gift for foreseeing air disasters. She sensed her mother thought the same thing as whenever planes, flying or airports ever came up in conversation, which admittedly was rare, Rhona's mother would quickly change the subject in case this might incite some other awful premonition and event.

What changed everything was when she dreamt of a man being shot in a big, shiny, open top car as it drove along a road with lots of happy and smiling people all waving. Next to him sat a pretty woman, wearing a pink dress and hat who tried to help, and for some reason, ended up crawling out the back of the car.

It was a terrifying dream. The man seemed very important and she felt sad seeing him get shot. She knew it had been a vision when she awoke and was not a normal dream. Like previous visions it seemed to play in her mind like she was watching a newsreel in the cinema. Images on a big screen of people she would soon come to recognise.

When she soon saw pictures of John F Kennedy and his wife in her father's newspaper, she knew she had dreamed about him and he was the man who was to be shot. She told her mother about her vision when Kennedy was elected President of America in 1960.

She couldn't stay quiet. She realised, now she was older and wiser and knew who she had dreamed about, that she could maybe warn Mr Kennedy and save this man's life. She told her mother what she had seen. How it had been violent, scary and it had woken her up like a nightmare. Her mother's face had tightened, and she instructed Rhona not to tell anyone else about this. Apparently, her mother didn't want to warn President Kennedy about her daughter's dream and save his life.

For three years nothing was said but then, when Kennedy was assassinated her mother broke down and cried. Her father thought she was just crying because Kennedy was popular in Ireland and had been a good Catholic. Rhona wanted to tell her father about what she had seen three years before. How she and her mother knew this was going to happen. And how it also meant that instead of a vision of a tragedy days before the event, like the Busby Babes and Buddy Holly had been, this dream had occurred years ago. But she didn't say a word as her mother now seemed to grow colder towards her.

These visions seemed to terrify her mother. Unwanted and uninvited words disturbed and confused everything she knew and believed. According to Father Hurley they were not a gift from God. Then what were they then?

Her mother began to look at Rhona as if she might bite at any minute. Fear replaced the little love she had shown Rhona and Rhona quickly realised that saying nothing about these visions was the best course of action if she wished for any affection at all from her mother.

Her mother continued to shun her, so Rhona made sure to stop telling her about her dreams. She didn't mention seeing four young men with funny haircuts stood waving on the steps of a Pan Am plane which she soon realised were the Beatles. For years she thought they too might perish in an air disaster, as a plane had one again appeared in her vision, but she came to realise that her dreams weren't confined to foreseeing tragic plane crashes or presidential assassinations.

It seemed as though, as she got older, she started seeing a wider variety of future events. She dreamt of Vietnam, Winston Churchill dying and riots in American cities between Negroes and the police. She said nothing about any of this and slowly her mother appeared to soften and tentatively show her more attention although nothing close to what could be described as love.

In 1966 Rhona had a vision of a mountain of black mud collapsing and a school being buried beneath it. Children died. Lots of children. She heard their screams and saw the panic in their faces. She saw the name on a street sign where this catastrophe was to take place. Aberfan. She looked it up. It was in Wales. She wanted to tell her mother. She was desperate to. This vision haunted her like no other vision before it. But she kept silent in case she might once again lose her mother's affections.

On 21st October 1966, one hundred and sixteen children and twenty-eight adults died when a tip slid down a mountain after heavy rain and engulfed Pantglas Junior School. Guilt consumed Rhona. She even prayed to God for forgiveness. If only she had said something maybe she could have prevented all of it.

Rhona and her parents listened to the news on the radio. Rhona felt her mother watching her, scrutinising her, and she could tell her mother was deliberating as to whether her daughter had any inkling this awful event was going to happen. Rhona hid her emotions well and hugged her mother tightly. As she did she promised herself that as soon as she was old enough she would leave Kilbaha as she didn't deserve her mother's love.

In 1969 at the age of eighteen, she left for England and went to London. She arrived in Kilburn with an address of a female cousin she had arranged to stay with. She initially got a job as a cleaner for an insurance company based near the City.

Back in Ireland she had continued to have visions as she slept. She saw Bobby Kennedy get shot. And Martin Luther King. And just after she arrived in London she saw men land on the moon. She said nothing about these visions and prayed they would end. She didn't want this gift, if that is what it was.

When she wasn't working she explored London's streets and sights. It opened her eyes to life beyond what she had ever experienced in her small village in Ireland. She soon got her own place and took an evening course in shorthand at the local college and eventually got a job at the *London Irish Daily*, a newspaper aimed at the Irish population based in the city. The position was a step up. She was to be a junior secretary, which was a nice way of saying 'someone who filed or found files for the journalists or made people cups of tea'.

She liked this job better than being a cleaner. It was better money and she was in an environment she realised she liked even though all she ever seemed to say was 'would you like tea or coffee?'.

The editor had instructed her to say this as often as possible in the hope that more caffeine increased the work rate and prevented tiredness although he forgot about increased loo breaks. It was here she decided she wanted to be a writer and soon started the first of what would be four unpublished novels.

And now here she was, in her flat one evening having been told by a man she met in a café to write about her visions after her own attempts of success had been a failure.

Perhaps writing about her deepest secret would mean success. Perhaps she could save people instead of watching them die. Perhaps this was what she was meant to do.

She went to bed and slept a dreamless sleep.

CHAPTER SEVEN

2019

JOE

Joe and Samantha talked for a while and Joe jotted down notes. The first thing he had asked her was if she knew where Lee's passport was. She had it so Lee hadn't gone abroad at least. By the end of their chat Joe felt he had some facts and places to begin his search like where Lee lived, worked and who his girlfriend was but little else. He knew Lee had split up with his girlfriend, who was called Rose, and it seemed Lee was having problems around this time due to the split up and he'd been drinking a lot.

He periodically stayed at Samantha's and then, when he must have felt like he had outstayed his welcome, he had stayed at other places, although Samantha didn't know where. Normally she didn't see much of him but she did see him after he'd been beaten up. He'd been to the Six Bells pub and came home battered and blue. He had refused to say what had happened. She said she knew something was very wrong in Lee's life and this was why she was especially concerned when a week later Lee's phone was turned off and he stopped responding to emails and Facebook messages. She went to the police and when they seemed unconcerned she remembered Lee's instructions about contacting Joe.

After they talked Samantha had called Lee's girlfriend and told her about Joe. She said he was helping out and asked if he could come by to ask her some questions. She agreed and so a meeting was set for later that morning.

When Samantha called Joe back to confirm all of this Joe realised he felt nervous, and for the first time, out of his depth. He still hadn't thought about what he might ask the girlfriend. *So, you've lost Lee? Where was the last place you saw him? Have you looked there?*

Joe needed to come up with a game plan and come across like he knew what he was doing. The first thing he had to consider though was what to wear. He didn't want to wear a suit but maybe that's what she'd expect. Joe dismissed this idea and decided on just looking smart. After all, he told himself, first impressions last.

Joe went into his bedroom and opened the cupboard. He took one look at his sorry-looking suit and closed the cupboard door. He didn't really go in for suits and it showed. He was happy he hadn't been forced to go for that option. He realised his suit must have looked okay at some point. That must have been some years ago now and the shortage of weddings these days, as well as the fortunate lack of funerals, meant there was no real incentive to buy a new one.

If you had to wear a suit for friends' divorces though, Joe would look sharp. He and his peers were at that age where all the weddings and kids had happened and now there was just the painful separations and the low key second marriages as they slid towards middle-age.

Joe paused for a second as he acknowledged the fact he'd never been married or had kids. The feeling felt like a pain tugging deep within him. He sensed a sudden wave of sadness washing over him and he quickly swept it away. He took a deep breath and decided that after he had found Lee he would purchase a new suit at least.

His thoughts turned back to the meeting. He decided on smart casual. He put a shirt on he sometimes wore for work. It was light blue and from GAP then added his black jeans and cream Harrington jacket. Shoe-wise he decided on his white Converse Chuck Taylor All Stars.

He looked at himself in the mirror. This would have to do. After all, Colombo had his old mac and no one complained about that. He drove over to the girlfriend's house making sure he took his notebook and pen with him. On the way, he listened to his F.J. Mahon album and hummed along to relax himself.

Lee's girlfriend lived on the Townsend estate which was down near the Castlepoint Shopping Centre. It was made up mainly of 1970s era council housing and numbered around fifteen hundred homes.

In the past the estate had suffered a bad reputation, and at various points had been labelled a 'ghetto' or a 'no-go-area', mainly by the local paper looking for a headline or local politicians looking for re-election. Today the area didn't seem intimidating at all and was even somewhat peaceful. The absence of tower blocks and the homes being a decent size by today's standards made Joe speculate if at some point this area would become gentrified, if it wasn't already. Whilst other low-cost areas in other towns and cities like London were now witnessing an influx of affluent young professionals desperate to get onto the housing ladder, Bournemouth had yet to really experience this phenomenon.

Southbourne, another suburb of Bournemouth, was home to a lot of people who had moved out of the capital and the new cafes and bars was evidence of this. But it seemed none of this had yet to reach Townsend.

Joe found the house, parked up and got out. He noted the garden was well kept as he rang the doorbell and waited. The door was opened by a woman of about forty with short brown hair who stood expectantly at the door. She was dressed in jeans and T-shirt.

'Hi, are you Rose?' he asked.

'And you're Joe?'

'Yes.'

Rose left it a beat before opening the door to let him in. She let him walk past her before closing the door. Inside Joe could smell fresh laundered clothes.

'Samantha says you're helping her look for Lee.'

Joe paused in the hallway. 'Yeah, I'm just helping her out.'

'So, you're a friend of Lee's?'

'I was. I knew him. But I haven't seen him for ages.'

Joe cringed at his choice of words.

'I meant I haven't seen him for years.'

'Are you a policeman or ex-policeman?'

'No.'

'Are you a private investigator?'

'No.'

'You're just *helping*?' she asked.

'Yeah.'

Rose nodded and led him through to the tidy and spacious lounge. Joe followed behind realising it hadn't been the best of starts. She indicated for Joe to sit down on the sofa whilst she sat opposite him on an armchair. As he looked at her Joe could almost see a slight smile hover across her face.

'Out of interest did Lee ever mention me?' asked Joe, his hands nervously clasped together in his lap.

'No, I don't think so. Why?'

Because I haven't seen him in over twenty years and he singled me out to help find him.

'No reason. I just wondered.'

It might be too complicated to explain. Too weird. He unclasped his hands.

'Are you looking for Lee as well?' Joe asked deciding to get straight down to business.

'We're not together anymore.'

'Samantha said you'd separated but I wondered if you still… maybe it was a temporary thing.'

'No. We split up a while back.'

'But you were engaged?'

'We were.'

Joe nodded thoughtfully.

'What do you do then?' she asked. 'When you're not *helping*?'

'I work in a bar.'

She smiled. Joe thought maybe he should have lied. Her smile didn't make Joe feel uncomfortable exactly, like she was humouring him or being condescending towards him even though maybe she was. It was more like she was just smiling at the fact that Samantha had got this guy, who was now sat in her lounge, to even bother trying to find Lee when he was just a barman. If that was what she was thinking, then Joe was thinking the same thing as he got his notebook and pen out, knowing this would only potentially add even more amateur gravitas to the effect he was probably creating, but Joe felt it was a sink or swim situation. Either he tries to act like he knows what he's doing or she really will point a finger at him very soon and shout 'Faking it'. He just hoped she wouldn't laugh.

'When was the last time you saw Lee?'

'My birthday. In June. He came round with loads of expensive jewellery. He wanted us to get back together but it was over. I didn't accept the presents.'

'And how long before that had you split up?'

'About six weeks. Look, Lee is a lovely guy but we weren't getting on. He was drinking. He had his own problems and I just couldn't go on. Don't get me wrong, I loved him once but...' She let the sentence hang.

'He was living here before you split up, right?'

She nodded.

'Samantha said she didn't know where he often stayed when he had left. You have any idea?'

'I don't know. Couch surfing. Airbnb. Hotels. I have no idea either. He packed a bag and went.'

'What about friends? Could you help me out there?'

She shook her head. 'He would go out to meet people. But I didn't know who or have any of their numbers. I never met any of his friends really. And then towards the end he'd just stay in and drink every evening.'

'You said he had problems? Besides the drink?'

'Mental health problems.'

He waited for her to elaborate. She spoke slowly and carefully.

'He said things that weren't true. Couldn't be true.'

She looked uncomfortable. Joe nodded, getting a vibe she didn't want to divulge any more details on the matter. He asked himself if perhaps Lee was a jealous type and had accused her of seeing someone else. But that, if anything, was just a guess.

'It got pretty bad?'

'When I look back, and if I'm honest with myself, I knew he was probably drinking too much years ago. But he managed to function. And then he just went downhill a few months ago. Around February.'

'Why do you think that was?'

'I had my second miscarriage.' She stared at him when she said this as though she dared him to show pity.

'I'm sorry.'

'It's okay. You say you used to know Lee years ago?'

Joe nodded. 'From when we were teenagers really. You not from down here?'

'No. Bristol originally. What was he like when you were teenagers?'

'Sound. Nice bloke. I don't remember him drinking a lot back then but this was years ago?'

'So, what else do you want to know?'

'I'm still trying to get a feel for Lee if I'm honest. He seemed okay when you saw him on your birthday?'

'Yeah. He hadn't drunk much and he was trying to be nice. To be sober. Said he'd got a bonus at work.'

'He must have been functional to some extent to have kept his job.'

'Yeah. I suppose.'

'Lee leave much here in the way of personal items? Anything that might help me?'

Rose got up. She went over to the corner and picked up a cardboard box that Joe hadn't noticed was there. She came back with it and put it down next to Joe. Joe looked through it. He picked up various comics, mostly graphic novels aimed at adults. Some were quite old which suggested that Lee was a collector. Joe wasn't a graphic novel reader but he'd read *Watchmen* by

Alan Moore a few years ago when the film had come out and enjoyed it.

As he dug deeper he found graffiti sketches in pencil as though Lee had some artwork planned. 'He still sprayed?'

'Sometimes. That's why I held onto them. I thought he might want them.'

The pieces were mainly Lee's tag which was *Skiver* and on a few of the pages were outlines of the words *Who Cares Wins* in various drafts and detail. The words made Joe wince. It had been a kind of motto an old girlfriend of his used to use. He pushed the thought out of his mind and moved on.

The sketches were all in pencil without colour but showed that Lee still possessed the artistic skills that Joe remembered from their youth. Joe made a mental note to check out the old school graffiti artists still in Bournemouth as possible leads. At the bottom of the box was a notebook. Joe lifted it out and flipped through it. Most of the pages had been ripped out but on one page he found three mobile phone numbers scrawled down with no names next to them.

'Is this Lee's writing?' He held up a sheet of paper.

'Yeah but I don't know whose numbers they are.'

'You phoned them?'

Rose let out a small sigh. 'Keep it if you want. You phone them. Keep the whole box.'

'You think he's just gone off?'

'I do. I think he's turned his phone off because he doesn't want to speak to Samantha and is probably drunk somewhere. He used to do that to me if I moaned at him. He'd run away and hide.'

'Samantha try and get him to stop drinking?'

She nodded.

'It's a losing battle. I appreciate Samantha is his sister but I just can't keep caring about someone who doesn't seem to care about themselves. It's not good for me you understand?'

'I do understand.'

Sensing the meeting had come to an end Joe got up. Rose did the same.

'I hope you find him and I'm sorry I couldn't be more help, but I haven't seen him for quite a while anyway, and that's how I'd prefer it.'

'I get it. I do. Thanks for everything.'

She showed him out. Joe walked back to his car and got in, placing the box on the passenger seat. It was then he realised he hadn't written anything down in his notebook.

He sat for a while and contemplated the meeting. The thought he hadn't really come away with much gnawed at him and the feeling that he was just playing at this made him feel uneasy. Perhaps he should phone Samantha and suggest she pressure the police to do more and actually take an interest in Lee's disappearance. It felt like an attractive option. Then he could give this up before he wasted any more time.

He'd made a mistake by agreeing to help. Delving into the lives of people and their pain and problems wasn't something Joe felt comfortable with. He'd had a taste of that during his bar work over the years. Customers, with a drink in their hands, would readily open up their hearts and souls and tell you their problems, not looking for answers but just looking for someone to talk to as their loneliness surfaced with melancholic predictability after that taste of alcohol.

Joe had never liked that aspect of the job although he knew they were just trying to connect and he tried to be the good guy who listened patiently when this occurred. But now here he was trying to find someone who perhaps didn't want to be found. A someone who had stood by whilst his fiancé had two miscarriages and their relationship had fallen apart. A someone who had sought refuge in the bottle but only, it seemed, found further unhappiness.

His phone rang. It was his sister, Eva. Joe answered. 'Hi, everything okay?'

'I can't get hold of Mum. Are you nearby?'

'Yeah, I can pop over. I'm about ten minutes away. I'm sure she's okay.'

'Call me when you get there okay?'

'Sure. Speak in a bit. Don't worry.'

Joe hung up and started the car.

CHAPTER EIGHT

2001

AMY

To: Andrew Hunter

From: Amy Greene

Date: October 5th 2001

Subject: Rhona O'Shea

Dear Mr Hunter,

I hope you are well. I wrote last week requesting a short interview regarding the work of your colleague, Rhona O'Shea, in relation to my article for the *Observer Magazine* on 'books that predicted the future'. I am writing to see if you have had a chance to consider my request?

I am keen to discuss her work with you as my article is coming along very well. Whilst I could comment myself on Rhona's novels your input would be invaluable and add substance to a fascinating genre of literature. I am very excited on the prospect of meeting you.

My contact details are below and I am happy to meet you wherever and whenever is convenient. I look forward to hearing from you.

Kind Regards,

Amy Greene

CHAPTER NINE

1975

RHONA

Any plot. Any genre. You need to dress them up a bit. That's what he had said.

Rhona sat eating toast and sipping tea for her breakfast the next morning as she thought about what the man had told her. The funk had passed, the clouds lifted to hover elsewhere until next time. As daylight once again shone Rhona began to see a new avenue to explore. New possibilities. It was true, she wasn't getting anywhere writing about the subjects she had written about so far so perhaps a change of direction was needed. Perhaps she should write about her visions. Take his advice. What was the worst that could happen? Another unpublished novel?

Rhona warmed to the idea. This could be her way of warning people. Her way of saving lives. Her way of making up for Aberfan. She would not be keeping quiet any longer. She would be doing the right thing. The question now was what to write about and how to frame what she had seen in some kind of consistent narrative without it being a sermon or just some kind of glorified sandwich board proclaiming 'the end of the world is nigh'.

She sighed and realised she was back to square one again, scratching around for inspiration. Devoid of ideas. But perhaps she needed to rethink how she came at it this time. Up until now she had seen herself as a serious novelist who wrote, or at least attempted to write, about the human condition with dramatic and heart wrenching plots set against historic or real events. She saw herself as a novelist that would go on to win important and prestigious prizes and who would, eventually, very eventually perhaps, be appreciated by not just the masses but other novelists and intellectuals. But maybe she had set her expectations just a little too high and needed to come at it differently.

Genre, Rhona decided, would be the first change.

'You're thinking of writing a science fiction novel?'

'Yes. I thought, why not?'

Andrew Hunter nodded his approval. He sat on his chair with Rhona perched on his desk. Andrew worked at the *London Irish Daily* or *the LID* as some called it. He was a Junior Reporter, which at the *London Irish Daily* meant he did all the reporting that no one else wanted to do. He wrote little read reports on non-league Irish football matches, obituaries of unknown Irish people, pleas to find missing Irish cats and anything else the more Senior Reporters decided was beneath them.

He didn't mind. In fact, he loved his job and saw it as an opportunity to learn. Unlike the majority of the staff at *the LID* Andrew was English born with no family links to Ireland. Some had seen his appointment as an affront to the ethos of the paper which was surely to report and promote Irish events and its people by Irish journalists and not hire privileged Englishmen to take their jobs.

But Mick, the Editor-in-Chief at the time, a self-confessed Marxist who liked nothing better than to drink numerous pints of ale at lunchtime in the local (Irish) pub and lecture anyone in earshot on the inequalities of the crypto-fascist capitalist system, went against the grain when he said he saw in Andrew a chance to 'break them from the inside' as though his plan was to groom Andrew in Marxist ideology. And then, when the time was right, he would set him loose amongst the British national newspapers to wreak havoc with politically provocative pro-left leaning reporting, arguing that an Irishman would never have that opportunity in this horribly corrupt country. Andrew decided not to mention he had never voted and happily came on board whilst others who worked for the paper never mentioned that Mick probably just fancied Andrew.

'Why not indeed but I didn't think science fiction was your thing.'

'Well I felt like a change.'

'Haven't you just finished a novel?'

Rhona played with a pen on Andrew's desk.

'I want to keep writing and I want to write sci-fi so for research what should I read, Andrew? Just answer the question.'

'Well, what science fiction books have you read so far?'

Rhona looked out of the window.

'None.'

Andrew nodded. 'Okay, well that's a start.'

'Don't be sarcastic. I'm a blank canvas. Help me out here.'

Andrew thought for a moment and held up his hands in mock surrender.

'Let me have a think and perhaps we could meet later? After work, for coffee?'

'It's a deal.'

Andrew watched Rhona walk away and back down to the basement to the filing room. He had met her soon after he started at the paper when he went to root out an old obituary of a local Irish councillor whose wife has just passed away. He wasn't sure what the procedure was for requesting clippings and Rhona had been the first person he had run into. She had smiled at him and he had taken in her short black hair and soft Irish accent. He'd been smitten ever since.

He had asked her out for a drink soon after and she had politely declined. After a short period of painful embarrassment where he tried to avoid her, he returned to work one day and acted as though the invite for a drink had never been offered which seemed to work as they now had and maintained a friendly, purely platonic relationship that existed solely at work. Their friendship had further improved when they both discovered they wanted to write. Rhona was serious literary fiction and Andrew was science and historical fiction. Andrew turned back to the work on his desk and wished for the day to speed by.

'The thing about good science fiction is that it isn't just spaceships on futuristic planets,' Andrew said passionately as he swirled the coffee around his cup.

'Well, what is it then?' Rhona was seated across from him in the café holding a cigarette in one hand and a pen in the other. It was as though she were interviewing him like he was an expert on the subject, which at this point he supposed he was.

'Good science fiction holds a mirror up to society. It can explore political or technological ideas and how humans interact with each other and new technology. There's so much to it.'

Andrew noticed Rhona still hadn't written anything in her notebook.

'I still don't get why you want to write in this genre.'

'What books do you recommend then?'

Andrew smiled and took out a list he had worked on throughout the day.

'Right, well you definitely need to read Kurt Vonnegut. *Slaughterhouse Five* is probably a good place to start and I personally loved *The Sirens of Titan*.'

'*Slaughterhouse Five* I've heard of.'

Andrew watched as she wrote quickly.

'Well that's good. I also recommend Samuel Delany. Read *Babel 17*. Philip K Dick. He's exceptional. Ursula K. Le Guin. She's a woman.'

'I guessed that.'

'Well her book *The Left Hand of Darkness* was brilliant.'

'That's enough.'

Andrew looked up from his list. Rhona had already put down her pen and was sipping her coffee.

'I've got more.'

'I can't read them all.'

'No, but you might, over time.'

'I'll see how I get on with what you've given me.'

'Right, okay. Well good luck.'

He folded up his list and put it back into his pocket. He had ten authors written down. His top ten he'd spent some time compiling. He decided he wouldn't throw the list away. She might ask for more recommendations in the future. If not her then maybe someone else. Maybe.

'Have you got a plot or anything?'

'Not yet. But I'm working on it.'

Rhona visited the library the next day. The list from Andrew had been helpful and she knew he might be useful again as she embarked on her new venture. He was a big sci-fi enthusiast or a big science fiction enthusiast as he would call it. Andrew drew a distinction between sci-fi and science fiction, the former being a pulpy, mass market and devoid of intelligent ideas kind of writing compared to the more weighty, thoughtful and challenging latter. As for her own opinion and preference she had still to differentiate one from the other but obviously, if asked, she would say she intended to write science fiction of course.

Rhona was unable to find any of the books Andrew had recommended but did find another book by one of the authors. It was Philip K Dick's *The Man in the High Castle.* To that she added Arthur C. Clarke's *2001.* She wondered why Andrew hadn't recommended Arthur C. Clarke as, after all, he was probably the most famous science fiction author there was. Even Rhona had heard of him.

She recalled going to the cinema to see the film of *2001* a few years previously with a young man called Kenny who insisted they lie down in front of the cinema and stare up at the screen. Ideally, he had told her, they should have 'dropped acid' for the 'ultimate experience', but unable to procure the substance, they had to make do with a gin and tonic in the cinema bar before the screening. Unfortunately, she found the film rather laborious and fell asleep which seemed to embarrass Kenny, especially when she started snoring which drew laughs from the other patrons who may or may not have been on LSD at the time.

Rhona borrowed books from the library and headed home, pleased she was being proactive. She was still unsure science fiction would be the best way to present the visions but she felt it made sense as a start. The visions were about future events. However you write about that it surely comes across as science fiction.

At home she fixed herself a cheese sandwich and pondered which book to read first. She finally decided on *The Man in the*

High Castle and sat down and started on her research, confident this time she would come prepared to a subject.

After about an hour she had to put the book down. It wasn't because the book was boring her, which she had to admit it was a bit, but rather that it seemed to fail to inspire any creative spark. It came across as a standard story although one that happened to be set in an alternative timeline when the Nazis had won the war. Perhaps she just wasn't in the mood or perhaps she should have started with *2001* which she felt at least offered spaceships and the future which were more typical and expected elements for a science fiction book. Promising herself she would start *2001* the next morning over breakfast, she went to bed early.

That night her dream turned into a vision. The vision was like a dream. Afterwards, Rhona awoke, wide awake immediately, unsure what she had experienced. She had seen something. Glimpses. She had felt it. But what it had been she wasn't sure. It hadn't been like a blurry newsreel this time but something different. Something new. The vision was more of a story. Not an event but a roadmap.

A boy meets a stranded alien. An extra-terrestrial. For some reason that name was important. The alien is small with long fingers and made odd noises. They become friends and the boy tries to help the alien go home. The alien becomes ill and the boy saves the alien from bad government agents. They escape on bikes. They fly. An image comes to Rhona as she lay in bed and remembered it. The boy on his bike. The alien in the basket on the front of the bike covered by a sheet. They're flying. Silhouetted against a full moon.

What an image thought Rhona as she reached over to grab a pen and note paper to quickly write down what she had seen. What an image.

Andrew read the sheet of A4 and turned it over expecting to find more writing on the back. When he saw one side was all there was, he looked up at Rhona who sat waiting expectantly opposite him, her hands clasped tightly together on her lap.

'Interesting,' Andrew said carefully.

'Interesting? What does that mean? Interesting what?'

'Well it's…'

'What do you think of the story?'

'Okay well, I get the boy in Ireland who meets an alien who has been stranded on Earth. They befriend each other. Yes, all good.' Andrew quickly re-read sections of the page of A4 Rhona had handed him that morning at work. 'But then the alien and the boy go on a sort of quest to save Elvis Presley from… dying on the toilet.'

'Yes?'

'Well… That just comes across as odd. I'm sorry.'

'The alien has these visions of what will happen in the future which he puts in the boy's head. They're trying to save Elvis. What's odd about that? It's just science fiction isn't it?'

'Well, apart from being strangely specific about the nature of Elvis Presley's death don't you think of all the things the alien could have seen or warned the boy about this is a bit... unimportant?'

'It's what the alien has seen. He doesn't get to choose what he sees.'

'Yes but... I mean, surely Elvis Presley and Colonel Parker might have something to say about all this if anything. You're basically saying Elvis is going to die on a toilet. It's undignified to say the least.'

'I can change his name but still make it obvious it's Elvis.'

'But why Elvis? And why a toilet?'

'The boy's mother loves Elvis.'

Andrew closed his eyes for a moment. Rhona smiled at his face, so serious and thoughtful.

'So, the boy is doing it for his mother?'

'Yes, I suppose so.'

'So this is what the book is really going to be about isn't it? A boy trying to please his mother. A boy wanting his mother's love perhaps?'

Rhona went quiet for a moment.

'You're very clever aren't you,' she said quietly.

She wrote the book in seven weeks. She called it Extra Terrestrial. Even working full-time, she managed a first draft in that period and shocked herself. It felt so easy. So enjoyable. So free. The other books had been like doing homework. Painful but necessary.

She got up an hour early each morning and worked then returned to the Olivetti when she got home at night from her day job. She didn't go out and stayed in at the weekends. By the end of it she had a book, a bin full of cigarette ends and a sore throat. Throughout this period, she said nothing to Andrew. He asked on occasion how it was going and whether she had read any of the books he had recommended to her, but her stock answer had been *it's coming along* and *I haven't had a chance to read any of the books yet.* Rhona felt guilty at his somewhat crestfallen expression after each of her confessions and promised herself she'd tackle at least one of the books soon. To please Andrew.

Seven weeks and four days later Andrew sat in her flat with the manuscript on his lap and an almost finished bottle of red wine on the table. Rhona sat cross-legged across from him half-drunk from the wine, waiting and watching intently, as he read the last few pages. She had made him come to her flat to read the last chapter. She wanted to see his expression when he finished. She had served him a dinner and opened wine when he had arrived. Her way of thanking him for the time he had given up reading her work.

She had made pork chops with green beans and new potatoes. They had not mentioned the book but talked about work and gossiped about their colleagues. Andrew seemed relaxed but she picked up a subtle nervous energy which she anticipated was the coming list of criticisms he had no doubt written on a carefully folded piece of paper he would produce at the right moment.

When they had finished eating, the conversation ceased as she produced the manuscript and Andrew read, as she had requested. Eventually he looked up and placed the book on the table. He took a sip of wine, thinking.

'Well? Put me out of my misery please?'

'It's… It's bloody good, Rhona. I mean that.'

Rhona clapped her hands together.

'You'd better not be lying.'

'I'm not. I'm being honest. I mean, there are some typos and I'd clean up a few bits but bloody hell, for someone who's never read any science fiction it's very good. So visual. The bit where they fly across the moon. I loved that bit. And the plot. It works. It does work. I thought, when you told me about Elvis or Ray as you've called him, dying like he does, I thought it wouldn't work but it does. Although I am positive whoever wants to publish this will probably want the toilet part changed. But that's just cosmetic. But it is good. So good. Sorry, am I going on?'

'You're making me go red.'

'Someone once told me to accept compliments because we don't get many. Well, I don't anyway.'

Rhona jumped up and put her arms around Andrew.

'Well I think you're brilliant. Thank you for your help. Your support. For reading it.'

She kissed Andrew on the lips. Andrew tensed up. Rhona, for a split second, froze. And then she kissed him again.

CHAPTER TEN

2001

AMY

Amy checked her emails to see if Andrew Hunter had sent a reply but found he hadn't. She closed her laptop and lit a cigarette and stared across her cluttered desk trying to decide on her next move, knowing he would not respond. She considered door-stepping him if she could find him but realised this would probably result in no cooperation at all. This wasn't what she wanted. That wasn't the kind of article she was after. At least not yet.

She leaned back in her chair and picked up the worn graphic novel that sat beside her and thought back to the morning she had arrived at the second-hand comic shop in Islington, beckoned by a friend of a friend to come and see what he had found. She leafed through its pages still amazed at what she was looking at, still unsettled on what it could mean. A piece of work that raised far too many frightening questions. And the only person who could answer them it seemed, was Rhona O'Shea.

CHAPTER ELEVEN

2019

JOE

Joe drove round to his mother's house in Winton. He managed to park outside which was rare owing to the large student numbers in the area who all seemed to own cars. Getting out of his vehicle he immediately realised why his Mum wasn't answering her phone. In the garden, he could hear the lawn mower in action. He let himself into her house with his own key, went out back, and waved. His Mum stopped mowing.

'Hello. Everything okay?'

'Eva was worried. She couldn't get through. I'll let her know you're okay.'

'Sorry. I've been out here all morning and can't hear the phone.'

'Do you want me to finish it off for you?'

'No, I'm fine. It won't take long'

'Do you want a cup of tea?'

'That would be lovely.'

Joe went back into the house and into the kitchen to boil the kettle. He texted his sister to let her know their mother was fine while waiting for the water to boil. He watched his seventy-year old mother through the window and reflected that she too had lived with a man who drank too much, and she too had left him.

That man had been Joe's father who Joe hadn't seen for many years. Joe rarely talked about him as it was hard to explain the kind of man he was to anyone outside the family. An Italian, an alcoholic, and a violent person who seemed to find a fault in everything and everyone. Someone who was angry at the world and ultimately at himself.

Joe thought of Lee. He drank too much but didn't seem the angry type. Maybe just the type not equipped with the skills to deal with the grief of losing two unborn children. The type who hoped for the best but failed to prepare for life's worst.

Joe and his mother had a cup of tea. He ended up staying for lunch and had scrambled eggs, beans and bacon. They spoke about his work, her garden, her book club and German lessons with the inevitable question of whether Joe had found a girlfriend yet. Joe told his mother, again, he had yet to find a girlfriend but hadn't given up trying. She seemed pleased and he was happy he had a close, strong relationship with his mother.

She had been through a lot when they had been younger and had looked after Joe and his two older siblings when things looked bleak. They had existed in poverty, mainly due to his father disappearing one day soon after their divorce, leaving lots of debts for Joe's mother to deal with.

After lunch Joe drove over to Lee's workplace which was a warehouse situated on the West Howe Industrial Estate. Lee worked for a sweet distribution company, sending out parcels and boxes to various sellers across the south. As far as Rose had understood it, he was just one of the guys who drove a forklift.

Joe found the place easily and parked up. This time he was determined to make a better go of things and appear like he knew what he was doing. He walked over to the warehouse feeling more confident. The shutter doors were up, and he could see various men, all in green jumpers and black trousers, going about their work carting boxes to and fro. As he walked in he got a few looks from some of the men but they soon turned away as though he wasn't there. He could smell the sweet aroma of the boxed-up sweets all around him. He paused inside and waited to catch someone's eye long enough until he couldn't be ignored.

'Can I help you?'

Joe turned to his left to see a man of about fifty-five stand there. He was in black trousers, a shirt, and black jumper.

'I'm looking for the manager.'

'I'm the manager.'

Joe held out his hand. 'Hi, my name's Joe Zuccu and I'm here to ask you about Lee Melis.'

The manager took his hand and shook it weakly. 'Sorry, what's your name?'

'Joe Zuccu.'

'Zuccu?'

'It's Italian. Well, Sardinian actually.'

'Zuccu. I've never heard of a name like that before.'

'Well, it's quite rare over here.'

'Zuccu. Sounds a bit like Zorro.'

'I used to get called Zorro when I was younger. Anyway, I'm here to talk about Lee Melis.'

'Lee Melis?'

'Yes. He's gone missing.'

'Are you a policeman?'

'No. Just a friend.'

'Are the police involved if he's gone missing?'

'No. Not yet. But that may change.'

'Well what do you want to know about him? You understand I can't give out any personal information if you're not a policeman?'

'I'm interested to find out who his friends are here. How he was? Have you spoken to him recently? I'm guessing he hasn't been in?'

Joe pulled his notebook and pen out.

'I haven't spoken to him for months,' said the manager.

Joe paused and looked up. 'For months? But he works here right?

'He did work here until I was forced to sack him.'

'You sacked him?'

'I had to.'

'Can I ask why?'

The manager hesitated. 'He came in drunk. You can't drive a forklift like that. You'll kill someone. I had no choice.'

Joe glanced around the warehouse.

'When? When was this?'

'February the fifteenth. I remember as it was the day after Valentine's night and I'd gone out with the wife.'

'Was that the first time Lee had been drunk at work?'

The manager looked around and crossed his arms. 'I shouldn't really be discussing this with you if I'm honest.'

'Okay I understand. I didn't know he had stopped working here. Are any of his friends around?'

'How about you write down your contact details and I'll ask the guys when they're on a break. I'll ask them to call you if they think they can help.'

'Thank you. I appreciate that.'

Joe wrote down his name and number.

'He was a nice bloke,' said the manager. 'I didn't want to sack him you understand, but if I'd let that go and kept it quiet, it could have come back on me if something had happened. Health and safety.'

'No, I get it.' Joe handed him his details. The manager smiled.

They shook hands and Joe left. He went back to his car and drove away. Once he was off the industrial estate he pulled over to the side of the road and got out his notebook and pen. He drew out a rough timeline that went backwards.

Three weeks ago was point one. Lee had disappeared with his phone turned off and no contact. Point two was a week before that when Samantha saw Lee after he'd been beaten up after being at the Six Bells Pub. Point three was two months prior to that when Rose had seen him for the last time on her birthday in June. He would need to get that exact date. Rose had said they had split up six weeks prior to that which put it around May. That was point four. Point five was Lee's sacking which was February. He guessed that tied in with Rose's miscarriage.

Joe put the notebook down. Lee hadn't worked since February so how could he afford the jewellery Rose said he came around with on her birthday? In fact, how could he afford anything unless he was surviving on benefits, but that still didn't explain the jewellery. He'd either stolen them, borrowed money, had some savings, or had another job. One he didn't tell anyone about. Joe called Rose. She picked up after four rings. He told her about Lee getting sacked back in February. She went silent. Joe waited.

'The fifteenth. I remember that. It was a couple of days after my miscarriage.'

Joe had been right.

'I'm sorry. Did Lee have any money stashed away or did you know if he had another job?'

'Lee had no savings. As far as I know he didn't have another job either. Do you know what the weird thing is? He never told me he got sacked and he still got up every day and went to work as normal then came home again in the evening. All that time he was lying. What sort of person does that?'

Joe didn't answer. He pictured her wiping a tear away. Or maybe she was just too resigned now for something like that. Maybe she was shocked but not all that surprised.

'You never sensed he may have been short of money?'

'No.'

'Okay. One last question. What date is your birthday?'

'Twelfth of June. Why?'

'I just need to make sure I got a proper timeline.'

'Sounds like you're getting organised.'

'I'm trying.'

'Well good luck with that.'

She said goodbye and hung up. Joe stared out through the windscreen sensing that finding Lee would involve answering a lot more questions.

He started up the car and drove to work for his late shift at the bar. Sergio was there and was in a talkative mood. He was around fifty years old and Portuguese. He liked to wear expensive white shirts with the top two buttons undone. His chest hair could be seen amongst the silver chains and crucifix he wore. As he spoke he would run his hand through his slicked back hair and today he was speaking fast.

Catalina was there and raised her eyebrows to Joe as Sergio complained about the quality of the food at some restaurant he'd been to in Poole, the town next to Bournemouth. Joe guessed Sergio had been snorting cocaine again. His eyes were glassy and hungry in the way he looked at Catalina.

With Joe now there though he couldn't be so obvious, so after his rant he went back to his office, probably to carve out another line on his desk and stare at the silent CCTV screens he had in there.

'You okay?' asked Catalina.

'Yeah, fine.'

'You look like you have something on your mind.'

He considered telling her all about Lee Melis but decided against it.

'I just slept badly last night.'

'Don't work too hard.'

She touched his cheek with her fingertips as she picked up her bag and went around the bar.

'See you soon.'

She left and didn't look back. Joe surveyed the bar. It would fill up soon, but for now, he just had his thoughts to entertain him. He glanced up at the security camera above the optics and speculated whether Sergio was watching him.

CHAPTER TWELVE

1975

RHONA

Polishing the novel took some time. Andrew helped, circling typos and possible improvements in grammar but made no comment on structure, plot or characters. He seemed to enjoy helping.

After the evening at Rhona's when he had finished reading her novel, he had stayed the night. Rhona was content to acknowledge they were now lovers. To herself she was also happy to admit he was the best lover she had ever had. Her love life up until that point had been uneventful. She had remained a virgin until more than six months of being in London and although not traumatised by the thought of sex, as so many of the girls she had known back in Ireland seemed to be, the reality of it had been less than stimulating when at last she experienced it.

Her first time had been with a young man called Tony who she met through her cousin. He had taken her to the cinema three times before suggesting they walk home one evening through the park. After kissing for some time and some awkward gropes, it seemed he could no longer hold on. He produced a condom and romantically suggested they 'do it'. She had considered saying no but decided this may be the time to finally experience what she had heard so much about. And so Rhona found herself losing her virginity under a rhododendron tree.

The experience lasted under a minute. Afterwards, Tony lay panting alongside her like he had run a marathon. Over a period of four weeks they had sex three more times under different trees in the park before Rhona decided she'd had enough of looking up at branches and leaves. She finished with him as gently as she could but not gently enough for him to not break down in tears and tell her he loved her.

Her second lover had initially seemed to have more potential. He was called Pete and said he had been in the army. He was older, nearly thirty, and said he had travelled a lot and had been all over the world when he was a soldier. They had met when Rhona had started at the paper and she had gone to lunch in a nearby café where he chatted her up.

He worked at Covent Garden Market, which had recently relocated to Nine Elms, where he stacked fruit and veg all day. It had improved his physique if not his conversation. When they made love they did it in a bed, always at her flat which should have rung alarm bells. His member, Rhona recalled, looked like it had run into some French doors whilst excited and had been bent out of shape, like a plant always desperately angling for the sun.

They saw each other for about three months before he confessed that he was married. Rhona should have walked away then but didn't. What did make her finish their relationship was when they got into a discussion on immigration one night in a pub and he happily advocated 'kicking all the pakis out' and revealed he supported the National Front. She got up and left much to his surprise. He tried to call her a few times but Rhona always hung up on him and he gave up in the end.

Her third and final lover before Andrew had been called Ralph. They had met about a year ago at a birthday party for a member of staff. Ralph worked in finance somewhere in the city and was a brother of one of the husbands of one of the secretaries. He had apparently come to the party against his will when he visited his sibling that evening, having got it confused with the next day, and then been forced to come along.

An overly complicated set up it was, but that is how fate sometimes works, thought Rhona. They chatted over cheese and onion crisps, and warm cider until Ralph suggested they 'ditch the party' for somewhere quieter. Rhona smiled and they ended up in an empty bar down the road.

Rhona enjoyed his company. He made her laugh. They started seeing each other. He was fun, easy going, and intelligent. He tried to introduce her to fine dining and high culture, symbols that in his mind befitted his salary whilst she tutored him on repressive Catholic practices and beliefs, and beans on toast. He often took her to eat in the West End and shunned Soho for being too common and shady.

She told him she wanted to be a writer and talked about her books. He seemed interested but asked no questions. She let him read the first few chapters of her last effort which he politely did but offered no critique or encouragement.

'I'm not much of a reader if truth be told,' he said.

Rhona left it at that. It was after this exchange that Rhona began to notice Ralph was far happier talking about himself and what he thought than about anything else. The tendency had been there all along, Rhona realised, but she had just chosen to ignore it. He would talk at you but not with you, and whilst he had an opinion on everything if you ventured any thought to a subject, he would give a condescending look and continue with whatever his viewpoint was as if you had not even spoken. Rhona, against her better judgment, continued seeing him even though slowly, and very slowly it was, he ground down her self-esteem.

He was an energetic lover though and Rhona was content in their relationship, in a self-denying kind of way, until one day a few months after they had been seeing each other they met for lunch and he finished with her. He said it wasn't working as he held her hands across a table. Rhona asked what wasn't working and he shrugged and told her she just 'wasn't the one'.

She should have gone home, cried, and been heartbroken. She should have gone into one of her funks. She should have been in love with him. But she neither cried or was heartbroken. Or was in love. A little let down would be how she would have described her feelings. A few days later she berated herself for even going out with him in the first place.

Andrew, meanwhile, was proving promising. He was a generous lover, happy to give her pleasure rather than satisfying his own needs, which surprised Rhona. One night they lay in bed listening to the rain outside.

'Do you mind if I ask you something?' asked Rhona.

'Ask away.'

'How many women have you been with?'

'Two, not including you.'

'Two? Is that all?'

'What did you expect? Sorry, I have let you down for not sleeping with more women or something?'

'No, it's just you seem to know what you're doing. Which is no complaint I should add.'

'Well thank you. I had a good teacher.'

Rhona frowned. Andrew smiled.

'I might as well tell you. My first… encounter… was with a friend of my mother's.'

'What?'

'Yes, I know. Sounds awful. Very Mrs Robinson I know.'

'How old were you?'

'Seventeen. Old enough but still… too young for her. She taught me everything I know.'

'My God. What about the second person? It wasn't another of your mother's pals was it?'

'No. No. Just a girl. A girl my age. One night. One drunken night.'

'You're a dark horse.'

Andrew laughed. '*I'm* a dark horse? So?'

'So what?'

'So, I throw the question back at you.'

'Three.'

'Three?'

'Three.'

'Hmm.'

Together they got Rhona's book to a stage where she was happy to send it out to agents. Using *The Writers' and Artists' Yearbook* she selected five agents and sent off the required first four chapters and short biographies, or whatever they asked for, and waited.

Seven weeks and three rejections later Rhona received a letter from an agent called Shirley Verne requesting the entire book. Another four weeks went by and then Rhona received a second letter from Shirley Verne requesting she contact her office to arrange a meeting regarding her manuscript. Rhona called from the phone box at the end of her street whilst an impatient elderly lady with blue hair waited outside. Rhona spoke to Shirley Verne's secretary and arranged to see her that Friday at 10am.

'Well done,' said Andrew with genuine warmth when Rhona told him.

'I'm nervous. I've never got this far before.'

'She must be interested so be positive. It's a good thing. Shirley Verne represents Dan Mills you know.'

'Who's Dan Mills?'

'A leading science fiction writer. One of the reasons you, we… me selected her to send your book to.'

'Oh right.'

'For Christ's sake, please pretend you know who he is at least, if she asks.'

'I will. Don't worry.'

Rhona expected Shirley's office to be awash with manuscripts with heaps of unpublished novels on her desk. Instead she was shown into a large, tidy, clean and rather sparse office with windows overlooking Cavendish Square Gardens near Oxford Street. Shirley, a smartly dressed woman in her late forties with strong blue eyes, got up from behind her desk to meet her as the secretary made the introductions and left.

'Do sit down, please.'

Rhona sat at the desk. Shirley sat back on her seat and picked up Rhona's book.

'I like this. That's why you're here.'

'Thank you.'

'How long have you been writing?'

'All my life.'

'Just science fiction?'

'No, various types of stories. But this one I'm most proud of.'

'You've found your voice.'

'Sorry?'

Shirley began flicking through Rhona's manuscript.

'Sometimes a writer needs to write for a while before they can express themselves in their own voice. Often a new writer copies another style or another writer. So, what do you do Rhona?'

'I work for the London Irish Daily.'

'You're a journalist. That's fantastic.'

'Well, I'm sort of a journalist.'

Shirley looked up.

'This book. Tell me about it.'

Rhona didn't know what to say.

'It's about an alien who tells the boy about the future.'

'And they try to save Elvis. I know he's called Ray in here but it's modelled on Elvis, correct?'

'Yes.'

'Why did you not just call him Elvis? It's so obvious it's him.'

'In case he sues me or something.'

'In case Elvis Presley sues you? If he did that you would sell a lot more books I can tell you. But Elvis won't sue you. I very much doubt he will read this and nor will anyone in his team. Don't take that the wrong way.'

'You mentioned selling books. Is that a hypothetical situation?'

'In what way?'

'Well, why am I here I suppose? Do you like the book?'

'Yes I do.'

'So do you think you can get it published?'

'Yes. But it needs some work. The dying on the actual toilet will have to go. Too vulgar me thinks. But I want you to meet Monty. He's a book editor. He edits all of Dan Mills' books. Have you read Dan Mills?'

'Yes, of course.'

'Which is your favourite of his out of interest?'

'Erm… The last one.'

'Really? Hmm. Anyway, Monty will work with you to polish it up and then leave it with me. Monty is very good at his job. His real name is Robert, which you must call him by the way. Not Monty. That's what people in the office call him. He fought in the war and sometimes it feels like he's still fighting it.'

'So you're taking me on as a client?'

'I am.'

Rhona smiled and felt warm inside.

'I forgot to ask,' said Shirley. 'Would you like a tea or coffee?'

'She made you a cup of tea?'

'Not her but she offered me one. That's my point. It was nice. It's usually me doing that when I'm here,' Rhona said, waving her hand around the *London Irish Daily* office.

Andrew sat at his desk holding a mug of coffee with both hands. Rhona had her usual position, perched on his desk, clutching a file in case anyone senior should come by so she could jump off and pretend to be working.

'So what else did you talk about?'

'My life in Ireland. She seemed interested in that. My influences, so I said I loved Kurt Vonnegut and Arthur C. Clarke. They're the only two sci-fi authors I could remember.'

Andrew gripped his mug just that bit tighter.

'Science fiction writers,' he said.

'Yeah, that's what I meant. And I told her I was making this book part of a trilogy.'

'What?'

'She asked me what I was working on next. I could hardly say nothing.'

'You could have done.'

'But I wanted to sound prolific. She loved it. Thought it was a great idea.'

'You'll be busy then.'

'Yeah, I suppose I will. I meet this Monty fella Thursday evening too. He's the book editor. Edits all the books for that Dan Mills you were talking about. And you were right, she doesn't want Elvis dying on the toilet.'

'Are we still on for tomorrow? Dinner?'

She got off his desk. 'Oh yeah. I forgot. Sure. See you later.'

Rhona walked off humming. She stopped and turned back to him.

'Something else I forgot too. Shirley wants me to go back to using Elvis Presley as the singer in the book. Not Ray.'

'Why?'

'Because he might sue me.'

Rhona walked off. Andrew turned back to his desk, suddenly feeling uneasy. Nothing ever stays the same, he reminded himself.

'That's the fucking problem with the youth of today. They don't know they're alive.'

Rhona loved listening to Monty talk. His voice was like an actor out of a Noel Coward film. Very English. Very posh. When he swore it sounded illicit, exciting and shocking. Like someone who spoke like that should be seeing married women off on trains with repressed feelings of love for them that he just couldn't articulate. In black and white. Certainly not saying 'fuck' a lot.

Monty, or Robert as Rhona kept having to remind herself to call him, was a tall, thin man in his fifties. He smoked a pipe and paced the office whilst Rhona sat dutifully at the desk with her manuscript before her. Red circles, lines and notes dotted the pages as Robert had already made his mark, and drawn blood with the thin rouge felt-tip he used. Now he was explaining to Rhona why young people shouldn't stay in and smoke pot but get out more. It transpired that he had a son who stayed in a lot. And never went out. And smoked pot.

'I mean, in my day we were all boozing. That or killing fucking Germans or Japs. But we got out, breathed in some fresh air once in a while. He doesn't even open the fucking windows. Anyway, where were we?'

'Chapter four.'

'Right.'

And that's how it went on. Rhona would come to Monty's office for an hour or so in the evenings and they would work slowly through the book, with regular breaks so Monty could swear profusely and complain about his son, and then Rhona would go away and rewrite that section. They got on well. Only once did they have a disagreement.

'I don't like the ending.'

'What don't you like about it?'

'They go to Las Vegas to warn Elvis that he needs to look after his health but they don't succeed. Elvis, who in your book is addicted to drugs, eats awful food, and just seems to go through the motions of these shows he is paid so well for, then just dies on the fucking toilet. I mean, bloody hell.'

'That's what happens.'

'Rather depressing though. It's not the toilet part, which we have agreed on we'll change, but why not let him be saved? Let him see the light, and the boy and the alien have then succeeded. Touch more upbeat to say the least don't you think?'

'But that's not what happens. He does die on the toilet.'

Monty gave her a funny look she couldn't read and puffed on his pipe. He looked away.

'Well at least have him die in the bath or something. Let him have his dignity at least.'

In three months they had completed a new polish and handed it over to Shirley to inspect.

'Go away and do something else for a while. I'll call you when I have something,' said Shirley.

Rhona went away.

About a month later Rhona and Andrew went to the cinema. They saw *Young Frankenstein*. Andrew laughed, guffawed, and sniggered all the way through it. Rhona hadn't seen the Universal Pictures *Frankenstein* or *Bride of Frankenstein* so many of the jokes were lost on her. So she didn't laugh so much. They went back to her flat afterwards, had satisfactory sex, and fell asleep.

Rhona dreamed that night. A dream that turned into a vision.

A bracelet. A pretty silver bracelet with crystals studded around it. A pretty silver bracelet on a woman. A naked woman in bed. She's making love. To another woman. The other woman moves her face. We can see her now. It is Rhona.

Rhona woke up. Troubled, unsettled and tense. She got up and fetched water from the tap in the kitchenette. The vision had been a vision. Not a dream. She knew that. But it wasn't the fact that she was sleeping with a woman that had really shocked her but that she herself was in the vision too. Rhona had never had a vision that had predicted her own future before. Up until now. She went back to bed and lay awake as dawn came.

Over breakfast she was quiet. Andrew sat opposite her and they ate toast and drank sugary tea. Andrew spoke about *Young Frankenstein* and she said little. Just as they had almost finished Andrew suddenly went quiet, reached into his jacket pocket then pulled out a notebook and pen. He scribbled away.

'What are you doing?' asked Rhona.

'I had an idea. I didn't want to forget it.'

'For what?'

'My book.'

'Your book?'

Andrew looked up.

'I did tell you. I've been working on my own book haven't I.'

Rhona tried to remember. Maybe he had mentioned it.

'I must have forgotten,' she said with a vague feeling of guilt now making itself felt.

Andrew nodded and went back to his notebook which made Rhona feel even more guilty.

He's just too fucking nice, she thought. And now she was sounding like Monty.

The telephone rang.

Rhona rose and went to get it. Andrew stayed seated but looked up at her and watched her talk to whoever it was on the telephone. He suddenly felt like weeping but didn't know why.

Rhona hung up and came back to the table. Her face was flushed.

'What?' asked Andrew, alarmed and preparing himself for bad news, possibly a family death.

'My book is going to be published. Shirley has signed a deal.'

CHAPTER THIRTEEN

1999

MANDY

Mandy awoke and took a few seconds to realise there was someone in the bed with her. It made her immediately bright eyed and on alert until she realised *that* someone was Joe Zuccu and it was her bed. He was still fast asleep.

She glanced around her bedroom and saw the mess of clothes scattered across the floor. Images flooded back from the night before of how they had both stumbled into her bedroom, undressed each other hastily, fumbling for belts and shirt buttons and bra straps, desperate not to lose the momentum that had started by her front door and led directly here within seconds. Joe had struggled whilst trying to fit the condom and Mandy helped as best she could and then they had quick, drunken sex. Afterwards they had smoked cigarettes and talked about something but she couldn't remember what it was.

She got out of bed and headed for the shower. She realised the only reason she felt so sprightly was that the alcohol was still probably sloshing around inside her and the inevitable hangover had yet to kick in. Whilst she washed she heard music come on but couldn't work out what it was until she came out. It was the Big Daddy Kane album *It's a Big Daddy Thing*. When she got back to her room Joe had his jeans on and was looking through her CD collection.

'You've got some good stuff here,' he said.

'That was Luc's music. I've got what he had on cassette, but I also got the CD in case it screwed up in a tape deck.'

Joe nodded. Luc had been an old friend of theirs who had died in a car crash years before back in Bournemouth.

'How you feeling?' she asked as she dried herself.

'Bit shit,' said Joe, watching her.

'So what the fuck happened last night? Did we have sex?'

'Er, yeah.'

'I don't remember.'

Mandy waited just enough time for Joe to look a bit crestfallen and then smiled.

'Had you there didn't I? Why don't you have a shower?'

Joe smiled back weakly and headed for the bathroom.

'Sorry,' she called after him. 'I couldn't resist it.'

After Joe's shower and after they had sex again, this time slower and far more satisfying, Mandy fried eggs in the kitchen. Joe sat at the table facing the window which looked out to the train platform at Tooting overground station.

'When I sit there in the morning I notice the same people stand in the same place on the platform. They must notice the same people too but they never seem to talk to each other,' said Mandy.

Joe shrugged. 'I guess that's living in a city for you.'

'Do you think that's what happens? You live here long enough and you just stop noticing other people?'

'Maybe they've already got enough friends so they don't have to talk to random people on train platforms.'

'That's not fair. I want to be the weirdo who strikes up conversations with people I don't know. Especially on tube trains where you sit and face people and everyone averts their eyes.'

'At least you'd get a carriage to yourself then.'

They ate egg on toast with orange juice and enjoyed a comfortable silence. Mandy was glad her two flatmates were both out and she had Joe to herself. She watched him devour the breakfast.

'Have you got any plans for the rest of the day?'

Joe shook his head. 'Nope.'

'Fancy a wander round Tooting?'

Joe nodded. 'Sounds good.'

They headed up to Tooting Broadway and made their way around the two indoor markets. Mandy took her camera and snapped Joe as he walked along. It was a second-hand Pentax and she loved the feel of the silver metal body. Joe stopped and smiled awkwardly by a stall selling plastic tubs. Mandy realised they were both still sizing each other up, each wondering whether the night before had been a one off or a start of something potentially more serious.

'They're going to be ones to put on the wall,' he said drily.

They had lukewarm coffee in the Castle, tempted to both have a pint but feeling it was too early, then had lunch over the road at Lahore Karahi where they both had spicy biryanis and talked about old friends back in Bournemouth, their hometown.

They had met up at a birthday party in Brixton the night before and ended up at the Bug Bar. Neither had known the other would be there or that they both lived in London. Drunk and on the dance floor they had danced together as sweat dripped off the ceiling and they came out with their T-shirts clinging to themselves. Whilst everyone tried to find taxis and night buses they had ended up snogging outside the Ritzy and jumping into an illegal cab back to Tooting. The driver was a middle Eastern guy who couldn't stop talking as he chewed on Khat. He even offered them some but they politely declined.

Mandy lifted her camera up and took a photo of Joe as he watched people walk past outside.

'This is the perfect place for you. You can watch people all day from here,' she said.

The restaurant had glass walls on two sides so you could see the whole street depending on where you sit.

'What do you mean?' he asked.

'You like to sit and watch. Like the train station at mine. You were mesmerised.'

'You're the one with the camera.'

'But I like to get in people's faces.'

'Is that how you're going to make your millions then? Be a photographer?'

Earlier they had talked about their ambitions. Joe was working in Waterstones but had his sights on bar work and wanted to own his own place. He mentioned he had spent part of his childhood in his dad's restaurant, but those places were full of 'alcoholics and perfectionists'.

Mandy meanwhile was torn. She had come to the city over three years ago, like most people, to escape their small towns and limited ambitions. She loved being in a place where you didn't have to queue behind a row of people all buying *The Daily*

Mail. And now she was here she was confused at what to do. She was working in GAP in Covent Garden at the moment which was great to be in the centre of things but it wasn't a career or at least the career she wanted. She didn't answer his question and they finished their food.

Two weeks later Joe called and said he had tickets to see The Charlatans at Brixton Academy. *Did she want to come?* Mandy didn't hesitate in deciding and they met at the Prince of Wales pub on Coldharbour Lane.

The last time they had been together Joe had gone back to West Norwood after their lunch in Tooting. He was sharing a flat with two other guys and said he hated the area. It was only on an overground line and he felt cut off from places. He said that nothing ever went on in West Norwood. After he had left, Mandy spent the rest of the day mulling over Joe. He was quiet but in a confident way that made you wonder what he was thinking about. She hadn't really known him back in Bournemouth and he had been one of many in a large social circle of people who met at various clubs and bars by chance. She remembered him hanging outside McDonalds in the town centre years before when they had been about fourteen and recalled his red Chipie jeans and curly hair.

Since they had last seen each other he had called her twice and she had called him once. She was too careful to suggest they meet up when they had spoken and she got the sense they both had played it cool. Mandy was beginning to think Joe had just been a one-night stand and the calls would eventually end then they would go their separate ways.

The phone call out of the blue about tickets to see a band had, she realised, cheered her up, more so than she had expected. In the pub they both had a couple of pints and then headed down to the Academy and past the ticket touts. The place was packed and the crowd keen for a good night. The band were on a high with a new album just released. Joe had already got the album titled *Us and Us Only* and was familiar with the new songs that were going down well with their loyal fans. By the time the band started singing "North Country Boy" they were both dancing along with everyone else in the venue. Afterwards they went back to her flat and had sex. As they both lay in bed afterwards, Joe turned to her.

'So, would you go out with me?'

Mandy laughed.

'Yeah alright. Nothing better to do.'

CHAPTER FOURTEEN

1976

RHONA

Gracelands

Memphis

Tennessee

United States of America

13th May 1976

Dear Mr Presley,

I hope you are well. It has taken me some time to try and work out how I should word this letter as I am sure you are expecting a fan letter of sorts. I'm sure you get thousands of letters from fans and so you should. You are an amazing singer and singers today are not a patch on you. However, I am not writing to tell you how good you are.

Instead I am writing to warn you. This is not a threat as that wouldn't be very nice but a warning that your health is in danger. If I'm honest Mr Presley, you need to lose weight and eat healthily. I know you take a lot of pills that you say are helping you but deep down we both know that isn't true. If you maintain your current lifestyle then I'm afraid you will not survive.

I know that sounds awful but I have a certain skill in seeing things that happen and I've seen you take a tumble in your bathroom and you don't get up. I don't want to get into too much detail, but please trust me Elvis, if I can call you Elvis. I know you like to sing the song "If I Can Dream" and I've had a dream about you which ends badly and that is why I am writing this. I've been having it for a while now too, all the way back to when I saw you with Ann-Margret in *Viva Las Vegas*, which was a wonderful film. Get healthy Elvis and stop taking those pills before it is too late.

Yours very sincerely,

R

CHAPTER FIFTEEN

2019

JOE

Mike sat at the dining table sipping the Americano that Joe had just made him. He had already done his morning boxing classes and was now home, showered and hungry. Joe had slept in after another late shift, and over breakfast, had shared with Mike what he was up to in regards to locating Lee Melis. Mike had known Lee from years before as well although he'd never been a keen clubber. Back then he was like he was now; down at the gym, training, keeping fit and boxing.

'Maybe he's just done a runner. Gone off to London perhaps. Made a new start.'

'Then I'm never going to find him.'

'You getting paid for this?'

'I just said I'd ask around as a favour.'

'What the flip? You're doing this for nothing?'

Joe loved how Mike tried so hard not to swear. With two young children, he was keen never to use bad language around them although he would happily take them to the gym so they could watch their dad box someone's lights out in the ring. When they had first started sharing a house Mike had even introduced a swear jar to encourage Joe to tone down his language. He insisted Joe contribute one pound every time he swore when his children were over. Having lost almost ten pounds Joe found he had actually stopped swearing.

'I'm not really doing much and it doesn't look like I'm going to find him anyway. Better if she saved up and got a proper private detective involved or the police.'

'You sure she's not just making up the bit about Lee asking for you? That just sounds weird.'

Joe thought about this. He hadn't considered Samantha could be lying to him in desperation to find her brother. Maybe she had said the same thing to various people around town who had known him, and now dotted around Bournemouth were a lot of confused old ravers having the same conversation. But it just didn't add up.

'No, she's being straight up.'

'I wonder who beat him up then?'

'That's what I need to find out.'

Mike leaned back in his chair and folded his thick arms.

'I need to ask you a question.'

'What?'

'How do you make your Spaghetti Bolognese again?'

'You mean my ragu?'

'Ragu. Whatever. Run it through with me again?'

'Why?'

'That time you made it for the kids they loved it so I want to do it your way.'

'Won't taste the same.'

'Well I want to try.'

'Okay. You fry up some celery, carrot and onion. That's called the *soffritto*. Let it fry in olive oil for a while on a low heat, and when it's soft, you add some lamb mince.'

'Not beef?'

'I prefer lamb but use what you want.'

'Okay.'

'So you fry the mince and just as it all goes brown, spoon off the fat and add one can of passata. Give it a stir then season with sea salt. Be generous. Don't use table salt. It won't be as nice. Add half a teaspoon of sugar. Then add some tomato puree and some garlic.'

'You don't fry the garlic?'

'No. You don't need to and you run the risk of it burning. Just add it in after. And that's it. You can add a bay leaf if you want or some mushrooms but I like it like that. Then you let it bubble softly for a while. I like to put a lid on it and keep the heat on low for a bit. But leave it as long as you want or can.'

'I saw a program once and they don't us garlic, passata, or even spaghetti in Bologna when they make it.'

Joe sighed.

'That's the way they make their ragu in Bologna. I make it how my Nonna made it in Sardinia. Every place is different. Spaghetti Bolognese is not an Italian dish. It's a version of ragu called Spaghetti Bolognese probably invented by some Englishman or enterprising but desperate Italian.

'Imagine some Italian came over here and had a fry up in Birmingham that had black pudding. He then goes home and comes up with a dish called Bristol Fry-Up which every Italian thinks that's how every single English person has their fry-ups, especially in Bristol where the guy never even visited. Then imagine an Italian having that fry-up and then tasting yours and telling you you've got it all wrong because you're not using black pudding. You try to explain that everyone and every area has their own version of a decent fry-up. Like you said, they don't even eat Spaghetti Bolognese in Bologna. It's rubbish.'

'Wow, you're quite passionate about this.'

'Just call it ragu.'

Joe walked down to the Six Bells Pub. He'd left Mike at the house making ragu. He didn't want to stand over his shoulder and back seat cook. He knew he would if he had stayed. Joe did most of the cooking if he and Mike were in together which he didn't mind in the least and Mike certainly never complained. Mike himself was more of a traditional and conservative cook who stuck closely to conventional English recipes, so when it was his turn in the kitchen, Joe would invariably be offered sausage and chips, or chicken and potatoes. Joe didn't mind this at all, and because of his boxing, Mike did eat healthily. He was keen to ensure he got a lot of carbs and protein which was one of the main reasons he liked Joe's pasta dishes.

As he came down the hill the Six Bells came into view. Although it was the closest pub to his house, he hadn't been in it for years. He had spent a lot of his youth in this bar, playing on the pool tables and drinking with friends. Through the years it had a number of refits and make-overs with its latest look matching a lot of the other bars in Bournemouth with an almost shabby chic aesthetic meets Edwardian interior. It had a kind of upmarket Weatherspoon's feel with more expensive prices. The purple paint on the exterior certainly didn't work.

Joe entered and had a look around before approaching the bar. The place was almost full. It was a Saturday afternoon and a Premier League football match played on the screens. Pint glasses had begun to stack up on tables as the staff busily served customers and delivered food, hoping for a small reprieve before the evening crowd began to arrive and fill the pub further.

Back in the nineties the pub had still been divided into two sections – with the sports bar on the left and the more refined, carpeted section to the right. Nowadays it was all one, although one end retained a sports bar feel with the pool tables and Cherries shirts on the walls.

Sadly, Joe thought, the place still looked like every other bar owned by a major brewery and this was one of the things Joe missed from London. Individuality. Like the high streets that only featured well known branded shops that could be found on every other high street up and down the country, the British pub was also a victim of this mediocre make over serving the same beers with the same food in the same interior designed spaces. There were smaller ale houses popping up now in the town so Joe generally held off trying to come across as the clichéd grumpy old man he feared he might become. For now at least. Maybe there was hope yet.

At the bar Joe waited for service and shortly a tall, well-built barman came his way. Joe ordered a coke and pulled the photo of Lee, that Samantha had left him, out of his pocket. He held it up to the barman. 'Don't suppose you remember this bloke do you?'

The barman glanced at the photo of Lee. He tried to hide the recognition that flickered across his face as he shook his head.

'Sorry mate. Never seen him before.'

Joe kept the photo up. 'You sure? He used to drink in here.'

The barman finished pouring Joe's coke and placed it on the bar in front of him. Joe handed him a five-pound note. 'Never seen him mate. Sorry.'

'He's gone missing. He was reportedly in this pub a short time before his disappearance. Reports are he had been beaten up.'

He watched the barman get his change from the till. The guy was nervous, maybe figuring Joe as a policeman. He kept up the act.

'We have witnesses who say he was here.'

Joe looked up at the security camera above the bar just long enough for the barman to follow his eye-line. The barman came back and handed Joe his change. He stood back and puffed out his chest and gave Joe a hard *don't fuck with me* stare. Joe looked at him and pondered whether he was straining his muscles in the hope they'd show through his shirt. He wondered how long he could keep it up and whether he was holding his breath. Eventually he had to breathe.

'You're not a policeman, are you?' asked the barman.

'Nope.'

'Then why you trying to sound like one?'

Joe took a sip of his drink regretting wearing his Lacoste polo shirt. Caught out he decided to be honest. 'I'm just trying to find a friend.'

'Like I said, I've never seen him.'

This time he gave Joe a look like he'd be happy to fight him if he had a problem accepting this last statement. He rested his arm on the beer taps. Nice and casual like at any minute he'd grab Joe and suffocate him with his gym toned, protein shake muscles. Joe took another sip of coke and put the glass on the bar. He smiled at the barman as sincerely as he could and put a card down in front of him. He had written out a few earlier. They had Joe's name, number and email on it. A poor man's business card.

'If you remember anything then just call.'

He walked out. At the door, he glanced back and saw the barman throwing the card into the bin.

He walked on to his mum's house as he had been invited for lunch and used the opportunity to think. The Six Bells used to be a rough pub that had made an effort in the last few years to move towards more respectability. Like most pubs nowadays they were probably struggling financially so getting away from a reputation of violence and rowdiness was in their interests. They did food, ales and had big TV screens for football and other sporting events. Nothing unusual.

But that barman had recognised Lee. So there was a good chance Lee had been in there the day he was beaten up. Otherwise why deny it?

Was he beaten up there or outside though, Joe asked himself.

The CCTV may have caught the fight and if not the pub was on a main road so there would've been witnesses.

He left these thoughts to simmer as he knocked on his mum's door. She was pleased to see him and he went in, savouring the familiar, comforting smell of his old home. His sister Eva was there, reading a magazine in the lounge whilst her son, Luca played in the garden.

'You look well,' she said, getting up and kissing him on the cheek.

'How you been?'

'Okay. What about you?'

'Same old.'

'What you been up to?'

Joe sat down. 'A few things.' His mum came in with a cup of tea. He told them about Lee and how he was looking for him. He could see the quizzical looks on their faces as he told them what he had done so far.

Eva shifted in her seat, her legs bent underneath her with the magazine resting on her lap. 'But why are you looking for him? You said you didn't really know him?'

'He was good to me once when I was younger. Helped me out. I felt I owed him.'

'Sounds like this is something the police should be dealing with to be honest, Joe. Don't get involved if there might be trouble,' his mum said with characteristic concern.

'But it's interesting. I'm bored just working at the bar.'

Joe sipped his tea knowing he'd summed up how he had been feeling for a while. He *was* bored just working in a bar. He told people he had come back to Bournemouth because he wanted to save up for a deposit for a house.

With the high rents in the capital city this had made sense at the time. That had been what he'd said anyway if they asked. The real reason was one Joe hid from everyone and sometimes from himself as well. A failed relationship had eventually sent him scurrying home, but he didn't like to think about that and preferred the excuse of house prices which was a great way to deflect any more interest. No one could afford to buy a property anymore.

But moving out of a vibrant, cosmopolitan city where you have lived for almost twenty years and returning to a somewhat inward looking, seaside town had taken readjustment. He still missed the buzz of London. He was bored.

'Be careful then.'

'I will mum.'

They had lunch. His mum had made a roast. Afterwards they all took a walk along the beach. When he got home he cooked mushroom spaghetti for himself and Mike. Mike could never understand how Joe could have a roast dinner and then have a plate of pasta later on. In Mike's eyes one large meal a day was plenty. He would happily make do with a sandwich for tea after a cooked lunch. Joe saw it as an Italian thing. If he could, he would quite happily have a three-course lunch and a three-course dinner every day.

With an empty plate and a glass of Barolo in front of him, Joe picked up the box he had taken from Rose's house and put it on the table. He found the notebook with the phone numbers in it and flicked through it once again. And then he stopped. Something caught his eye.

He flipped back to a blank page and saw it. The page was indented where someone had written something on the previous page that had since been ripped out leaving the imprint that Joe was now staring at.

Joe got up and grabbed a pencil then came back. He had seen this done in some old black and white film once. Probably a

Charlie Chan movie or one of those Sherlock Holmes films with Basil Rathbone. He remembered repeating the trick as a kid and being surprised it actually worked.

He gently moved the side of the pencil across the imprint to reveal writing. It was an address. Joe felt a childlike excitement. He wondered if they still taught this to new police recruits. He held up the page. The address had a BH24 postcode. Using Google maps on his phone this told him it was an address in Ringwood, a small town just outside Bournemouth. Interesting. It might be nothing but it might be everything. Joe put the page to one side.

He flipped to the three mobile numbers scrawled by Lee Melis and called the first one.

It rang to the answerphone and without a personal 'please leave a message after the beep' recording. Joe said he was looking for Lee Melis. He left his number and asked whoever it was to call back. He moved down to the second number and punched in the digits. It rang four times and was answered.

'Hello?' It was a man. Possibly a southern accent or nearby.

'Hi, my name is Joe Zuccu and I'm phoning as I'm looking for Lee Melis. He had your number.'

There was a short pause as though his voice had to bounce off one satellite dish too many.

'Lee Melis?'

'Yes, do you know him?'

'I do. Why are you looking for him?'

Joe grabbed his pad and pen.

'I'm working for his sister. Lee has gone missing. I'm trying to find him.'

'Missing?'

'When was the last time you saw him?'

'Oh… A while ago. I didn't know he'd gone missing.'

'Could I ask you to confirm your name please?'

'It's Tom Martin.'

Joe wrote the name down.

'And could you tell me how you know Lee?'

Another pause. 'You're not a policeman then?'

Joe closed his eyes. He needed to work on his patter. Get the questions in sooner before people had time to think and begin to question his motives.

Joe would have been the same though, he thought. Don't trust anyone. He hoped not everyone was like him.

'No, I'm not. I'm a private investigator.' That was technically true. He was *investigating* Lee's disappearance *privately*. He would have to Google whether you needed a licence to be a private eye in England though or whether that was just in America or even just in the movies.

'I met him at the AA meetings.'

'Alcoholics Anonymous?'

'Yeah. You didn't know he went?'

'No I didn't.' Joe wrote down AA.

'He showed up a few months ago. We became friendly. We swapped numbers but I think Lee began to drink heavily again because he stopped coming to the meetings. The last time I saw him he looked pretty ill.'

'So when was that?'

'Oh ages ago. Two months maybe?'

'The last time you saw Lee was at a meeting?'

'Yeah. He was…. fucked.'

'Is there anyone you know who might know where Lee has gone?'

'No, not really. I only knew him through the AA. He might have gotten to know some other people there but he was quiet you know. Hardly spoke. Fighting his own demons like us all.'

'Yeah. How come you got friendly with him?'

'I don't know. We used to go and have a fag together. We got talking. Can I ask who you are?'

'My name is Joe Zuccu.'

'Okay. Great. Is there anything else you need to ask me? I'm a bit busy.'

'Not at the minute but I may call back if that's alright?'

'Sure and if I hear anything then I'll let you know. I hope he turns up.'

'So do I. Thanks for your help.'

They said goodbye and ended the call. Joe sipped his wine. Two months since Lee's last AA meeting. That would have put it around the time of Rose's birthday when Lee tried to shower her with expensive jewellery in an attempt to win her back. She said no and he never, it seemed, went back to AA.

Joe called the third number. On the second ring it was answered.

'Yeah?' said an irritated male voice.

'Hi, I'm looking for Lee Melis and he had your number.'

'Don't know him mate.'

'Well, could you tell me…'

Joe heard the other person hang up. He went to redial but stopped. He needed to start thinking a bit more long-term and strategically if he was going to do this properly. He was going to wait. He had the phone number. Joe figured the guy knew who Lee Melis was. He copied the numbers down in his notebook and decided he needed to start putting together a proper report with what he had been doing to give to Samantha. He got up to fetch his laptop when his phone rang. He didn't recognise the number and speculated if it could even be the guy he was just speaking to calling him back.

'Hello.'

'Hi, is that Joe Zuccu?'

'It is.'

'You came by the other day. To the depot where Lee worked. I might have some information for you. If Lee's still missing that is?'

'He is still missing.'

CHAPTER SIXTEEN

1976

RHONA

The book was published in June 1976. From then on Rhona found her life changing. As the publication date had approached Shirley had gently pressured Rhona to give some more detail about the planned trilogy.

Rhona had sat on the bus home from her office one afternoon desperately trying to think of how to expand on the story of *E.T.*, as her book was now called, the feeling being *Extra Terrestrial* was just a touch too long, too on the nose and *E.T.* as a title was far more *punchy*. The only plot point Rhona could come up with was that the boy had moved out of Ireland and possibly to a city. London perhaps.

At work one morning she was also asked to go and see Mike, the editor, in his office.

'I heard you're going to be a published author,' he said with genuine enthusiasm as he stood by the window sipping coffee. 'Congratulations.'

'Thank you,' Rhona said, standing awkwardly by his desk.

'Andrew has told me all about it. Do you have any plans to leave us, if I may ask?'

'No.' Rhona was being honest, but was still unsure how long the money she had been paid would last.

'Well we can't have you down in the basement finding files and fetching tea and coffee for people now, can we? Not if you're going to be famous. How does Senior Reporter sound? Get your own desk. Perhaps you could specialise on the arts section of the paper.'

'I wasn't aware we had an arts section.'

'Well we can have one now.'

'I don't know if I'd be any good. I don't know if I deserve it. What about Andrew as you mention him? He'd make a good Senior Reporter.'

'He might and I do see a lot of potential in that young boy. But I don't see that he's got a novel about to be published now do I?'

She also met the hugely successful and the very celebrated science fiction writer also represented by the Shirley Verne Literary Agency, Dan Mills. It was at a pre-launch drinks evening that Shirley had arranged to encourage Rhona to network.

'It's not what you know but who you know after all,' she said. 'Or even better. It's what you know about who you know.'

Rhona had arrived and clutched her glass of champagne nervously as Shirley marched her round and introduced her to various agents, writers, publishers, and journalists she had corralled together for the evening. Rhona tried her best but felt on display and scrutinised. Eventually Shirley got bored of showing Rhona off and left her with Monty smoking his pipe whilst she networked elsewhere and alone.

When Dan Mills arrived, he did so by coming through the door and stopping like a model on a catwalk for obvious maximum effect. He wore a tailored suit with flared trousers and a red cravat in place of a tie. Rhona had only ever seen someone wear a cravat on television. There was enough head turning, nods to colleagues that 'he's here' and conversations suddenly at a lower volume to suggest that someone close to royalty had arrived.

If nothing else, thought Rhona, Dan had certainly mastered the art of an entrance. To Rhona, and perhaps others too, his entrance also had an air of theatrical horror about it as Dan Mills, for all his literary skills, looked like the spitting image of Herman Munster from *The Munsters*. Or so Rhona thought anyway as he walked, or lumbered as Rhona would have described it, towards the nearest waiter carrying a tray of drinks.

Taking a glass with his little finger testing the direction of the wind and surveying the gathering like an angry husband looking for his wife's lover Dan moved around the room, dispensing nods to those he came across. Rhona and Monty stood transfixed at his performance and even more so when he spotted them and strode over with the confidence of a man who knew his place in the world.

'Are you Rhona O'Shea?' he asked with a bluntness that made even Monty blush.

'I am,' replied Rhona, strangely feeling calm and uncharacteristically in control whilst noting Dan Mills' slight lisp.

'Shirley insisted I come. So here I am.'

He looked Rhona over as if she was for sale and was considering making a bid. Monty, sensing trouble, took the pipe out of his mouth and was about to enter the conversation when Dan continued.

'I read your book. Tell me, do you read much science fiction?'

'Not much.'

'Hmm. And do you research? By that I mean do you keep abreast of new technology and developments? Keep tabs on NASA or what the Russians are up to? That sort of thing.'

'I can't say that I do.'

'Hmm. I thought not. Your book, you see, lacks believability. I'm sorry if this sounds harsh but I never fail to be honest in my opinion.'

'I can see that.'

'And I can deduce that the only selling point you really have is to suggest that your main characters believe Elvis Presley is to die. Which, if that is the only unique angle you bring to this genre, it is not a very original one. In short, I can't say I liked your book and I can't say you are a very good writer.'

'Steady on old man,' said Monty. 'That's no way to speak to a lady.'

Dan smiled, which was more of a smirk, like Monty had just set him up with the punchline, which in Dan's mind, he had.

'Unfortunately, I don't think she is much of a lady. Now, I hope you're not going to cry.'

Rhona stepped forward so she was close to Dan.

'I agree,' said Rhona softly with a voice full of hurt.

At this Dan smiled. He had hit the target.

'You do?'

'Yes. I am not much of a lady.'

With that she kneed Dan Mills as hard as she could in his balls.

Dan bent over and let out a gasp of pain. Rhona smiled and turned to Monty.

'I'd better be off. Lovely talking to you both.'

She walked away leaving Monty laughing and Dan still bent over holding his aching balls and unable to talk. The rest of the room meanwhile, whose occupants had witnessed the assault, watched her float out of the room with a mixture of shock and envy. She had also hit her target.

Rhona got to the entrance of the hotel, pausing on the steps and was just about to search for the nearest bus stop when Shirley caught up with her.

'Hold it right there,' she said, out of breath and with an unsteadiness that suggested she had been enjoying the drinks trays.

Rhona turned.

'Did you just knee Dan Mills in the balls?'

'I did. He was rather rude.'

For a second Rhona thought she may have crossed the line and gone from a soon-to-be published author to a never-to-be published author. Instead Shirley put her hands in the air in delight.

'Yes! I can't stand that conceited arsehole.'

Shirley hugged her as if she'd just won a race.

'You know, I'll have to say you were drunk or something don't you? Otherwise he might walk and he does bring in quite a lot of money.'

'I understand.'

'Where are you going?'

'Home.'

'Don't go home yet.'

'I can hardly come back in.'

'Well come to mine... Have a drink.'

It was the tone that made Rhona look down at Shirley's wrist and see what she knew would be there. The silver bracelet. The one with crystals studded around it. The one she had already seen in her dreams.

The next morning Rhona left Shirley's apartment. It was definitely an apartment and not a flat. Rhona felt that using the American term captured the sheer size, wealth and style of Shirley's home which differentiates it from the more humble, unambitious and small sounding word *flat*. Shirley had woken up hungover and embarrassed. She swore she never slept with clients and Rhona swore she never slept with women.

'So why did you then?' asked Shirley.

Rhona shrugged. 'For the new experience I suppose.'

Shirley shooed her out of her apartment as politely but as quickly as she could. Rhona got the bus home feeling no remorse or guilt for what she had done. She would not tell Andrew and she would not question her own motivations.

When she got home she did go to the phone booth and call her mother in Ireland, which she had not done now for some considerable time.

'So how have you been?' asked her mother.

'I've written a book. It's going to be published.'

'Oh is it now? What's it about?'

'About a boy who meets an alien and they try to save Elvis from dying on the toilet.'

There was silence on the other end of the line.

'I hope you know what you're doing?' came the eventual reply.

Rhona didn't have an answer for that.

CHAPTER SEVENTEEN

2001

AMY

Amy paused outside the building to check she had the right address. It was a converted warehouse off Brick Lane and around the back of the Old Truman Brewery. Amy hadn't been in this area for some time, especially after the bombing a couple of years before. She had always associated the area for its curry houses, but as she had walked from Aldgate East station, she detected signs of change and a hipper, younger, and whiter crowd on the streets no doubt attracted by the cheaper rents in this part of the city. She remembered that Gilbert and George also lived somewhere nearby which perhaps confirmed the developing artistic atmosphere.

She rang the buzzer with the crudely hand drawn name, Ash Comix, underneath it and waited. The door buzzed and she soon found herself inside and at the bottom of a worn, unpainted staircase with an old cage lift running up through it. Not trusting the lift she began to ascend the stairs, pausing on each floor outside thick doors naming various new media companies or photographic agencies. The scene reminded her of Soho where she had once worked as a runner for a post-production company before she got her break in journalism. There she had gone back and forth dropping off tapes and film cans and seen behind the curtain of many a production company and the crummy offices they kept amongst the brothels, sex shops and drug dealers. She had loved that job.

By the time she got to the fifth floor she was feeling both sweaty and elated like she had gone for a run, which was rare. She paused to calm her breathing before knocking on the door. When no answer came she turned the door handle and entered.

The starkness of the staircase was in direct contrast to the loud, colourful and spacious interior of Ash Comix. High value, collector item comics hung on the white walls in black frames. They surrounded four desks with a collection of drawing desks at the end and three Apple Macintosh computers in the corner. Somewhere a radio played Coldplay. All but one of the desks was unoccupied and in the occupied one sat a bearded man in his early thirties wearing a green T-shirt with a 1940s era Superman on the front. He was leaning back in the chair on his phone with his feet up on the desk. He saw Amy and gave the signal to hold on.

Amy moved towards his desk as he continued his conversation.

'Well that's not going to work is it? Quite frankly mate I don't know what to say. Tuesday I said and it's Thursday now so can you see where I'm at. Not a happy place is it?'

His accent was educated, hidden behind a put-on London twang. Amy had heard these accents a lot since arriving in London as the middle-classes tried to hide their backgrounds in the hope of gaining some working-class credibility, believing it would validate them in some way and lend them authenticity.

Amy had come from a family of farmers who were by no means rich and had struggled to maintain their land. She spoke posh, as people liked to tell her, even though she had been educated in the state system as that's how people spoke where she had lived. And there was no way she was going to start talking Cockney if that's what they hoped.

'Look I got to go. Just sort it out mate will you. See you.'

He hung up and gave her a look that said, *what's a man got to do?*

'Sorry about that.'

He stood up and extended his hand. Amy shook it.

'I'm Amy Greene. You must be Rob? We spoke on the phone.'

'Yes, of course. I am he. Sorry.' He glanced at his watch as he came around and grabbed a chair from behind one of the empty desks. He wheeled it over next to Amy. 'Can I get you a tea? Coffee? We only have instant though.'

Amy sat down. 'I'm fine.'

Rob smoothed his hair down then sat back behind his desk and appraised Amy. She wondered if men realised they were so obvious when they did this.

'If I may say, you don't look like a journalist.'

Amy smiled politely and took out the graphic novel she had in her handbag, the one that had led her to this man. She held it up to him.

'So, like I said on the phone, I've come to talk about this.'

Rob seemed surprised. He reached out for the book and Amy handed it to him. He held it carefully in his hands. On the front cover, below the title *The Warning* by Trey Griffin, a passenger airliner was about to impact into one of two tall skyscrapers in a city that was unmistakably New York City. And unmistakably the World Trade Centre. The image mirrored the reality of what had just happened. An event that shook the entire world. The only puzzle was that the graphic novel was published by Ash Comix back in 1999.

'I'm surprised you actually have a copy. We only printed two hundred you know. How did you get this?'

'A friend.'

It had actually been a friend of a friend who contacted her. *Had she heard of this graphic novel? She has got to read it?*

'I've already had calls about it but most people think it's a wind up. They can't accept it was published two years ago. Some people have asked I reprint it, but you know, that would be bad taste. Wouldn't it? But it is tempting.'

'Can you tell me about how it got published?'

Rob sat back.

'We've got nothing to do with what happened. You understand that?'

'Of course. I just want some background.'

'It was when we were just getting started. We had put out a few comics aimed at the *2000AD* market but it's hard to break in you know. Hard to get those readers. And this series was made up of reader contributors. Our ethos was to find the next generation of graphic artists so it made sense to open it up, see what was out there. We put them out as novels which, economically, was a really stupid idea. We should have mixed them up and serialised them in retrospect. Spread the risk.

'But anyway... This came through. At the time we just appreciated the artwork and story. It was all there. Usually you get the artist but not the storyteller and you have to put them together, but with this, we had both. It made our lives easier.'

'So who was the author? I can't find anything on Trey Griffin.'

Rob bit his lip.

'Can I ask where this is going?'

'Well isn't that obvious? We've just had a major terrorist attack and you have a novel here that seems to have predicted that attack, but it was published two years ago. I'm a journalist. I want the story.'

'Yes I understand but we actually own the copyright to this. It was a buyout, so I think I'm allowed to ask. And I might have more offers. Exclusive offers.'

'I just want to interview whoever wrote it, drew it. Find out more.'

'It's a struggle this business you know. We're only small. I had to let a couple of people go a few months back. Internet is taking over these days. You go online and it screws advertising figures.'

'I don't intend to make you look bad. In fact, you'll get some free publicity.'

Rob nodded, warming to the idea.

'Okay, okay. I only met Trey Griffin once. He came in to get the money for the book.'

'It was a man? And you only met him once?'

'Everything was done by email. He said he lived outside London. We just edited it a bit but what you see is what we got. It was very straightforward and didn't warrant lots of meetings. Everything, like I said, was done by email.'

'What about a phone number or home address?'

'Just his email address. And before you ask, I did email him after you phoned and it bounced back as it's not being used anymore apparently.'

'What about his bank details?'

Rob squirmed a little.

'I don't actually want them,' said Amy. 'But the sort code would tell me which bank it is and where it's based.'

'I was still getting my head around it all at the time, so I paid him in cash. Made the paperwork easier if you know what I mean.'

'I see. What did he look like then?'

'Young. Early twenties. Blonde hair. It was a while ago.'

Amy waited for more.

'That's all I remember about his face. It's not easy describing someone's face if they just look normal. Have you tried it?'

Amy considered her next question but Rob continued.

'The only reason I really remember him was because he said he had a taxi waiting outside and needed to get a move on.'

Amy frowned.

'Okay. Imagine you tell a young, struggling artist you're going to publish their first story or book even. A bloody graphic novel. Most are over the moon. They want to wallow in it. Enjoy the limelight. They can't get enough of it. And they're getting paid. We weren't paying much but we were... are... a decent company. All the other artists were here loads.

'But this guy comes in, hardly says a word, gets his cash, and leaves. It stuck in my mind. I mean, some of these types are a bit introverted, shall we say, so maybe that explains it. But I don't know. And I'm not even sure he was actually called Trey Griffin anyway.'

'What do you mean?'

'He had to sign for the cash. And when he did he paused, like he had to remember his own name.'

'You remembered that?'

'Yes. Like I said he was a bit odd. And then he left and got driven off by some woman.'

Amy leaned forward.

'Say again? The taxi driver was a woman?'

'If it was a taxi. I went to the window when he left. He got into a car, Volvo I think, and I could just make out the driver's face. It looked like a woman. But I can't be sure. And they were gone.'

'Is there anything else at all you can tell me?'

'No, not really. Sorry.'

Amy stood up and took the book back from Rob.

'Are you going?'

'I suppose so. Bit of a dead end isn't it.'

'If I'd known what would happen then it would be a different story I can assure you.'

'I expect it would be. You don't have any more information?'

Rob stared into space for a moment, his mouth hanging slightly open. Amy decided it must be his thinking face.

'I can show you the files and emails. There's nothing there though that would help you find him.'

Amy glanced at her watch. She had time.

'If I'm here I might as well take a look.'

CHAPTER EIGHTEEN

1977

RHONA

The book was published and it proved a moderate success with modest reviews. Many reviewers remarked how visual some parts of the story were. Shirley, who never spoke of their night together again, was happy enough to pressure Rhona on details of the second book in the promised trilogy. By this point Rhona was ready.

'The alien and boy discover there is a rogue alien on planet Earth who plans to start a revolution in Iran. This is complicated by the fact that they befriend a girl whose father works in Iran and he becomes one of the sixty-three Americans who'll be held hostage at the American Embassy. So it's a sort of race against time with a personal angle.'

Shirley chewed her pen.

'I see. That's an... interesting plot.'

'It's going to happen so they need to save the father and warn people.'

Shirley nodded.

'Well get me a draft as soon as possible. How far have you got?'

Rhona hadn't started. The visions had only come days before. Images of thousands of people marching carrying massive placards of an old man with a white beard and black hat merged with tanks on the streets and ambulances racing past. And then she had seen the American Embassy being stormed and then Americans with their hands tied behind their backs with white blindfolds on. The images had scored her dreams for two days running. She had other visions but none she found was as startling and dramatic as these images. She'd also seen Russian tanks in some mountainous country but didn't know where it was. She also saw Margaret Thatcher becoming Prime Minister but she wasn't really sure if people needed to be warned about her yet.

'I'm quite far in. Just need time to finish it.'

'Well that's brilliant.'

When she was leaving Rhona contemplated whether she should write a letter to someone like she had to Elvis. To warn them that people would die. To tell them that what she had seen would come true. But who could she write to?

'She wants it soon.'

'What about Sardinia?'

'We can still go. I can finish it there.'

Rhona and Andrew were in Rhona's office at the *London Irish Daily*. It looked out across the main office as well as Andrews desk. Rhona's office had windows. Andrew had a view of a filing cabinet with his back to Rhona so he never knew if she was watching him. Since taking her own office Rhona had detected a shift in their relationship. Andrew was no longer the mentor figure he had perhaps been and even made a joke of it, or a kind of joke.

'I'm like Robert Duvall in the *Godfather II* when Michael takes over and doesn't need him anymore,' he had said.

Rhona had smiled at the analogy but also remembered that in the movie, Michael, who Andrew was suggesting she was in some kind of way, was a mafia boss who had his brother Fredo murdered and even passively threatened Hagen, who Robert Duvall had played. Andrew had always liked to use film references to make a point which at times annoyed her if she hadn't seen them. He even referred to Rhona's now infamous kneeing of Dan Mills in the balls as *a great movie moment*.

'What's that?' asked Rhona for the first time noticing the thick manuscript in Andrew's hands.

'It's my book. I've finished it.'

He placed it tenderly on her desk.

'That's brilliant. Well done.'

'Thanks. Well, when you get the odd spare week to have a read I would greatly appreciate it.'

'I'll read it in Sardinia.'

Gianluca heated the coffee in an old coffee maker on a stove in the kitchen of the ancient house in the ancient village. He crossed his arms and patiently waited for the water to boil and steam through the coffee, ignoring Rhona who sat at the kitchen table behind him watching. Rhona and Andrew had been in Sardinia for two weeks now and they were becoming accustomed to the daily rituals and routines of the people and the village.

They were staying with Helen and Gianluca. Helen was Andrew's older sister, Gianluca her husband and whose village they now lived in with their one-year old daughter, Michela. Gianluca had been a waiter in London but now worked with his father travelling from village to village selling fruit and vegetables off the back of a lorry.

Rhona quickly found Sardinian life similar in many ways to the rural Ireland she had been brought up in and appreciated the challenging life the people here led. Meanwhile Andrew, she believed, only saw the romantic side of their existence. Whilst Andrew saw stoicism, integrity, hard work, family values and happiness, Rhona saw near hunger, desperation, exhaustion, resignation and the willingness to embrace vendettas as a form of justice.

The dirt roads, the intermittent water and electricity supply, and the financial precariousness of the people only made Andrew believe he was in some kind of neo-realist Italian cinematic fable. Apart from the realities of life in Sardinia Rhona admitted they were having a nice time.

Once across the channel they travelled down to Genoa by train, taken a boat crossing to Olbia in northern Sardinia and driven down to Milis, a small village in the Oristano region on the western side of the island. So far Helen had taken them to the beach on a number of occasions, only twenty minutes away by car, and to the main town, Oristano, for shopping. They had also enjoyed multiple lunches and dinners at various homes of relatives that had gone on for hours.

Rhona and Andrew had never eaten so much pasta. They had also enjoyed lots of potato soup that was a kind of a local minestrone, which was something Gianluca's mother seemed to make as often as ragu, that to Rhona was spaghetti bolognese. They had also eaten lasagnes, suckling pig on occasion, fish, pig's brains, which the locals gave to the children as a treat and last of all, worm cheese.

The worm cheese, Rhona was horrified to discover, was a pecorino with live maggots in it which the men of the village proudly treated as a delicacy. Andrew did try it, as a badge of honour rather than genuine gastronomic curiosity, and feigned enjoyment which the locals, in their good humour and seeing straight through his English polite reserve and honest effort, laughed heartily at.

They also drank a lot of homemade wine and something called *Aqua Vita*, which was a kind of after dinner fire water that Rhona also noticed the local old men sipping in the early mornings in the village square with their espressos.

Helen seemed genuinely happy here with her life having been a secretary in London before they had moved to Sardinia and started a family. She had learnt Italian and was picking up the local dialect which most people spoke. It seemed to be a mixture of Latin, Italian, Spanish and some other ancient tongue which made Rhona think it must be like an Italian landing in Wales, expecting English to be spoken only to hear Welsh.

Gianluca was sociable and enjoyed taking Andrew out for drinks in the village bars and his family were hospitable and welcoming. The bars were purely for men which Rhona found annoying.

One day Rhona was a little bored and walked through the village without a bra on under her T-shirt. She made sure to wander past the bar Andrew and Gianluca were in. The men of the village stood or sat transfixed and ogled, unused to this sight. Andrew went red. Gianluca laughed. Rhona smiled and waved innocently at them and wandered back to the house.

'Do you know DH Lawrence came here in the early twenties?' said Andrew as they all sat in the orchard of one of Gianluca's relatives one night and sipped wine while letting another substantial meal digest. He had taken out his now familiar notebook that he always kept with him to jot down ideas. He opened it up and read.

'He said this land resembles no other place. Sardinia is something else. Enchanting spaces and distances to travel - nothing is finished, nothing definitive. It is like freedom itself.'

Gianluca translated to his family as best as he could and they all nodded back politely, probably wondering who DH Lawrence was and what Andrew was on about.

'He also said Sardinia is out of time and history,' said Helen who sat next to Gianluca with a sleepy Michela on her lap.

'What did he mean by that?'

'Can't you see?'

Rhona smiled to herself and pondered how she would describe what she saw here but could only come up with generic clichés at that moment. Rugged, sweltering, sparse, ancient, and beautiful.

She was thinking the same thing some days later as Gianluca heated up his coffee and she sat in his kitchen. Helen and Andrew had gone to the shop with Michela leaving them alone for the first time.

'You have written a book?' he asked suddenly, his back still to her as he watched the coffee pot intently.

Rhona came out of her daydream.

'Er, yes.'

He turned to her.

'It's about aliens?'

'Sort of.'

He nodded. The coffee began to bubble. After waiting a few seconds more he took it off the heat and poured them both espressos, or just coffee as Gianluca called it, into small yet beautifully decorated coffee cups.

'I saw aliens once,' he said adding sugar to his drink.

'Really? When?'

'When I was a boy. We went and camped in the mountains and one night I woke up and saw this space ship in the sky, just... er, floating there.'

'Wow. What do think they wanted?'

Gianluca thought for a few seconds.

'Nothing. They just wanted us to know they were there.'

He saw the confusion on Rhona's face.

'We are all connected. People, things, places, everything. Even aliens in the sky. All connected. Everything for a reason.'

With that he shrugged and then wandered off with his coffee.

In between visits to the beach, eating and socialising, Rhona attempted to start her second novel. She succeeded finally by getting up one morning, locking herself away, and just forcing herself to throw words onto a page. She drank strong coffee, smoked Italian cigarettes and ate panini.

A sequel to a story is sometimes harder than just starting again she realised. It was like a relationship you needed to work on and compromise with rather than finding someone new and exciting, hoping that will work.

After two chapters she stopped. She sat back in her chair and smoked, wondering what she was doing. Her thoughts went back to the man in the café, playing with his Zippo lighter.

I'm here to tell you to write about the visions, he had said.

It felt like an age away now. Like a dream. Like a vision itself.

She leaned forward and wrote.

She managed to average a thousand words a day although that slowed when she noticed Andrew taking an interest in what she was doing with her time and her typewriter.

'Just writing in there?' he asked, his eyes full of hope.

She read his book. She read it alone on a small balcony overlooking the backyard and with a view out to the hills surrounding the village. She ordered Andrew not to disturb her. It was just her, his manuscript, and the sounds of village life.

A few days later they were on the outskirts of the village in the late morning, slowly heading back to the house before the heat became too hot. They were taking a stroll by the orange groves.

'I finished it,' she said.

Andrew stopped immediately.

'And?'

'And I think it needs work.'

'You didn't like it?'

'I didn't say that.'

'Did you like it then?'

'It's not really my thing. It's quite heavy isn't it? I thought it would be science fiction?'

'You didn't like it?'

'I'm trying to be objective.'

'You can't be objective over a book.'

'Yes you can.'

'Why didn't you like it?'

'Why does it matter whether I liked it or not?'

'It doesn't matter. Well, it does actually. I wanted you to like it. That was all.'

'It's quite heavy is all I thought.'

Rhona often queried how his tastes in film seemed to be in contrast to his taste in books. Andrew loved to read weighty novels and dense literature as well as thoughtful science fiction, but then he'd watch light comedies and mass market entertainment. He would be quite happy with *War and Peace* on his lap and a Doris Day film on the television.

'Heavy? What does that mean?'

She wasn't quite sure.

'Do you mean you didn't understand it?'

Maybe that was it.

'No. We just have different tastes,' she said.

Andrew froze, suddenly finding another meaning within her book critique.

'Different tastes.'

He said it slowly as though he had never said it before.

'What?'

'I sometimes wonder what you see in me.'

'Andrew.'

'No, really. What did you see in me?'

She saw kindness, love, security and honesty.

She stayed silent.

Andrew walked off.

They came back to England on August 15th 1977.

The next day Elvis Presley died.

CHAPTER NINETEEN

2001

AMY

Amy met Shirley Verne in a coffee shop near Shirley's home in St John's Wood. For a woman who must now be in her seventies, Amy noted Shirley had aged remarkably well and dressed fashionably, wearing black jeans, a warm expensive looking jacket and brand new looking boots as she came in and made her way to Amy's table. With the coffee shop at this time in the morning, in this busy area with well-off mums sipping lattes and talking about recent holidays to Saint Tropez, Amy decided Shirley could easily have been the glamorous granny with the Midas touch who would no doubt have stopped a crying baby with one look from those cool, elegant blue eyes.

She was on time and asked for her *usual* from the person behind the counter which Amy soon found out was a chamomile tea. She took off her black leather gloves, placed them on the table, and regarded Amy's mini-tape recorder with suspicion.

'I do hope you're not going to tape this?'

'Would you prefer if I didn't?'

Shirley considered this for a minute, or at least for enough time for her tea to be brought to the table.

'Well I suppose it's okay.'

Amy thanked her and Shirley watched as Amy checked the recorder had a tape in it.

'I read some of your work,' she said. 'Rather good. How long have you worked for *The Observer*?'

'A few years.'

'How old are you then? If you don't mind me asking?'

'Thirty-two.'

'Hmm. You look younger.'

'Thank you.'

'Mind you. At my age everyone looks young. I really can't tell anymore. Tell me then, what can I reveal about Rhona O'Shea that you don't already know?'

Amy pressed record on her machine and waited a couple of seconds to see the tape going around.

'Well you say that as though there's a lot of information out there about her but there's not as much as you might think. She's a writer with a somewhat cult following who has an air of mystery surrounding her.'

'An air of mystery. Yes, yes I suppose she has.'

'Tell me about her?'

'I thought you wanted to discuss her work?'

'I do. But the more I've looked into her life the more fascinated I become about her. I'm trying to secure an interview with Andrew Hunter and besides him you're the only other person I've tracked down who worked with her.'

'Andrew Hunter. I've not seen him for years.'

'Can you remember your first meeting with Rhona?'

'Vaguely. She sent in her first book and I took her on as a client. She was young then. Naïve and ambitious.'

'And beautiful.'

'Yes but I wasn't a modelling agency, dear.'

It was only then that Amy realised how piercing Shirley's stare was. She seemed annoyed at Amy's comment and was not afraid to make it obvious. Amy blushed. She felt she had let her side down. Her feminist credentials were in tatters. She had a point. She got back on track.

'What impressed you about her first book as we see Rhona now as a writer who had an uncanny ability to predict certain events, but then of course, you were judging her purely on her writing ability?'

'She was always judged on her writing ability. Or she should have been.'

'But what were your first impressions?'

'On *E.T.*? It wasn't called that then of course. It was a strange book. Suitable for its genre and original. It had some striking imagery and the whole idea of this boy and alien trying to save a rock star was just... odd I suppose. But compelling.'

'They try and save Elvis Presley from dying.'

'Yes.'

'What did you initially think of that?'

'Like I say, odd. Somewhat bad taste. Original. Edgy. Sellable.'

Amy laughed.

Shirley smiled. Her teeth were all white and they looked new. Some unkind person, Amy thought, might say false teeth never looked so good. If they were false of course.

'And then Elvis Presley did die.'

'Did you know in the first draft he died in the bathroom? On the toilet.'

'No I didn't.'

Amy felt the hairs on the back of her neck go up.

'Well that was odd. In hindsight I wished we had kept that in but taste prevailed. I remember watching the news of his death on the television, and then thinking, *hang on*. A couple of days later we started getting calls and letters from readers and all sorts. Some of the letters were very strange. It did increase sales so no one was complaining.'

'Did you talk to Rhona about it?'

'Well yes, of course. I remember she had just come back from a holiday in Sardinia. She came to my office to talk about her second book shortly after his death, and I just said 'where in heavens did you get the idea of Elvis dying like that'. I remember she smiled then shrugged.

'Writers are creative. They have imaginations. At that point I just thought it was a very, very odd and sad coincidence.'

'Rhona wrote two books that were published. I read somewhere she'd written a third,' said Amy.

For the second time that morning Amy felt Shirley's eyes bore into her.

'Where did you hear that?'

'In an old science fiction magazine.'

'You have done your homework.'

'Did you ever read the book?'

Shirley shifted position in her seat and took a sip of her tea.

'No. I heard she was writing another book but she never put it forward to me to represent.'

'And then she disappeared into obscurity.'

'Yes, rather odd again. God how many times have I said odd in conjunction with Rhona O'Shea? She really wasn't odd you know. She was very normal in most ways.'

'I would love to speak to Rhona. I don't suppose you have her contact details?'

'What?'

Amy suddenly felt awkward. Like she'd been found out.

'I know she stopped giving interviews a long time ago and I know she's a hermit of sorts. It's obvious she values her privacy but I would love to request a meeting. A short interview. I've found it impossible to find anything to indicate where she lives now.'

Shirley looked at Amy with a heavy, sorrowful frown. Amy felt her eyes interrogating her yet again.

'I would have asked in my email but I didn't want to jump in.'

Shirley Verne shook her head.

'My dear. You didn't know?'

'Didn't know what?'

'Rhona O'Shea died years ago.'

CHAPTER TWENTY

1980

RHONA

Since the publication of *E.T.* back in the early summer of 1977 life had, arguably, been good for Rhona. The book increased in sales following the death of Elvis Presley, and whilst there had been awkward ripples and questions asked, the general conclusion was that Rhona's prediction of his death had been a coincidence. Rhona felt conflicting emotions about all this. She hadn't prevented his death. She was just profiting from it.

In one rare interview Rhona denied she had any special gift and said how sorry it was to lose the King of Rock 'n' Roll. She said she'd dreamt the plot, which wasn't a lie. The only person who wasn't persuaded was Monty.

'I'm only going to ask you once Rhona but how on earth did you fucking know that would happen to Elvis?' he had asked.

'I didn't,' she had said or words to that effect. By this point, and now familiar with repeated denial, she said it with real emotion so much so that she almost convinced herself she was telling the truth. She felt his eyes scrutinising her as he sucked on his pipe. He went back to her second book that they were working on and never said another word about it.

Her second book proved more problematic. Predicting a revolution in Iran and a hostage crisis proved harder to explain away as a mere coincidence.

When the revolution occurred with the hostages taken that November, her readers and some journalists had recognised the obvious parallels, and she had experienced her first brush with genuine fame. It had been fleeting.

She found herself pursued down streets by photographers. Her flat was besieged by fans and journalists who all wanted a comment of some kind. Many wanted to know what would happen to the hostages. Some of her fans just wanted to touch her as though she was divine. They were not just her fans now of course, they were her followers.

Shirley put out a press release denying any special talents for divining the future. Rhona O'Shea was merely a gifted writer. Merely. And her latest novel is available in all good bookshops.

Rhona stopped giving interviews altogether and became reclusive. She moved flats and changed her telephone number.

The second book sold well. It seemed more than just science fiction fans were taking notice. Shirley was happy. Rhona was lonely. She wondered what Andrew was doing.

They had split up after coming back from Sardinia. Not straight away but they had begun to drift apart like all couples do when there is nowhere to go. Rhona spent her evenings writing and did not want to be disturbed. Andrew left her to it, perhaps rewriting his own novel. Rhona didn't know as she didn't ask.

And then Andrew got a new job at *The Sun* as a sports reporter so they ceased seeing each other in the day. Rhona didn't miss seeing his back as he sat at his desk. She herself wrote in her spare time and moved again to a bigger flat in Stockwell. She still lived alone but now had an extra bedroom which she turned into her office. She sold her 2CV and bought a Mini. She let her hair grow and changed her wardrobe. She wore more dresses and bought an expensive necklace which was a present to herself.

Once she had finished her second novel and planned her third she met up with Andrew. They still had not officially separated as up until then Rhona had her excuse of a book deadline and Andrew had football games to attend and match reports to write up, so they couldn't possibly see each other.

They finally went to see a show in the West End. *The Dresser* with Tom Courtney. They sat next to each other in silence and

Rhona felt neither of them were taking in the production or enjoying it in any way. It was simply a prelude of what was to come.

In the taxi on the way home Andrew spoke.

'You finished the book. So what now?'

'Rest and then start on my next book.'

'Busy. What's it about?'

'John Lennon and Ronald Reagan get shot. Lennon dies and Reagan survives. I haven't worked out the plot yet.'

'Ronald Reagan?'

'He becomes President of the United States.'

The silence made Rhona turn to him. He was staring at her.

'What? Why are you looking at me like that?'

But she knew why. She hated herself for it. So blasé about death. She didn't even attempt to hide it. He looked at her like she was the one pulling the trigger.

'How do you know these things?'

'I just made it up.'

'We both know that isn't true.'

Rhona looked out the window.

'Let's talk about something else, shall we?'

'No. I don't want to. I want to talk about this. Why do you do it? If you know these awful things are going to happen so why don't you do something?'

'I'm a writer, Andrew. Just a writer.'

'I love you.'

Rhona looked away. Anywhere but at Andrew. She watched the London streets flash past.

Andrew stared at the floor and said what he had to say.

'I love you but I can't go on like this.'

He stopped the taxi and got out without saying another word. It struck Rhona that he may have been waiting for her to jump in and stop him when he was saying he loved her, expecting and hoping she would tell him that she loved him too. But she didn't. She let him continue. Finishing them. And she had stayed silent and let him get out without doing anything about it.

Going home that night Rhona sat at her dining table and smoked cigarettes. When the sun finally came up she went to bed.

Rhona immersed herself in writing and rewriting her third novel. She went out occasionally with Shirley who was now seeing a man who looked and sounded like a gangster because he was a gangster. His name was George Frenton and he liked to wear tailored suits and expensive shirts and have his hair cut every week.

A few years previously, a gunfight in a snooker club in Catford had made its way into the tabloids and George and his friends, who were all involved, had briefly become infamous before they were carted off by the police to spend some years at Her Majesty's Pleasure. He had a scar across his throat where someone had once stabbed him with a broken bottle in an attempt to decapitate him. They hadn't succeeded and Rhona did speculate on occasion what had happened to the person who had tried to kill him but she never asked.

He had 'interests' in various clubs and casinos in the West End and Soho and he liked to eat at expensive restaurants. He was very civil to Rhona and always treated her nicely and with respect. He liked her because she was Irish, like his grandparents had been. Shirley called him her Cockney and he always took exception to this. He reminded them he wasn't technically a Cockney but a south Londoner from 'the Elephant'. He mixed well amongst celebrities and was discreet about his occupation.

He almost let the cat out of the bag once at a dinner party when people around the table were drunkenly comparing lists of famous people they had met. When George was asked this question, his answer had been 'Well I met Meyer Lansky once' which was met by a confused silence from the guests and giggles from Rhona.

On the completion of her third novel Rhona realised she was lonely and lost. She went into one of her funks which lasted four days. She had not gone out and had stayed in her flat with the curtains shut whilst leaving the television on with the volume turned up.

She thought of her mother. She questioned everything she had achieved and came up with no answers. On the fifth day she was feeling a little better when men in suits knocked on her door. Men who had questions. Men who she knew would never leave her alone. And now here she was. A woman who had followed her dream and was now being chased by a nightmare.

CHAPTER TWENTY-ONE

2019

JOE

They met at a Costa coffee shop in Kinson near the Tesco's. The man, who still hadn't given Joe his name, had asked to meet the next morning.

Joe turned up at ten o'clock and parked in the supermarket car park. When he walked in he paused by the door. The cafe was half full of mothers and babies, the odd jogger and a few pensioners. One guy sat in the corner with his back against the wall. He was looking at Joe with a coffee in front of him. He gave a slight nod and Joe walked over.

'Hi, I'm Joe. Are you the guy who called?'

'I am. I'm John.' He was about thirty-five with ink creeping up his neck and had short dark hair. He wore an old blue Regatta jacket zipped up like he was cold.

Joe held out his hand.

'Nice to meet you.'

The guy half rose out of his seat to shake Joe's hand. 'And you.'

Joe sat down.

'You not getting coffee?' asked John.

'No I'm fine.'

'It's not bad coffee here. Not as good at Nero's but for Kinson it's not bad.'

'Yeah, you can't complain. Thanks for getting in contact.'

'Listen, Derrek would have probably been a bit more forthcoming, but as you weren't Old Bill, he was playing it by the book.'

'Yeah I got that.'

'He's a decent bloke. Not a bad boss. The bloke we had before was a complete twat which you don't need up there. Know what I'm saying?'

'I can imagine.'

'So you a mate of Lee's?'

'Sort of. I knew him from back in the day.'

'I thought I recognised you. Did you used to go to The Manor?'

'Yeah I did.'

'Thought so. Some heads up there weren't there?'

Joe smiled and nodded. 'Yep.'

The Manor had been a nightclub back in the nineties at a place called Matchams just out of town.

'So you and Lee are mates?'

'Yeah, just from work like but we used to have a cheeky spliff at lunch and that. I recognised him from way back too but I was a bit young back then. My brother Kieran was about your age so that's how I sort of knew everyone. You remember him? Kieran Spencer?'

'Yeah I remember Kieran. But you said *was*?'

'You didn't know? He died.'

'Shit, I'm sorry.'

'Nah. It was a while back now. It was a car crash up near Southampton.'

'Shit.' Joe remembered Kieran. A big guy. Looking at John he could see the likeness.

'I'm sorry you didn't know.'

'I moved out of Bournemouth for years. I lost touch with a lot of people. I lost a friend in car crash a few years back.'

'Oh right. Sorry.'

'So am I. So with Lee, what can you tell me?'

John took a small sip of his coffee.

'I'm telling you this because I know who you are and I know you're kosher right. But I don't want my name anywhere near this if it gets nasty or anything.'

'Why would it get nasty?'

'Lee was a dealer.'

'Okay. What did he sell?'

'Charlie.'

'Did he sell it at work?'

'Nah. Nah. Let me rewind here and fill you in. So Lee gets sacked from work because he turned up drunk. I think he'd had an argument with his missus but I don't know. He never talked about anything like that. But he liked his booze. To be honest Lee had a few issues.'

'I heard that. What kind of issues?'

'Depression. He was self-medicating with the booze if you asked me. He wasn't a happy chappy. I asked him what he actually wanted to do as he hated work. He said he wanted to save the world.

'Fucking hell, what an answer. I told him to fuck off and join Greenpeace but not till he finished his shift otherwise I'd be stitched. But he kept it together most of the time. We used to all go out on Fridays after work sometimes and Lee would be knocking back the shots. I couldn't handle it. Not these days anyway. More of a weed man you know.'

Joe nodded and thought of taking out his notebook but decided not to. He wanted John to keep talking.

'Anyway, he gets sacked. Derek feels out of order doing it but we all get it. You don't turn up fucking pissed to work do you? So I go and see Lee and he's in a bad way. On the slide. I could tell.

'A few of my mates have become alchis. All yellow and fucked. Awful. I told Lee he needs to sort it out and I don't know if he listened. About a month later he calls me again and we meet. This time he's sober and he seems okay. Told me he talked to his aunt and she sorted his head out. But he's telling me he stopped drinking and is now selling coke.

'I'm like what the fuck? At your age? Who wants the stress serving up? His aunt obviously didn't do a very good job if that's supposed to be sorting his head out either. But he's telling me he's not a street dealer and he's not on top. He's already moved up a rung or two and is selling to dealers.'

'Was he using coke himself?'

'When I knew him at work it was just the weed and the tinnies. When I see him this time he didn't look like he was on anything. He looked clean.'

'Do you know how he got into it?'

John shrugged. 'A few old faces are still in the game I suppose. Dunno.'

'But to sell to dealers? Where was he scoring from?'

'Well that's what I'm saying. That's why it was a shock. He's already jumped ahead and had all the readies.'

'But he didn't sell to the people at your work?'

'Nah. No one there. You don't shit on your own doorstep, do you?'

'Do you know any of his customers?'

'No one I knew. Most people at our age had given up. Lightweights.'

Joe smiled although he didn't find it funny.

'So he was earning a lot of money then you think?'

'Fuck yeah. I'd lent him fifty quid way back. He gives me back two hundred. Told me the extra was interest. He didn't give me any Charlie though the tight fucker.'

John laughed giving Joe a good look at his rotting teeth. Joe smiled and tried to laugh back.

'When was the last time you saw him?'

'A couple of months ago. He seemed okay then but he looked a bit worn out.'

'How do you mean?'

'I reckon he'd been drinking the night before. You can see it in the eyes and he had a little bit of a shake. I reckon he was back on it.'

'Where did you meet?'

'He popped round mine. A few of us were chipping in for some rare powder for the weekend and Lee sorted me out for a favour.'

'You ever go to the Six Bells with Lee?'

'No. But weird you mention that place.'

'Why?'

'When I called him up that's where he was. I even offered to come down there and pick it up over a pint but he said he'd come to me. I doubt he dealt down there though.'

'Why not?'

'Cameras. Too on top serving up in most pubs. Too many faces. Don't know who's watching you, do you?'

Joe leant back in his chair. 'Any idea where Lee has gone?'

'Maybe he's done a runner. Maybe he owes people money. I've heard loads of mushes from London are selling gear down here now. County lines they call it isn't it? Mostly kids though innit. Maybe he fucking ripped one of them off and now they're on the war path.'

Joe looked out the window and watched the traffic go past. John finished his coffee.

'I better be going. Gotta get my haircut today. Anything else you want to know?'

'Not for now.'

'Call me if you have any more questions mate and let me know when he turns up okay?'

'Yeah. Thanks for the info. Have a good haircut.'

'Any time mate.'

They shook hands and John walked out.

Joe drove home and typed up all the information he had on his laptop with the intention of sending it in an email to Samantha. What he had made Joe think the police should be involved. A guy becomes a drug dealer, gets beaten up and shortly afterwards disappears. But what would the police say? They would look for evidence if they even cared or had the time to look into it. What Joe had was second hand. Conjecture was the right word wasn't it?

Maybe Lee had made it all up about being the next Pablo Escobar to impress John and hide the fact he was a man struggling with alcoholism. People lied all the time. Joe had met many of them from working in bars. Maybe Lee had just run off. But the drug dealer angle bothered Joe if it was true. To deal drugs successfully you needed a number of talents but one thing was crucial and that was the threat of violence. If you can't protect your stash or make sure debts are repaid you are in trouble as a drug dealer. You need to be either physically and mentally capable yourself to carry out your threats or have someone on hand to do it for you. If you haven't got this then you are a potential victim and it's only a matter of time before someone recognises this flaw and takes advantage.

Lee wasn't a fighter by any means, so if he had back up, why was he beaten up? Maybe he was beaten up and Lee was trying to take revenge and it all went wrong?

Conjecture again, Joe thought. That was the word he was becoming familiar with. He got up and swooped up his car keys. Before he left the house he knocked on Mike's door.

PART TWO

CHAPTER TWENTY-TWO

1991

LEE

When we get round they've already locked the special needs kid in the cupboard. The cupboard is in the hallway under the stairs, so as soon as you walk in, you can hear the crying and hammering from inside. AJ and Keith stand smiling as me, Adam and his brother, Darren, troop in wondering what is going on.

It was supposed to be a party we were coming to but it isn't. AJ had invited us. It was actually Dave Elgin's house, but Dave's parents have gone away and AJ and Keith Palmer had got wind of it and were trying to organise a party round there, whether Dave wanted one or not.

Dave is a nice guy. He's in the year above us at school, in the first year of sixth form, but even we know we can fuck him over and he doesn't have the balls to do anything about it. So he's not going to stand up to two overbearing brothers with a reputation for violence who've come round his house and told him he's having a party.

It's still light when we get round. A lovely summer evening where everything seems shiny and yellow. A bit of a contrast to what is going on in the house which is fucking dark. The special needs kid is called Steve but everyone calls him Shit Steve. He's one of Keith's mates, if you can call it that.

Keith Palmer is two years older than us and lives in a bedsit in town and sells shit drugs. Personally, I find him annoying, but I usually get on okay with AJ so I put up with him. When Keith's not around AJ can be sound but tonight is not one of those occasions.

People, weird people, have a habit of attaching themselves to Keith. People like Barry the Fish who seems to have no neck and is from the Midlands or Max, a small, black American bloke who tells everyone he is an ex-marine which everyone knows is bullshit. And people like One-Eyed Sam who had his face stoved in when he was on remand and now has a glass eye. And of course, people like poor Shit Steve.

Maybe it was the drugs Keith gives them and the spiel about how hard and big time he is and they lap it up or need to lap it up. Lap up anything and go along with anything that might give them some street cred, some protection, some kind of salvation from how cruel people can be. Cruel like Keith Palmer. Apart from Steve though, none of Keith's weird mates are here tonight which is something I suppose. Maybe they've already been round and can't stomach what we're witnessing.

And then AJ tells us what else they've done.

'We spiked him with acid. He's fucked,'

We hear more hammering from the cupboard and the anguished, frightened cries from Steve. When I was a kid we'd called people like Steve spastics and you didn't see them much except on buses. You were told to be nice to spastics. But no one is being nice to him now.

Dave comes out of the lounge with a look on his face that says he knows things are getting out of hand. He doesn't say much. Too traumatised to talk. It certainly wasn't a party. In fact, it was just the Palmers, Dave and us so God knows if anyone else is coming.

AJ opens the cupboard and lets Steve out. He stumbles out and looks round like he's never seen the house before. Tears are coming down his face. He's terrified. AJ is laughing along with Keith. It is sick but we do fuck all. Just stare at him. Not believing this is actually happening. And then they throw him back in. The small, dark cupboard under the stairs, sharing the space with the hoover and shoes. It's as though AJ just got him out to show him to us.

We move from the hallway and sit down at the breakfast table in the kitchen. You can still see the hallway from where we sit. Dave goes to hide back in the lounge. It's a nice house. Large, airy and middle-class. Dave's parents would probably disown him if they knew what their son was doing right now. I glance at Adam and Darren but like me they don't know what to say so, as mad as it sounds, we skin up as AJ and Keith scream at Shit Steve through the cupboard door.

We light our joints and watch the show like some sick spectators, giving each other looks as we tap ash into a 'I love London' cup. Eventually I find myself saying something.

'Maybe you should let him out.'

'Yeah good idea, Lee,' AJ replies.

He comes in and opens a kitchen cabinet then pulls out a pepper pot. He's on a roll. Like we were his audience and he wants to impress us. Keith tugs of his own joint but doesn't say much, happy for his younger brother to take the lead. We all watch AJ sprinkle some of the pepper into his palm and go and unlock the cupboard.

Steve spills out blubbering and incoherent into the early evening light.

'Quick, snort this Steve and you'll be fine,' says AJ, holding out his palm. 'Go on. I promise this will help.' He speaks really slowly, like Steve can't understand English or something.

AJ is a good liar but by this point Steve would probably do anything to stop what the acid is doing to his brain.

Steve leans down and snorts the pepper like it is speed. Just like that. It is that easy. Like giving water to a man who's been in the desert for a week.

Almost immediately Steve starts sneezing violently. He doesn't have time to do anything else before AJ grabs him by the cuff and pushes him back in the cupboard, shutting the door and laughing as he locks it.

All this time Keith says nothing. He just laughs too. Maybe deep-down AJ is just trying to impress his brother, but I can't be sure. Maybe they're both on acid too.

Is this how the Germans killed so many Jews, I wonder. People just watching and doing nothing? I feel like a cunt but I'm stoned now and Keith is a lairy fucker. So we bottle it.

And we leave soon after. We don't discuss it. Just a mutual nod and understanding. *Let's get the fuck out of here.*

We finish our joints and say we'll be back soon as we need to buy some booze. We're out the door and we leave Shit Steve in his hell hole as the Palmer brothers enjoy their little party and the scared shitless Dave, who looks like he wants to come with us, stays hiding in the lounge.

We walk home in silence and I feel awful. I want to talk about it. How shocking it was. Maybe go back and do something. But we say and do fuck all.

That night I lay in bed and think about it some more, and when I go to sleep, I have nightmares again. This time they're more vivid, violent and real and I think it's a kind of punishment for doing nothing. For being a bystander.

CHAPTER TWENTY-THREE

1980

RHONA

Both men, in their early thirties, were clean shaven and smartly dressed in tailored suits. One was American and the other English. They held briefcases by their sides as they politely asked if they could come in and ask her some questions. Rhona, stood at her front door, politely asked for some kind of identification. The Englishman produced a card revealing himself to be MI5. The American stayed silent.

Rhona let them in. They settled on the sofa and surveyed her lounge. They had placed their briefcases on the floor and seemed relaxed, at odds with Rhona's uneasiness. She sat down opposite them on an armchair and waited for what was to come but they seemed to be in no hurry to initiate conversation.

Perhaps they were waiting for her to offer them tea or coffee but she was not going to do that. Eventually, after having a good look at the room, the Englishman picked up his briefcase and pulled out Rhona's two novels, *E.T.* and *The Return,* which he placed on the sofa between himself and his colleague. And then there was another pause as they watched Rhona and her reaction to the two books being placed there. At last the Englishman spoke.

'Do you know why we're here?'

His voice was pleasant enough. Oxbridge intonation. Non-threatening. Rhona could picture him saying things like *well, that was jolly nice* and *splendid* a lot.

Rhona glanced at the novels on the sofa.

'My books? I take it you don't want me to autograph them for you?'

The Englishman laughed like he genuinely found her comment funny. He picked up *The Return* and turned it over in his hands as the American stayed silent.

'No, I'm afraid not. However, it is your books we would like to discuss.'

Rhona shrugged with as much innocence as she could muster.

The American spoke up.

'Your first book, in the version you presented to your agent, you said Elvis Presley would die whilst he sat on his toilet. That's kind of an odd thing to write, don't you think?'

Rhona immediately realised she had now been in some way investigated if they had sourced the book's first draft.

'Depends on what you define as being odd.'

The American seemed to tense up at being challenged, like a dog straining on the leash.

'Unusual might be a more suitable word then don't you think?' asked the Englishman.

Rhona shrugged again.

'And then a few months after your book was published Elvis did die in his bathroom, on his toilet. Now, that's not just an unusual situation you created in your book but also an unusual coincidence. Would you agree?'

'I suppose so,' answered Rhona.

'And then in your second book you have a revolution in Iran. And that happened too. Now that's interesting too. Don't you think?' said the American.

'Perhaps you could tell us where your inspiration comes from?' asked the Englishman, still all smiles whilst his colleague was all crossed arms.

'I just made it up.'

The American leaned forward, his whole body strained as he tried to match his colleague's politeness, but was visibly finding it somewhat hard.

'I'm sure you are aware, especially as you talked about the event in your most recent book as well, but we currently have sixty-three American citizens being held hostage in Iran. We'd like them back. So what can you tell us about that?' he asked.

'I just made that up as well. I couldn't believe it when it happened.'

'Just made up sixty-three hostages being taken? Which was the exact number that were taken.'

Rhona shrugged.

Now it was the American's turn to pick his briefcase up and open it on his lap. He pulled something thick from it. It was a manuscript. Rhona recognised it immediately. The American kept it on his lap as he put the briefcase back on the floor.

'Where did you get that from?' Rhona asked.

'This is, is it not, the galley proof as you call it, of your new, unpublished book?'

'It is.'

'Titled *The Girl Who Walked Off The Moon*. Strange title.'

'If you can think of a better one then let me know.'

The Englishman smiled. The American didn't.

'About some kind of alien from the Moon who comes to Earth and takes on the body of a dead girl. And then she tries do good things but it all kind of goes wrong.'

'That's one way of looking at it.'

'Tell me another way.'

'It's about someone who is different from everyone else trying to fit in and find happiness, but her powers kind of have an opposite effect to what she had intended. She wanted to help people but instead she just causes chaos and unhappiness.'

Rhona felt the sudden urge to cry. She held it in and stared at the two men definitely. The Englishman watched her, sensing some kind of shift in her mood. The American flicked through the pages of the manuscript, oblivious of her emotion.

'Well it was an interesting read you could say. You have another rock star dying. This time he's shot outside his apartment building in New York, and later on, you also have an American President targeted for assassination as he leaves a hotel. They're not real people this time though which I thought was odd. What I mean by that is you don't use real names. Why was that?'

'My agent decided it might be…'

'Bad taste?'

'Perhaps.'

'But you named Elvis Presley in your first book?' said the Englishman, looking genuinely confused which Rhona now realised was just a deceptive mask that hid his true intentions and skills at interrogation. Because that was what this was. An interrogation.

'I was unknown when that was published.'

The American jumped on this straight away.

'But now you are known. Known for making predictions in your books that come true.'

Rhona stayed silent. She didn't know what to say.

'The rock star, is that John Lennon? It's pretty obvious it is.'

'Have I done something wrong?'

'And the President. Are you referring to Ronald Reagan because that's how he's described which is kind of fascinating as he hasn't been elected yet?'

'I ask again. Have I done something wrong?'

'Did you really think we wouldn't ask you about this?'

'Well I know he's from MI5 but who are you exactly?'

Stone faced stares came back her way.

'I'm just a writer,' said Rhona.

'Are you?' asked the American.

'I just made it up.'

'Is the future President of the United States really going to get shot?'

'I don't know. I really can't help you. It's all coincidences. I just made it up.'

She was speaking too quickly now.

The Englishman spoke.

'You keep saying you just make it up. But I ask you, let's just say if you did have some knowledge of future events, and you knew or even had an indication or strong inclination that harm would come to an individual or individuals, then would you not agree it is your moral obligation to try as best as you could to prevent any harm coming to those people?'

Rhona thought of Aberfan. The mud coming down the hill. The screams.

'I really don't know what to say. I'm just a writer.'

The two men exchanged looks and packed away their briefcases. Rhona watched her manuscript disappear and felt a dread rise up from her stomach. The two men got up.

'Well, as you are unable to help us, we'll leave you to it. Thank you for your time,' said the Englishman.

Rhona showed them to the door. The Englishman stepped out onto the street and the American went to follow but paused. He was facing Rhona and was close enough so she could smell his cologne.

'Do your dreams tell you what will happen?'

Rhona's mouth dropped open. The American smiled and spoke in a whisper. Soft and slow.

'Do you really think you're the only one?'

CHAPTER TWENTY-FOUR

2019

JOE

Joe walked into the Six Bells pub and straight up to the bar. The place was virtually empty. The barman he had met before was talking to a customer. By the way he was casually leaning against the bar Joe guessed it was a regular. The barman looked up and immediately recognised Joe. He stood up and came over. Slowly.

'Just having a drink?'

'No. Actually I wanted to ask you about Lee Melis again. We got off on the wrong foot last time and I thought you might have something to tell me.'

'Shame to waste your time, but like I said, I do not know that man.'

'I know Lee drank here, okay? So why lie to me because I know you are lying? Why don't you just tell me what you know and I'll go?'

'I don't need to tell you shit.'

'You don't. That is true I suppose.'

'And I don't have to serve you or allow you in this pub. So how shall I put this politely? Oops, I can't. Fuck off.'

'Wow. Good line.' Joe tried to remember which Guy Ritchie film he'd heard it in.

'No. I mean it. Fuck off.'

'What's the problem? You know Lee. I know you do. Do you know where he is? Did he pay you to deal in here?'

The barman tensed up. Joe had touched a nerve. A guy his size was usually listened to and obeyed by others. But now Joe was calling his bluff and making an accusation that the barman had to react to. With a regular sitting right there at the bar, who would report to everyone else what had happened that day, the barman needed to control the narrative.

The barman walked around the bar and towards Joe. His face was set on confrontation and his eyes were popping. Joe recognised all the signals.

'Hey, I don't want to fight you. I'm just looking for a mate.'

Joe scanned the room and took a couple of steps away from the bar. The regular who sat on the stool had jumped off and was backing away like he was in some wild west saloon. Besides him there were only three other customers in there and they hadn't even noticed what was unravelling. The barman was three feet away when Joe half raised his arms in surrender but moved his feet into a boxer's stance.

'Hang on mate.'

The barman launched a right hand. It was slow and signposted. Joe blocked it with his left forearm and simultaneously punched the barman in the face with his right. It was a stun shot as Joe was unable to put his full force behind it.

Without missing a beat Joe grabbed behind the barman's neck with his right hand and moved his left arm under the barman's shoulder and over onto his back. With the barman now stunned and locked in place, Joe pulled him downward whilst bringing his right knee up into his midsection.

The barman jolted upward in pain. Joe kneed him twice more in quick succession and then tugged onto the guy's neck to bring him down onto the floor. The barman lay on the ground, catching his breath. Joe stood over him.

If he tried to get up to carry on the fight Joe was ready to kick him in the face. He'd been kind up until now. Joe looked over at the regular. He was still stood there, fixed to the spot. He met Joe's look for a fraction of a second and then looked away, telling Joe he was just a witness but not a threat.

The barman slowly raised himself to his knees and looked up at Joe. He put his arm up. He'd had enough. He was tapping out.

Joe grabbed him, hauled him up and sat him on a bar stool. He was heavy.

That was the problem with guys who worked out in gyms for the big muscles. They were slow. They needed too much oxygen to operate and ran out of gas too quickly in confrontations. Most weren't fighters either but just guys who found their self-esteem and confidence improve with their muscle mass. But some thought they could do both without the necessary training. And that was a mistake. Joe had seen thin, weedy guys with boxing, BBJ, MMA or Krav-Maga experience defend themselves against big, muscle bound men with inflated egos and win easily for those very reasons.

Joe turned to the regular.

'Show's over. You going to finish your drink then?'

The regular nodded and retook his place at the bar, making sure to look straight ahead and not in Joe's direction. Joe turned back to the barman.

'So now are you going to tell me about Lee Melis?'

The barman looked ashamed and kept his eyes on the floor. He'd let himself down.

'Look, I got lucky okay. I don't want to fight you. Just tell me about Lee,' said Joe.

'He used to drink here. I knew him. He didn't deal here though but just come in.'

'But you knew he dealt?'

The barman nodded.

'And what about when he got beaten up?'

'It wasn't here. I swear. He came in early one evening and then ordered a taxi. He said he was going to a party. He goes off and then comes back a couple of hours later all beaten up.'

'What did he say?'

'He just wanted a drink. I was offering to go round and help him sort out whoever did it but he didn't tell me anything. He just had a drink and stormed off. That's when he stopped coming in.'

'And that's it?'

'Yeah, that's fucking it.'

'So why the attitude? Sure you didn't let him deal and then take a cut?'

The barman shook his head.

'I promise you, he wasn't dealing. Not in here. I wouldn't let him.'

'So why?'

'I let him crash here occasionally. He'd sort me out as a kind of payment. That's all.'

'Any of his stuff here?'

'No, nothing.'

'How much would he sort you out?'

'Does it matter?'

'Was it a few lines? Or was it a few grams?'

The barman stared at Joe, speculating why he wanted specifics.

'A few grams. Every couple of weeks if he crashed here. It wasn't all the time.'

Joe had his verification. Lee was dealing and enough to be able to pay for lodging with coke. He had one more question.

'Do you know what taxi company Lee used on the night of the party?'

Joe walked out of the pub and started up the hill. He heard footsteps behind him and glanced back. It was Mike. He caught up with Joe and walked alongside him.

'Thanks for the back-up, mate.'

'You didn't need me.'

Mike had gone into the bar twenty minutes before Joe to scope it out. He'd sat at the back by the windows and silently watched the confrontation, with instructions from Joe to step in if Joe was losing whatever went down or if any of the barman's friends decided to jump in.

'Still good having you there though.'

'No worries. Nice block and hook mate.'

'Thanks.'

'Obviously don't use knees in my thing but an effective move nonetheless.'

'Cheers.'

They walked the rest of the way home in silence.

Joe decided to send Samantha an email update later that evening after his shift at the bar. Wording it took a while. He had never really done this before and it took some time trying to keep to a formal, factual reporting style. Finally, he opted to just stick to the facts in bullet points. He completed a draft aiming to check it when he came in or first thing in the morning over coffee.

Work at the bar was more fun than he had anticipated. Catalina stuck around after her shift and the place was busier than normal. Sergio came in with some family to eat and was in a good mood. They had a young guy in the corner with his guitar performing some classic covers which improved the atmosphere and mood. He found himself forgetting all about Lee Melis for a few hours as he lost himself in the music and work.

At around ten in the evening Claudio and Matteo came in. Claudio and Matteo were two brothers around Joe's age who he had grown up with. Their father, Aldo, had worked for Joe's dad when he had run one of the first Italian restaurants in Bournemouth back in the seventies.

When Joe's dad had made himself scarce, Aldo had struck out by himself and opened a small restaurant in Springbourne, a neighbourhood of Bournemouth couched between Boscombe and Southbourne. He called it La Bella and it had proved a success with its Anglo-Italian menu of Spaghetti Bolognese and prawn cocktails. He had been there ever since.

Claudio had gone to work for Aldo after leaving school whilst Matteo went to catering college and then onto London and Rome for valued work experience in a variety of kitchens. It left him with a hungry, ambitious plan to make his own mark on modern Italian cooking.

With Aldo now nearing retirement, the plan was for Matteo to take over as head chef at La Bella. From talking to him Joe knew Matteo was intent on modernising the menu in an attempt to educate Bournemouth on what Italian cuisine had become in Italy and places like London. The town still hadn't got much further than the prawn cocktails served up in the seventies and eighties and was far behind the times.

'Well this makes a nice surprise,' shouted Joe over the music, shaking their hands as they took up position at the bar.

'We thought we'd pop in. We were at the Richmond.'

The Richmond was a nearby pub along the high street.

'And Valentina hasn't seen you in years.'

It was only then that he realised there was a third person with them. Claudio and Matteo made some space and Valentina moved in between them.

'Hi Joe. Remember me?'

'Oh my God,' said Joe, leaning over the bar to give her a hug and a peck on the cheek.

'You remember our cousin then?' asked Matteo.

'Yeah. Course I do. You look great,' said Joe.

Joe took in her dark hair and eyes and a wave of instant attraction surged through him. She was in her thirties now, and the last time Joe had seen her, it must have been nearly twenty years ago.

'How come you never looked me up? I've just heard you were in London,' she said.

'You were in London too?'

'For a time. I was working in the City.'

'I never knew.'

'Joe disappeared off the radar for a number of years, didn't you?' said Claudio. 'We didn't even know where he was.'

'Well I'm here now. What can I get you all?'

Joe served drinks and made small talk. Valentina was down with her mother and father visiting family. She now lived in Woking near her parents who ran an Italian deli there amongst the large Italian community. Valentina, who had worked for a law firm in the City, was now a consultant of some kind who was able to work from home the majority of the time. Home sounded like an expensive apartment in the nice part of town.

'What are you doing tomorrow?' asked Matteo.

'Nothing I believe.'

'Want to come to Sunday lunch at ours? Dad's cooking.'

'I'd love to. Will you be there?'

Joe looked at Valentina. She smiled.

'Yeah.'

'Well we can have a proper catch up then.'

'How come you came back to Bournemouth, Joe?' she asked.

Joe shrugged. He couldn't help but feel embarrassed.

'Couldn't afford London. How come you left the City?'

'Wanted a new start.'

Joe nodded and looked into her eyes, detecting an edge of sadness.

They stayed for two drinks and then left. It was difficult to hold a conversation with them whilst working so Joe was thankful for the invite to visit tomorrow.

He finished around two in the morning. Sergio cashed up whilst Joe restocked and cleaned the bar. Both men headed out onto the street at around three. The high street was still busy and Joe was careful to steer clear of the obligatory drunk young men who, with one look, would be happy to start a fight.

Joe thought it was odd that in all the years he spent in London he never had any trouble, but yet in Bournemouth, he found a nightlife on the edge with people happy to resort to violence easily and often. Maybe it was frustration, Joe thought, as he crossed the road to go down a side street to get to his car.

On the way to his vehicle Joe thought again about Valentina's question. *How come you came back to Bournemouth, Joe?* He had felt embarrassed and he knew why.

The answer was that he had left Bournemouth vowing not to return. He wanted to travel the world, see places, meet people, and experience other cultures. The usual youthful ambition. Bournemouth had bored him, stifled him and made him long to escape.

He had moved up with little money and got a job at Waterstones bookshop on King's Road. He loved it. He got friendly with an older Iranian guy who had fought in the Iran/Iraq war a few years earlier and was full of stories. He remembered his tale about the delivery of a load of tanks from the Russians that turned out to be German tanks captured in World War Two, and how they had to fight the Iraqis in them with the German crosses still on the sides.

Joe had then gone into bar work with the aim of becoming a manager. But it just hadn't happened. And however many reasons Joe could come up with of why it hadn't worked out and why he had returned, he still felt and knew it came back to the simple fact that he had failed. And that failure was because he was still haunted by his love for a woman he would never see again.

He had fallen in love, screwed it up and had lost her forever. He would never recapture those days or moments that had made him so happy. All he had left was the memories which lingered each passing day, refusing to let him move on and heal. He should have stayed and struggled some more. Not given in so easily. Sought help if it was affecting him so badly.

Better to have loved and lost than never loved at all, he said to himself, but he wasn't convinced.

He had made a mess of things. And now he was approaching middle-age and still felt like he hadn't got started. The problem was he lacked a plan.

He kicked the thoughts out of his mind. Things can change he told himself.

As he got near his Honda Jazz he got his keys out. He was the first to admit his car wasn't the most impressive of vehicles for a single man over forty years of age but cars had never meant much to him. It had never been the status symbol that many of his peers had seemed to obsess about. For him a car was for getting from A to B. When he had been offered the vehicle at a good price from a friend who was selling it for his mother, he had happily accepted.

Joe pinged the locks open and heard a rustle in the front garden behind him. He turned and saw the outline of a small bat emerge from the darkness, swinging round towards him at head height. He didn't have time to react as it struck the side of his head, sending a sharp shot of pain through his skull. He stumbled backwards and managed to lift his forearm to deflect the second swing as the bat came crashing down toward his head. At the same time he felt someone punch him in the ribs and hoped it was a fist and not a knife. In pain and dizziness he staggered back against his car, trying to move out of range, realising he was being attacked by more than one person.

The worst thing to do in any confrontation is end up on the ground, especially if there are multiple attackers involved. So Joe pushed himself off his car and charged at the guy who had punched him, lifting his elbow up across his face as he did as both a defensive and offensive move.

The man he ran into, about six feet tall, was wearing some kind of black mask which may have been the type cyclists wear. Joe was sure he heard the guy's nose break as his elbow collided with the attacker's face. The guy squealed with pain and shuddered as Joe attempted to both push him back and spin him round to use him as a shield against the other attacker who held the bat.

As he did Joe could see the empty street to his side and a clear path to safety as long as he could run. But then he felt a pain in the back of his head and everything went black.

CHAPTER TWENTY-FIVE

1980

RHONA

Questions overwhelmed her. *Why not just tell the truth? What harm could it do? The Englishman had a point surely?* She did have a moral obligation. That had been the whole point. *Hadn't it?* She had thought writing about it was enough. *But what did that achieve?* Elvis still died. Even after her heartfelt letter of warning to Graceland. Iran still had a revolution. *Was it just the success she craved at whatever cost?*

The men in suits and their questions.

Rhona's thoughts twisted and turned as she paced her living room. She was agitated and not thinking clearly now. She was in a state of panic. They had scared and unsettled her. The American. And the Englishman with his sweet smiles. *Do you think you're the only one?*

What did they know? What was she doing?

She had changed the names in her new book because she feared the publicity. Because she was becoming too well known.

Because what made her would now break her.

Because she did nothing to help.

People were listening. People were making the connections. And people were scared.

She had become dangerous.

Rhona tried to calm herself. She stopped pacing, sat down, closed her eyes, and concentrated on her breathing. She started to feel better.

Thinking about it now and taking deep breaths, Rhona was pleased she had said nothing. *What had they done to the others who admitted their dreams?* The ones who came out and said yes, they had dreams that foretold events. Dreams that invaded their minds and took over their lives. Dreams that haunted them in their waking hours. Like children being buried alive. Dreams that you would never wake up from.

But John Lennon and Ronald Reagan would be shot. And once that happened they would come for her again and they would not accept her denials another time. They were probably watching her right now. Probably had her phone tapped. Her mail intercepted. Her life dissected, analysed and appraised. Rhona felt the panic returning. They would come for her. It was November 1980. *How much longer did she have?*

'Can you stop it going out to anyone?'

'Rhona, what has gotten into you?'

'Can you stop it going out to publishers? I don't want it read.'

It was dark. Rhona stood in a phone box in Leicester Square. She had got on and off buses, hopped on tubes, and gone up and down streets before coming here all the while looking over her shoulder in case she was followed. She was soaked through and tired. Her eyes darted about amongst the tourists around her, looking for undercover policemen or spies but all she saw were people moving quickly through the busy square to get out of the rain. She wondered if they were listening to this call. Perhaps they had tapped Shirley Verne's telephone too. Shirley sounded unamused.

'The short answer is no. Far too late, dear. I've sent copies out already. And why on earth would we want to stop it being read?'

'I have to go.'

Rhona went back to her flat. She packed a bag and her passport, still unsure of where she was going to go but sure she just had to get away. She paused in her living room and stared at her typewriter set up on her dining room table. That would stay.

She locked her front door and came outside. It was dark. She looked up and down the street then headed for the tube station. As she made her way down the street a car drew up ahead of her and stopped at the kerb. It was black and polished. Official looking. The passenger door opened and the Englishman who had come to her flat with the American got out and held the door open.

Rhona slowed down and stopped.

'Are you off somewhere?' he asked.

'Is that any of your business?'

The Englishman smiled.

'We've got a couple more questions we'd like to put to you.'

'I don't want to come.'

'Do you really think we were just going to let you run away? Especially after that call to your agent. Come on Rhona, get in. Be a good girl.'

Rhona hesitated and glanced behind her. Two men lingered a few yards up the road. She had been right. They had been watching her and her own panic had revealed her guilt. And now it had come to this. She was trapped.

She reluctantly got into the car. The Englishman got in next to her, closed the door and the car drove away.

Rhona stayed silent as they crawled through the city streets. They drove towards Vauxhall and headed over the bridge. The Englishman stared out the window. Eventually he turned to her.

'Don't worry. You're going to be just fine.'

Rhona said nothing as they drove towards Westminster. The streets became more crowded and the car slowed as traffic jammed the roads. Up ahead some traffic lights were turning red. Rhona glanced at the Englishman. He was looking out the window on his side, lost in thought.

The car stopped at the lights.

Rhona said a silent prayer and flung open the door and jumped out. The Englishman turned and tried to grab her. He missed and went to follow her out of the car. Rhona turned and slammed the door into him. She heard him yelp and swear as she took off down the street, heading into the crowds. She dodged and weaved and allowed herself one glance back.

She saw heads running her way. She darted down an alleyway and disappeared into the darkness until she found two Chinese waiters smoking outside an open door. She ran past them and into a hectic kitchen full of chefs, smells, and trays of food. She bolted through some swing doors and into a busy restaurant.

Some diners holding chopsticks looked up at the panicked woman who had just appeared. Rhona slowed and forced herself to walk as calmly as she could to the front door. She exited onto the street and saw a black cab drop off a happy couple right in front of her. A few paces more and she was in the taxi.

'Where to, love?'

'Just drive.'

CHAPTER TWENTY-SIX

2003

MANDY

16 February 2003

I start a diary today. This is it. Why today I hear you ask? Well, why not today? I have started diaries before but I never carried them on and I regret that now as when I look back at them and read about what I got up to, all the memories come back. Otherwise your experiences and memories fade over time, and if that's all we have, then a diary is not just a journal but a form of security. A blueprint of who we were, are and could be. A way to remind ourselves of our meaning to the world.

People die but diaries last. It can be our legacy that stretches through time. Samuel Pepys would not be remembered today if his diary had not survived. I'm not saying I'm Samuel Pepys or that anyone would be fascinated by reading my diary in four hundred years' time, but you get the idea. Okay, I'm getting carried away. More people should write a diary so here's mine.

My name is Mandy Smith, a boring name I know, but someone has to be called that. I'm twenty-seven years old and I live in Tooting, London. Yesterday I went on the anti-war march in central London to protest against the war with Iraq that Blair and Bush are about to start.

I don't want this to be all about politics though, but it will be on occasion as it's a scary time we're living in. Tony Blair seems to have gone mad and cosied up with George Bush. We're going to war and lots of people are going to be needlessly killed. It seems like a lot of people don't care. Which is wrong. And that's my motto really and one I tell people when I can. Who Cares Wins.

The march was amazing and it wasn't just in London that people demonstrated but protests happened all over the world. We started off at the Embankment and slowly made it to Hyde Park. It didn't rain which was good and we managed to hear a bit of Harold Pinter. Ben needed to poo so we slowly made our way back though London and stopped off at Gordon's Wine Bar in Villiers Street for a few drinks.

I wish more of our crowd had come along but excuses were made. It does make me wonder at what point people decide that a line has been crossed and action needs to be taken. Like back in Hitler's Germany there must have been so many occasions in the early days when people thought *wait up, this isn't right.* But they didn't do anything and before long it was too late. It makes me angry – people's apathy and indifference and how, as long as they're alright, they don't bother about anyone else. Who Cares Wins, eh?

Which brings me onto Joe. When I got home Joe was watching TV. He had his feet up on the sofa. It winds me up. He could have taken the day off work and come with us, but he didn't. It has taken me a while to realise that Joe is a cynic. He doesn't vote because he says he doesn't trust any politicians but fails to present any other alternative to improving things. Even going on the biggest protest march in history didn't interest him as he said it wouldn't change anything.

But how does he know that? Surely a government has to listen if enough people protest? They did when people protested against the Poll Tax didn't they? We've been going out for four years now and (I really hope he doesn't find this and read it) he has a lot of good things going for him but I'm not sure if we're going to continue much longer.

Good points – he's a great cook and lover. He's kind. He's enthusiastic about things if he's actually interested in them like when he started coming to my Krav class. He's good looking, of course but is he the one? Should there even be *the one*?

I came up here to find myself and experience new things but I'm now living with a guy who comes from my hometown. How did that happen?

Bad things – he doesn't read. I just don't get people who don't read books. Do they not realise what they're missing out on? I've got him to at least read *The Guardian* and his politics weren't Tory thank God but I don't think I'll ever see him in a Che Guevara T-shirt. I even considered buying him one for his birthday but I realised that would be a bit cruel. And he wouldn't wear it. And he's quiet.

Joe is one of those people who sits and listens rather than gets involved and I don't want that. I like to be challenged. Maybe that is his challenge to me? Passively resisting my attempts to politicise and enthuse him about new things.

I work for ActionAid. It's a worthwhile cause that helps women and girls living in poverty. I'm an Admin and Research Assistant. There's opportunities to progress. I feel like I'm making a difference.

But Joe is happy to stay working behind bars serving drinks to people all day and night. He's a clever guy though. He's been up here for quite a while now and I've hinted he needs to start thinking more about a career, but he doesn't seem to care.

Am I judging him? Yes. But I'm not getting any younger and I want to start thinking about buying a place soon which means mortgages and sharing a flat with someone since I can't afford a place to myself.

Is that with a boyfriend or a friend? I could ask Ben if things go pear shaped, but he's going out with some guy he says he's in love with, so that will mean they'll probably get a place eventually. Or do I go with Joe who just seems to drift through life without ambition. He's just too bloody laid back!!

Anyway, I get home and I think the catalyst is the feet up on the sofa. It sets me off and we have an argument. Or rather I have a go at Joe. He just doesn't get it and his inability to see what's making me so angry makes me even more angry, so I go upstairs which is good timing as Lee phones.

Poor Lee. He's a friend from Bournemouth that I keep in touch with. I haven't told Joe about Lee as he wouldn't really understand our relationship I think and he might get needlessly jealous. Lee is one of the only people I do keep in touch with from Bournemouth. He's a lost soul is Lee. He phones me and I phone him.

I've seen him a few times and things are either going okay or going really shit. He's going through a 'things are really shit' stage. I keep trying to get him to go to the doctor and get some antidepressants as he needs them and, to be honest, I don't feel like I'm getting the full picture with him sometimes. I sense he's not telling me everything, a bit like a drug addict who lies so much it's almost normal for them, and it gets so much you never really believe a word they say anymore.

He's seen the march on the TV and asks if I went. Of course I went I tell him. He seems happy about that and says he wished he could have come. I stop myself from saying *so what stopped you?* as some people you have to treat with kid gloves. Lee gets uncomfortable if you challenge or pry with him. Maybe one day he'll talk more and open up about his issues. I know he has had drug problems in the past and I hope he's moved on from that. He sounds normal and just wants to catch up which is nice.

He tells me he's reading *The Magus* by John Fowles which he picked up in a charity shop. He says I should read it and I note it down. Lee is one person I can talk books with. And to think he didn't even read books until a few years ago is amazing.

I eventually finish the call with Lee and sit on the bed wondering what to do when Joe knocks on the door and comes in all sheepish and apologies even though he doesn't actually know what he's saying sorry for. And now I feel guilty because I am judgemental, and I need to keep a lid on my temper sometimes and be more considerate. We hug and he offers to make me some dinner which I accept as the fillet-o-fish I had earlier wasn't enough. He tells me he loves me and I tell him I love him back. I used to mean it but now I'm not so sure.

CHAPTER TWENTY-SEVEN

1993

LEE

I meet Nathan at the Anchor pub in Springbourne on Sunday afternoon. It was a part of the town on the slide. Lots of bedsits and junkies overflowing from Boscombe. Nathan was from New Zealand and had come over a few years earlier and been at the same school as myself.

Weed brought like-minded people together there and we had got on. Nathan had only recently come out of hiding when we meet at the pub. He had started selling pills which, being six feet seven inches tall, meant he didn't get much hassle but stuck out like a sore thumb, especially with the accent. It was a shame to see him go downhill as the party lifestyle had taken hold, but then again, we all seemed to be in the same boat. Jobs seemed hard to keep if you had one and none of us ever put on any weight and only lost it.

Nathan had been in hiding because he had fucked up. He got too hungry for his own supply and ended up owing a dealer called Smiler a lot of money. Enough to not go out for a few months as he tried to clean up his act and clear his head. He got a job in a hotel and worked on the bar. It was a nice hotel, a place all the top snooker players stayed at when they played at the BIC which was the Bournemouth International Centre. One of his jobs was to restock the mini-bars in all the rooms.

One day he walked into a room where a Russian businessman was staying. On top of the TV was a stack of US dollars. A massive wad. Nathan pocketed the lot and checked the guy had enough vodka. The police were called when the Russian came back to his room and realised he'd been robbed and everyone was questioned but there was no evidence. Supposedly the Russian was going mental. Why he had left his money there in the first place beggared belief.

When Nathan counted it when he got home he had four thousand dollars. He then set about changing the dollars to pounds. I helped him out for a small fee and a few of us drove round all the places you could change up currencies. We went in with a few hundred dollars at a time, each armed with the story of just getting back from Florida if any conversations were started up. The last place I went into I bricked it. I handed the woman behind the screen the money and she took ages staring at the dollars. I started to sweat as I clocked the cameras all over the place. She went and got her manager who inspected the notes. I felt like legging it. Finally, after what seemed like ages, she came back and gave me the sterling.

'What was all that about?' I asked.

'We thought some of the notes might have been forgeries.'

'Wow. What would you have done then?'

'Called the police.'

That was the last time I changed any of the money up for Nathan.

A few weeks later and carrying a load of stolen dosh, Nathan met Smiler and paid him his money back plus interest. He made sure to meet him somewhere public in case it kicked off. And Smiler seemed contented, especially after Nathan gave him a big sob story about being such a fuck up and it wouldn't happen again. All was forgiven. Nathan started dealing again, but this time adding cocaine to the ecstasy he was already flogging.

When I meet Nathan in the pub he's on a come down and already on his second pint of Stella. It's just gone twelve and the pub has only just opened. We get drinks and play pool. It wasn't often I met Nathan without a load of us being there but he had called and I came out.

He was a sociable bloke and deep down a decent person. He was clever too and could talk about all sorts. We played a few games and sunk a few pints. Before long the regulars were piling in and Nathan is nipping off to do deals in the toilets and in the car park.

The pub is dodgy and a shit hole. I wouldn't have been surprised if half the clientele there were undercover coppers whilst the other half are drug addicts. At one point I play a guy called Horse at pool. I'd heard of this guy. As criminal as they come and dangerous. Long hair in a pony-tail. Baggy T-shirt and jeans that both needed a wash and thin, tattooed arms. He was probably in his mid-twenties but looked older. He knew Nathan so he was being nice with me as I beat him at pool. The drinks were still going down and Nathan is away more and more and I'm with these people who make me nervous. Eventually Nathan comes back over.

'Fancy a smoke?'

'Yeah go on then,' I say relieved to be leaving.

'Mickey has invited us round his place.'

I don't know who Mickey is but we're soon round at his flat that's five minutes away from the pub. Nathan is chatty and half pissed but I'm edgy, knowing the booze has made me a bit woozy and I can't think straight.

There are loads of people round Mickey's and I don't know any of them. It's a big flat with a big lounge, high ceilings, sofas, and bean bags. It's quite a tidy place to be honest and Mickey seems friendly enough as Nathan skins up.

I sit on a sofa and accept the spliffs being passed my way while making small talk with the people there who are all a bit older than me. I get the impression they're all on pills as they witter on. Mickey's phone rings which is soon passed to Nathan who, in clumsy code, makes arrangements to sell to whoever is on the other end some drugs. He finishes the call and gets up.

'Back in ten minutes, mate.'

And he leaves me there. I take some tokes on a spliff and someone hands me a can of Viborg, some kind of cheap extra strong ghetto lager. The liquid goes down though and takes the edge off.

'Fancy a hot knife?' asks Mickey.

I nod and follow him into his kitchen where four blokes are standing around the cooker with two knives heating up in the flames. I don't usually do hot knives. I associate them with an old school way of ingesting pot. My mates and I usually do 'lungs' which is a plastic bottle cut in half with a plastic bag wrapped around the bottom. You then heat pot up on some foil on the top where the lid would be and pull the bag down slowly, bringing the smoke into the bottle which you then suck in in one go. Hot knives look like too much faff with a chance of burning yourself.

I wait my turn as pot is squeezed between the knives and the smoke sucked up hungrily. It's my turn and I get a good pull and step back, keeping the smoke in my lungs as long as possible. I blow it out and wait for the hit to come.

'What's your name then?' asks the bloke standing next to me.

'Leon,' I say. There's no way I'm telling this guy my real name.

I wander back into the lounge but someone has taken my seat. I sit down on a beanbag next to a pile of records as the hot knife hits me. I start to feel spooned and regret accepting the offer of the knives. I begin to regret even coming round here as I go silent and retreat into my own world.

A funny smell lingers and I clock that one of the many dodgy fuckers surrounding me is now smoking heroin. I start losing it. Thoughts and fears start to bounce around my brain. I can feel my heart beating fast and I need some water but I have to make do with Viborg as I don't want to go back into the kitchen.

I need to get a job and stop all this. I need to be able to sleep and pray when I do the nightmares don't come. I'm proper fucked now. I feel myself sweating and I feel faint. I want to cry. I want to hold someone I can trust. I want my mum. I want to start all over again. Reset the clock as I hadn't been ready this time. Unprepared for life. I want some fucking meaning next time.

My vision swims and I know I can't even stand up. All that booze and the pot, which I know sends me loopy, has trapped me here. I know Nathan won't come back. He'll be off on one till the middle of the week now knowing him. He won't care. Nobody cares.

I try and focus on the records but they're all shiny and like I'm looking at black holes ready to suck me in. I'm acting a part now and pray no one speaks to me otherwise they'll see the terror in my eyes. I need to just wait. Wait until the pot wears off so I can get out of here and go home. Go home to lie down and cry.

CHAPTER TWENTY-EIGHT

1980 - 1982

RHONA

George Frenton studied Rhona sitting opposite him. They were in the Coach and Horses in Soho. George had been reading *The Telegraph* when she had rushed in. He had recognised the fear behind her eyes straight away and her relief when she saw him. She had gotten lucky. He was just about to leave. She repeated her question.

'I need a passport.'

George's face didn't register her words for the second time. He just sat there, looking at her. Blank faced. Like a face that had denied a thousand crimes in its time.

'The police are looking for me. I need to get out of the country.'

Finally, as though a decision, plan and its execution had all been worked out, George got up.

'Wait here.'

He went to the bar and made a call from the telephone on the counter. Rhona sat still and tried to stay calm. George came back shortly holding a glass of brown liquid.

'We need to get a photo done. You look like you need a drink.'

Rhona felt like crying as he handed her the glass. She sipped it and felt the strong taste of whisky slip down her throat.

'Thank you. I haven't got any money. Not at the moment.'

'You can owe me.'

'I expect you're wondering what I've done.'

'I don't want to know.'

George glanced at his watch.

'It's probably safer if we wait upstairs.'

Rhona nodded and got up. She turned to follow George as he headed to the bar and presumably out back to where the stairs were. It was then that both doors to the pub leapt open and policemen marched in. Rhona froze and turned slowly to George.

She had expected to see signs of shame and apology but George looked stone faced at the policeman as they were quickly surrounded. He turned to her.

'It wasn't me.'

The fact that the room was so mediocre unsettled Rhona. She had expected a dark room with a single bulb hanging low above a splintered desk. Perhaps a rusty lamp aimed straight at her terrified face whilst moody shadows roamed around her. She expected film noir but got *Dixon of Dock Green*.

She sat in an office with a table and chairs on both sides. Windows looked out onto central London traffic that filtered up and reminded her that life went on regardless of what happened here. She had been in her chair for an hour. She was curious as to whether it was a psychological ploy to unnerve her. She needed the toilet. Was this Scotland Yard she wondered? Or was it MI5?

The door opened and in walked a man in his fifties. He wore spectacles and a tweed three-piece suit with a file in his hand.

'You must be Rhona O'Shea. Sorry to keep you waiting.'

He sat down across the table from her and adjusted his glasses before flicking through the file.

'I'm Doctor Walker,' he said without looking up. 'I'll be taking care of you from now on.'

'What do you mean?'

'I run the study. Didn't they tell you? On precognition.'

He looked up. His face looked kindly like he smiled a lot.

'You do have that ability, don't you? That's what it says here.'

'I think there's been some mistake. I'm just a writer. I make stuff up.'

Walker smiled.

'The world is a cruel place isn't it? I mean at the minute we're in a ghastly Cold War with the Soviets. Imagine what life would be like if they took over? Have you ever really thought about that? It's a matter of trust with you isn't it? It's understandable. But we are the good guys. You can trust us.

'As much as it may not look like that right now, consider the alternative if they were to get their hands on you. And we need all the help we can get. Sometimes we have to be a little cruel to be kind.'

'I don't understand what you're saying.'

'Let me spell it out for you then. If you refuse to cooperate you'll never get out of here. It's as simple as that.'

'I'm an Irish citizen. You can't keep me here.'

'We won't keep you here. We have a hospital we're going to take you to. And whatever is on your passport means nothing to me. I let the suits handle all that. But think of your mother back in Ireland if it helps. Cooperate and you'll get out and be able to see her again. If you don't, she'll die wondering whatever happened to her daughter.'

Rhona stared out the window. She suddenly felt exhausted.

'Are there others like me?' she asked.

Walker smiled again and closed the file in front of him.

'Of course there are.'

They took her in blacked out windows to the hospital. Or what they called the hospital which was about an hour outside London. She wasn't sure as they had taken her watch. It was a big country house set within large grounds. She couldn't see or hear any traffic. She was led down wood panelled corridors to her room which was like a glorified prison cell only more clinical with white walls, a desk, and a chair. Bars on the window let in diffused light through frosted glass. She was given clothes and a meal which was left there as the door locked behind her.

She lay on the bed that night and cried.

The next morning it began. She didn't see Walker but instead a group of doctors, or at least people who looked and sounded like doctors, in their white coats with their crisp manner as they asked her countless questions. The questions and answers were recorded. They wanted to know everything.

When the visions started, what she had seen. At first it was just a conversation as she outlined her life's history. After a few days they wanted the detail. The colours, the smells, the sounds of her dreams. They asked if she could control her dreams, move around and perhaps influence events. They asked if she was a time traveller as if she could will herself into the future. She said she couldn't and pondered if others could.

All the time she saw no other people there besides the doctors. No other patients as they were no doubt called. She was limited to her room, a deserted canteen and supervised walks outside twice a day where she would look up at the sky and wished she could fly.

After they had exhausted her history they tried hypnosis. They said they wanted *just a bit more information.* She remembered nothing of these sessions, but the doctors seemed annoyed as though they didn't get what they wanted.

Next, they wired her head up to a machine that might have measured brain waves but looked like a big, cranial lie detector test as it whirred and spat out graphs as they asked her even more questions like *Imagine a street in Paris in 1985. What do you see?* and showed her pictures of political figures like Leonid Brezhnev and asked what she saw. They clutched clipboards and scribbled notes wearing serious faces. She couldn't give them much as she had never been to Paris and didn't really know who Leonid Brezhnev was.

And each morning came the same question. *Tell us what you dreamt about.*

But all the time there she had no visions. She slept nights filled with normal dreams. Dreams of her at home in Ireland, walking around London, having coffees in Soho, and nights alone with Andrew.

Rhona often wondered what he was doing as the seasons changed and she tried to guess how long she had been there for. She began to scratch a small line on the wall as each day passed and wished she had done this from the start. It felt like they wanted to disorientate her, and it was working. She thought of Steve McQueen in *The Great Escape* as he sat in the cooler with just his baseball for company. She knew how he felt. Except she had no baseball and no great escape planned.

And they waited. And she waited. Once she thought she heard carols being sung. Another day she smelt fresh paint. Another day the pipes rattled. Every event took on new meaning. One day she could swear she heard the other patients. Once she heard screams.

Time stretched on and all she could measure it by were the scratches on the wall and the leaves on the trees.

Eventually Doctor Walker came to her room and sat down heavily on the chair. He wasn't smiling.

'Rhona, there's a feeling amongst the staff you're holding out on us.'

'I'm not. I've told you everything I know.'

'If you don't cooperate how can I help you?'

'I am cooperating. I have cooperated.'

'John Lennon was killed. Did you know that?'

'No.'

'And President Reagan was shot. He survived. Did you know that?'

'How could I? I haven't seen a newspaper for God knows how long.'

'What about the Falklands?'

'What?'

'Tell me about the Falklands.'

'What are the Falklands?'

Doctor Walker shook his head and stood up.

'You're making my job harder. Do you realise that?'

'I don't know what you expect me to say. I've had no dreams or visions since I've been here.'

'Maybe you need a bit of help then.'

Rhona waited until nightfall for the sounds of the hospital to grow quiet as patients and staff either went home or went to bed. Night staff were basically a skeleton crew of Orderlies and a couple of doctors dotted around the hospital in case of an emergency. She had noticed the Orderlies at night were the least attentive and the least interested in their jobs.

Their uniforms were not so crisp and their eyes were usually heavy either through lack of sleep or from something else. The

Orderly who worked on her section was often a large man in his early thirties she had nicknamed Bod. They were not allowed to give you their real names so Bod he became.

He, like the rest of the staff, was uncommunicative and said very little. By now she knew the staff had to do their rounds. They were supposed to look in on each patient twice a night and she had often heard him enter her room whilst she had pretended to be asleep. She felt him watching her as she lay in her bed and heard his heavy breathing, hating to think what might be going through his mind. He always had a bottle of water on him that she suspected contained Vodka or suchlike as late into the night she had often heard him snoring outside her door or singing quietly as though in some drunken stupor that you could only really get away with if you worked alone.

That night she waited until there was only silence and waited some more until she heard Bod approach, going from room to room to do his usual first round of checks for the night. As he got closer she could finally hear him unlocking the door next to hers. She heard him open the door, and waited as he looked in on the poor patient next to her that she still hadn't met. He locked the door again.

At the very second he locked her door Rhona dropped the glass of water she had by her bedside onto the floor. It smashed, as she had hoped, into little pieces making a satisfying sound.

She wasn't even supposed to have glass in her room and had grabbed it earlier when she spotted it sitting under a bench when she had been allowed outside for her supervised walk, thereby giving her the nucleus of an idea for a plan she knew she had only one chance to make work. Failure would mean increased security and scrutiny. Failure would mean never getting out.

She sat and waited, looking at the broken glass on her floor and hoped nothing would prevent the next stage of her plan being put into action. As predicted Bod had heard the smash and hurriedly opened her door. He rushed in and Rhona jumped up.

'Look, look,' she shouted hysterically and pointed at the floor. 'Look at it, there's something there.'

Bod, puzzled now, flicked the light on and moved towards the breakage.

'Look, look at it,' said Rhona again, still pointing.

Bod bent down to inspect the ground, confused and unsettled by the disruption to his usual routine. At that moment Rhona leaned down and unclipped the bunch of keys on Bod's belt, pushed him to the floor and ran for the door. She came out into the corridor and slammed the door shut behind her. She only had seconds as she quickly found the silver key that she had noticed time and again was used to open her door. She pushed the key into the lock and prayed she had the right one as she turned it. It locked as Bod tried to open it from the other side. Rhona turned and ran with Bod already shouting for help.

She headed down the long corridor aiming for the door at the far end that led outside into the grounds. As she made it to the door she heard shouts behind her. Other staff members had arrived at her room, alerted by Bod's yells and they had now seen her.

Rhona tried the door. It was locked. She still held the bunch of keys and tried one in the lock, desperately hoping that one of the keys would give her access to freedom. Nothing. She tried another. Nothing.

A whistle echoed down the corridor. She glanced back. Another Orderly, the whistle in his mouth, was running towards her. She tried another key. It was still the wrong one. She tried another. The door unlocked. Rhona flung the door open and ran as lights started coming on all across the grounds. She ran down a gravel path and then onto the grass with the aim of making it to the woods nearby which she hoped led to a road. She could hear shouting behind her and feet on gravel. She prayed they didn't keep guard dogs on the grounds.

She made it to the woods and ran on stumbling through the undergrowth, careful and hoping not to fall. She allowed herself a glance back and could only see shadows now against the glare of the hospital security lights that had all been turned on and as though aimed towards her.

Rhona ran on, and within a minute, made it to a tall wire fence. She was about to jump onto it to scale it to the top when she recognised the yellow sign hanging off the wire with a bolt of lightning across it. The words *Electric Fence* ran under it, just in case the futility of the situation needed confirming. The words felt like a mixture of threat and challenge.

She swore at herself as she caught her breath. She hesitated for nothing more than a couple of seconds before taking off again. She ran on alongside the fence and away from the hospital hoping to find a gap somewhere but now she could hear the crunch of feet behind her. They were getting closer.

The lazy Orderlies she had hoped would be her pursuers now felt more like dedicated and trained staff, usually hidden from view of the patients and only brought out on occasions such as these. Realising time was running out Rhona ducked down behind a fallen tree and lay down as flat as she could and waited, holding her breath and properly praying to God for the first time in many years.

She heard male voices and saw torch beams sweep the woods. They got closer and closer as Rhona felt herself sink further into the dirt, willing herself to be devoured into whatever grave would take her. The voices moved on and Rhona waited. Finally, she allowed herself a sigh of relief and pondered her next move. Above she could see the stars through the trees, and for a second, enjoy the tranquil sight of space and its infinite possibilities. The next second she felt her feet being grabbed as she was dragged out from behind the tree and into the path of a powerful torch beam.

'Got you,' were the words she heard come from the darkness.

CHAPTER TWENTY-NINE

2019

JOE

Joe awoke in darkness. He was on the ground, half on the pavement and half on the road with his head resting on the pavement. He slowly turned himself over and briefly stared up at the stars. He ached all over. The smell of fast food mixed with the crisp air as he got his focus.

He felt the pain in his head and winced, still disoriented and confused. He turned to his side and lifted himself up then sat for a few seconds to let what had happened came back to him like waves. He looked at his watch. It was almost three fifteen. He must have been knocked out for seconds and not minutes which was good. He checked his pockets and found his wallet and phone were both there.

As far as he could tell he had no broken bones and concluded his attackers must have fled soon after they had knocked him out. Maybe they got spooked by a passing car or person. Or maybe they thought they had done him enough damage.

Joe slowly got to his feet and climbed into his car, realising he had been lucky. Other attackers would have carried on hitting him when he was unconscious. He could be a bloody mess now, quite possibly dead, but he wasn't. They had hit him a few times and gone. It looked to Joe like he had received a warning. He sat for a few seconds in the driver's seat, trying to decide on what to do. He started his car up.

'What? And you drove home and just went to bed?' asked Mike the next morning.

Joe had come home and had gone straight to bed. When he awoke he knew he should have gone to the hospital to get checked out. And now Mike was reminding him of that fact as he washed down some paracetamol.

Head injuries can seem minor but prove deadly. A hard knock like that from a bat could have caused bleeding and swelling on the brain and easily death. There was every chance he could have gone to sleep and not woken up again. At best he just had concussion.

'You need to get to hospital,' said Mike. As part of Mike's job in the boxing world was dealing with head injuries he knew the drill. 'I'll take you.'

Joe was still too shaky to complain. He was happy to be loaded into his own car and driven to the hospital by Mike. They sat side by side in A&E while Mike drank watery coffee from a plastic cup.

'You sure they were waiting for you?' Mike asked.

'They were in the front garden behind a hedge of the house where my car was parked.'

'So they knew where you worked and what car you drove.'

'I worked that out myself.'

'It has to be the barman.'

'Might be. How'd he know where I worked and what car I drove?'

'Googled you. Looked at your Facebook page. Or followed you. There are ways. You should go to the police mate. This Colombo gig you got going isn't a walk in the park is it?'

'I feel okay. I just got a bit of a headache.'

'But it could have been a lot worse.'

'Maybe it was just a mugging. Or they got the wrong guy.'

But Joe knew his own words didn't ring true. He hadn't been robbed. He had been targeted. He needed time to work through every possible cause.

'I very much doubt that. Someone had it in for you. And they still might.'

Joe was soon seen by a nurse and then a doctor who decided to do a CT scan and X-Ray. Joe told them he had been jumped by two drunks rather than two masked men who had stood and waited for him in the shadows. Nothing showed up on the scan, so by midday, Joe was persuading the doctor to discharge him to the care of Mike who promised that if Joe displayed any worrying symptoms, to get him back to hospital as soon as possible. The doctor, who wanted to keep Joe in longer for observation, acquiesced when Joe persuaded him he would be freeing up a much sought-after bed.

They walked out into the sunlight where Joe sent a text off. As they reached Joe's car he got a reply.

'You want to come to lunch at Claudio and Matteo's parents' place?' asked Joe.

'Aldo's?' Like Joe, Mike had also grown up with Claudio and Matteo and their family.

'Yeah. I got invited to lunch last night.'

'You're still going?'

'I'm hungry.'

Mike laughed.

'What a surprise. But I can hardly just come over.'

'They said it's fine. I've just texted them to ask.'

'That's good of you.'

'I can hardly bail out and leave you when you've done all this and I didn't want to cancel the lunch.'

Mike sniggered.

'Trust you to just be thinking of food.'

Joe smiled. He didn't want to tell him it was more to do with the fact that he wanted to see Valentina again.

After going back to their house to change they picked up a bottle of wine from the Co-Op and went over to Aldo and his wife Janet's place. They lived in a house in the Littledown area. It was a large, family home with a dining room that allowed space for a long oak table where Aldo could put on his banquets. Today though, they were informed, the Sunday roast and been predominantly cooked by Janet who met them at the front door.

'The English do the best roasts,' she said as though stating a fact.

Aldo, who stood behind her in the spacious hallway, shrugged and opened a bottle of wine as they were shown in. After kisses and hugs they were led into the lounge where Valentina's mother and father sat. Valentina's father, Paolo, looked like the spitting image of his brother, Aldo, and it was often thought that they were twins although Paolo was the elder by two years.

Claudio and Matteo soon joined them and small talk was made. Joe made no mention of the attack and put it out of his mind. His headache had almost gone and he felt okay if just a little tired. He looked around for Valentina and hoped she hadn't decided to head home early.

'You know when you get bored of that Spanish bar there's a place for you at the restaurant,' said Aldo after asking how Joe's work was going. He always said *the Spanish bar* and Joe was sure he got the nationality wrong on purpose. It was a familiar refrain he would always make when they met and Joe often wondered if the offer was a result of Joe's dad running off when he was just six years old.

Joe's dad and Aldo had known each other since childhood back in Sardinia and had come to England to work together. But whilst Aldo was a loving, generous husband and father, Joe's dad had been the opposite.

When he finally left, with an eighteen-year-old girl on his arm, Joe and his siblings had felt relieved, and whilst Joe had found it difficult growing up without a father, he also understood early on the alternative would have been far worse.

But he always suspected that Aldo may have felt some kind of guilt or responsibility over how Joe's dad had behaved, although there was no need. In some ways Joe would have liked to have worked in a familiar Italian restaurant but being good friends with Aldo was different to having him as your boss.

Aldo was well known to have a classic Italian temper and would often flare up in the kitchen when things weren't going right. Matteo, by contrast, was quieter. He was still as demanding as a head chef should be but he was calmer, making people think he took after his English mother's side. His brother Claudio, who was front of house as Maître D', had more of an Italian disposition and was known at school for solving any problems with his fists.

Joe thanked Aldo and said he would think about it. Aldo shrugged.

'Well here she is at last,' said Janet.

Joe looked up to see Valentina had entered the room. She had on a black jumper and jeans with her hair tied back. Joe smiled at her and tried to hide the attraction he felt. Valentina glanced his way and nodded. Joe wondered if he was blushing.

At the dinner table Valentina sat opposite Joe. Joe had been first to sit and he hoped she had chosen her place on purpose. As they tucked into the roast dinner Valentina glanced over at him and gave him a questioning look.

'Did you hit your head last night or something?'

Joe put his hand up to the large bruise at the back of his head that he had hoped no one would notice.

'I knocked it on the bar. How did you know?'

'When you got off the sofa you seemed to be massaging your head. Is it okay?'

Joe hadn't even realised he had done it. He decided to change the conversation.

'Yeah it's fine. What are your plans before you go back then?'

'I think we're going for a walk along the beach this afternoon but for the next few days I'm not sure. There's talk about visiting Corfe Castle and Studland.'

'That would be nice.'

'Are you working this week?'

Joe chewed his food slowly, making sure he was careful.

'Not all week,' he answered.

Valentina ate but her eyes remained on Joe. If Joe was going to do anything, it was now.

'Maybe we could hook up for a drink. I didn't really get a chance to speak to you last night,' he said.

Valentina didn't answer straight away, and for a moment, Joe worried that he had been too clumsy.

'That would be great,' she finally said, taking a sip of her wine.

Joe smiled at her and couldn't help but notice Claudio giving him a look that said he knew his game.

Joe drank his wine and enjoyed the meal.

They ate a feast. A full roast dinner was followed by cheese, ice-cream and liqueurs. Joe steered clear of alcohol besides half a glass of wine with his meal but Mike, who had no work obligations that day, was swooped up by the celebratory nature of Italian meal times. By the time they left he was giddily tipsy.

At the door they said goodbye.

'I'll call you,' said Joe, giving Valentina a farewell hug and kiss.

She hung onto him just a beat too long.

'You do that.'

Joe floated out of the house.

Later that evening Joe needed to do one last thing. He dropped Mike home and made espresso. Mike dozed on the sofa whilst Joe tidied and kept busy. When it got dark Joe put his coat on and walked down to the Six Bells pub.

He entered and made straight for the bar. The barman who he had a confrontation with was at the other end serving customers. He had his back to Joe as he took the nearest stool and ordered a coke from the girl also serving that evening.

Joe glanced around the pub. It was a Sunday, so it was quiet now since the majority of the lunch time crowd had returned home to the TV, sofa and the thought of work the next day. He could spot the people who had come in for lunch and then stayed as their flushed faces and glassy eyes nodded and swayed. They would suffer the next morning.

There was also a bunch of younger guys on the pool tables and the solitary drinkers warding off their loneliness with the warm, friendly fuzz of alcohol. Music played from some stereo hidden behind the bar. *Lady Gaga* on low volume. Joe thought slow jazz would have been more fitting.

He kept his eyes on the barman as he picked up a newspaper from the counter and raised it in front of him to partially hide his identity. The barman turned around. His face was unmarked so Joe can't have elbowed him the night before. Joe waited for the barman to work his way down towards him, and with just a few feet between them, Joe lowered the newspaper. The barman spotted Joe and did a double take, trying to hide his fright. Joe watched his eyes. The barman stood for a few seconds, confused and fearful. Joe wondered if it was an act and looked for tells. Eventually the barman came over to him and spoke quietly so no one else could hear.

'What the fuck do you want now?'

'I was just in the neighbourhood,' said Joe.

'I told you everything I know okay. Jesus. Can't you just leave me alone?'

'Relax. I just popped in.'

Joe searched his face and didn't find what he was looking for. The barman moved away warily, as though expecting Joe to vault over the bar and attack him at any second.

Joe finished his drink and left the pub knowing the barman had no part in the attack on him the night before.

CHAPTER THIRTY

1982 - 1986

RHONA

'Did you have a dream? Is that why you ran?'

'No.'

'Then why did you run?'

'I was scared. I want to go home.'

'You can't go home until you help us.'

'But I can't help you.'

'Then you can't go home.'

They tried to break her. Into what she wasn't really sure.

They started with drugs. They came and injected her one day and when she awoke they said she had been asleep for three days. She wasn't sure she believed them. They had even inserted a catheter for the occasion.

Then came the electro-shock treatment. Rhona still felt groggy from the drugs they had already given her. She was unsure how long she'd been lying in her bed when they came to fetch her. They put her on a cold, hard trolley and wheeled her off to a room that looked like an operating theatre. They strapped her down and plunged a rubber gag between her teeth before placing electrodes around her head that looked like metallic headphones.

When they turned a switch on the machine the electrodes were plugged into, electricity tore through her head and she had multiple convulsions. For those few seconds the world went black and white and she felt like her bones were melting. This went on twice a week for four weeks.

And then came the LSD. She guessed it was LSD but they never confirmed it. Whilst her bones had melted with the electro shock treatment, she felt her brain melt on this drug. They calmly observed her screaming and panicking as she saw things that were not there and experienced the walls, curtains, floor, table and chair melt, move, and swim around her.

One day an Orderly told her Stanley Kubrick lived nearby but she didn't know why.

She heard the word Project MK Ultra whispered by a doctor.

They once left her for three weeks in her room with just a tray of food each day, pushing it through a post box in the door.

Time slipped away. Days and months drifted and merged.

The isolation felt comforting at first and then mutated to terror. She suspected her food was being poisoned so refused to eat. Eventually they charged in and forced a tube down her throat to feed her. She gagged and lashed out as they forced her to live whilst she wept for death.

And then one night a vision came and Rhona wept in gratitude at the awfulness of it. She welcomed the horror with open arms. She saw deserted streets and empty homes. Towns abandoned and overfilled hospitals holding the sick with their arms held out for help and mercy as they cried out in pain and vomited onto the floors. She saw soldiers and panic. She saw people die and the earth become uninhabitable and she was so happy because she had a name, given to her first in whispers, then words and then a thousand screams. Chernobyl.

When she awoke she banged on the door and they came and took notes, asking her countless questions that she answered through tears of joy.

They let her out of the room and let her walk outside. They gave her food she could eat.

She felt so thankful for their kindness. They seemed happy. Doctor Walker even paid her a visit and smiled at her. He rubbed her arm and said *well done*. They were good people after all.

They let her watch TV in the evenings. She sat in an armchair in a room staring at the television transfixed. It felt so warm and good. She wanted to stay. And they let her stay for weeks. Maybe even months.

One evening a newsflash came on. Breaking news. They didn't usually let her watch the news. A disaster in Russia. A catastrophe. An accident at a nuclear power plant. In Chernobyl. Rhona watched her dream unfold on the television. She felt the swirl of betrayal grow within her. She sat up and saw the four walls around her. She asked to see Doctor Walker.

'You have to understand Rhona there are reasons we can't always share the information you give us. You don't understand these things.'

But she did understand. They let it happen. They wanted Russia to fail and for the entire planet to suffer so one ideology could be victor over another.

That night she heard a radio outside her room playing Buddy Holly's "Raining in My Heart". She listened as she tied the bedsheets from her bed around the bars on the window. She hummed as she moved her chair and stood up on it and tied the sheet around her throat. As tight as she could. And then she kicked the chair away and felt her life swim out of her to the gentle sounds of the song.

CHAPTER THIRTY-ONE

1995

LEE

I arrive at Mad Mandy's at midday. She lives in a flat near my college at the Lansdowne, which is where I'm heading after. I get off at the train station and walk across the main road by Asda and down past the chippie and strip club to her place. She lives in a flat opposite a bowling green on the first floor. She opens the door with a hug and a big smile and I follow her up the stairs. Her flat is titchy but clean and tidy. On the blank walls are two posters. *Pulp Fiction* and a Bob Marley one she has cut up so the spliff Bob is smoking is now upside down. The TV is on.

'Tea?'

'Go on then,' I say.

I sit down on the sofa as Mandy busies herself in the miniscule kitchen and the kettle boils. She grins as she holds up some biscuits.

'Lovely,' I say.

'How you been then?'

'Alright.'

'Alright? Everyone's always alright.'

I laugh. She's called Mad Mandy but she's not really mad at all really. Just different. Her hair is wild and curly like an afro and she wears tight blue denim jeans with a tucked in white T-shirt. It's like she's arrived from the 1980s and hasn't twigged fashions have changed. But she just doesn't care.

She comes and sits down next to me with the tea and biscuits. I get the pot out.

'Eighth wasn't it?' I ask.

'Yep.'

I put the pot on the table. She picks up some rizlas and starts building a spliff.

'What you watching?'

'Fuck knows. I just had it on. I was reading. Can I still pay you when I get my dole through?'

I look at her bookshelf. It's bursting with books.

'Yeah, sure,' I say.

She burns some pot onto the papers. It's soap so it's nice and crumbly.

'How's college then?' she asks.

'Alright.'

I'm retaking my maths and English GCSEs.

'Alright,' she repeats sarcastically. 'So what are you going to do after that?'

'Dunno.'

I sip the tea and dunk a biscuit. She lights the spliff. I get off the sofa and pretend to look at the books on her bookshelf but it's really that I want to keep clear of the smoke.

'Do I smell or something?'

'Nah.' I decide to be honest. 'I'm not smoking pot anymore.'

She blows out some smoke.

'Why?'

'I get panic attacks.'

I don't mind telling Mandy for some reason. I know she won't take the piss I suppose.

'Shit. When did they start?'

'A while back.'

'You okay now you've stopped?'

I nod.

'I'm sleeping better.'

'But you're still selling it?'

I shrug nonchalantly. 'Don't get high on your own supply.'

I wanted that to sound cool but it just sounded crap. For the first time I look at the books on her bookshelf properly.

'Did you rob a library or something?'

'What do you like to read then?'

'I don't read books.'

'What the fuck?' she says.

I turn back to Mandy.

'What?'

'You should. Books are a free education if you join a library. If I'm not reading I feel lost.'

'I've just never got into it. My sister Sam reads books.'

'You're an artist Lee, you should.'

No one has ever called me an artist before.

'Art is the lie that enables us to realise the truth,' she says as though she's talking to a crowd and not just me sitting on her floor.

'You what?'

'It's why you should read. You'll learn things. Things like that.'

Mandy gets off the sofa and sits next to me with the spliff in her mouth. She starts pulling books off the shelf. I can smell her perfume now, even with the pot smoke circulating. She hands me three books. I read the titles. *Trainspotting*, *Dice Man* and *The Electric Kool-Aid Acid Test*.

'That will get you started. They're all great.'

'Okay.'

Mandy picks up on my reluctance and takes the spliff out of her mouth.

'What films do you like to watch? I assume you watch films?'

'Yeah.' Now I'm having to think. I'm trying to remember what I watched recently. I saw *Deep Cover* the week before on VHS with Laurence Fishburne. Quality movie. And what else?

'Sci-Fi.' I'd seen *The Omega Man* on Channel 4 with Charlton Heston.

She pulls another book from the shelf and puts it on the pile.

'There we go.'

She smiles. I really like Mandy. She's cool, clever, and confident. I'm glad she's my friend. We had met years earlier when loads of us used to hang around downtown, outside McDonalds and at an under-eighteen nightclub called Chicos which changed its name to Galaxy. Everyone knew Mandy. I wish I could just stay here all afternoon, but I need to go soon.

I look at the last book she's put on my pile. It's called *E.T.* by Rhona O'Shea.

'That one's mental. People reckoned she could tell the future.'

I freeze. My heart rate shoots up as I stare at the book jacket.

'Read them, bring them back and I'll lend you some more.'

CHAPTER THIRTY-TWO

2019

JOE

Joe got a call from Samantha the next morning. He had forgotten he'd finally emailed her his report the night before. He had left out the part about being attacked, still unsure if it was connected to Lee Melis.

'I would have called last night but I didn't read it till late,' she said.

'That's okay. What did you think?'

'Well if he was dealing drugs then I think he's probably hiding from someone. Knowing Lee, he owes someone money.'

'That's one possibility. It would explain why he was beaten up.'

'But it fills in a bit of detail about his life and how he was managing to live.'

Joe still wasn't convinced. It sounded like it could be the case but Lee as a drug dealer just didn't fit. He still didn't have the full picture.

'Will you go to the police?' he asked.

'I don't know. I'm thinking that if they hear he was a drug dealer before he disappeared then they'll care even less.'

'Give me a bit more time. There's still a couple of things I can check out.'

'You sure?'

'Yeah.'

Joe was silent for a second. He stared out of the window.

'Do you remember the actual date you saw Lee when he came back from the Six Bells all beaten up?' he asked.

'Hang on.'

He could hear her rummaging around.

'I had to go the dentist that day so it's in my diary. Will it help if you know?'

'I hope so.'

She found the date and gave it to him.

The taxi firm office for the cab Lee had ordered from the Six Bells the day he got beaten up was off Winton high street. Lee parked in the nearby Waitrose car park and walked round. The office was small. On the right there were two plastic chairs for customers waiting for a taxi. The left side had the usual glass window and desk behind it was a constant ringing phone. Sat at the desk and on one of the phones was a middle-aged woman taking details. She held up her hand to Joe and smiled, giving him the *won't be a minute* look. Joe waited until she had despatched a driver somewhere and turned her attention to him.

'How can I help?'

'Hi, I think I left some belongings in one of your taxis.'

'When was this?'

Joe smiled like he knew it was a long shot.

'It was a while ago now. It was my work diary and I've only just realised that I might have actually left it in the cab. Sorry.'

Joe gave her the date Lee took the taxi from the Six Bells pub.

'It was around six in the evening.'

The woman tapped something into her computer.

'Where did you get the taxi from and where were you going, darling?'

'Six Bells pub. I'm not sure on the address as it was in the diary but if you have it then I'll know.'

She tapped on the keyboard some more.

'Name?'

'Lee Melis.'

She scoured what he guessed was some kind of database of call logs.

'Lee at the Six Bells at six fifteen going to nine Oak Park Road?'

'That's it.'

'It was a while ago. Can you describe the diary?'

'Small. A5. Black leather cover.'

'Wait here.'

She got off her chair and disappeared out to the back in what must have been a larger office for the manager and drivers waiting for jobs. Joe could have walked out of the office then. He had the address he needed and getting it had been simpler than he had thought but he waited, keen to see the charade through to the end just in case he might need to come back at any point.

The woman came back after a few minutes.

'Sorry darling. I had a look through our lost property and it's not there. Our drivers are very honest though, so they would have brought it in and we always try to contact our customers if we can.'

'No problem then. I must have dropped it somewhere else. It was a long shot. Thanks for your help.'

Joe said goodbye, smiled and walked out. He went back to his car and looked up Oak Park Road on his sat-nav. The address was in Talbot Woods, an expensive part of the town where the wealthy resided. The houses around there were mini mansions in

Joe's eyes, most built at the beginning of the twentieth century amongst newly planted pine trees. The neighbourhood of Winton, where Joe currently was, which was far more middle and lower class, was right next to Talbot Woods, and the sat-nav gave the location as a mere five minutes away. Joe decided to check it out.

Minutes later he sat across the road from the house which was situated along a tree lined road. Probably built around 1920 it was surrounded by trees and shrubbery with a high, open gate that led onto a small gravel drive then to the double front door built into the centre of the house. Joe guessed it would have at least five bedrooms if not more, and whoever owned it, looked after the place with a well tendered front garden, clean windows, and a spotless black Porsche Cayman 2011 that sat out front. The house recently had grey PVC storm cladding fitted which had become popular over the last couple of years.

Joe got out of his car, self-conscious at the very unfashionable and very cheap car he drove in a neighbourhood like this. He felt like he was being watched and he probably was.

He walked across the road and up to the front door. The gravel from the drive scrunched under his feet. He rang the doorbell and waited, admiring the car even though he had no interest in it. The door was opened by a plump, balding man aged about forty, wearing a blue, open necked shirt and cream shorts. He held his mobile phone in his hand and looked like he was in the middle of something.

'Yes?' he asked as if time was money.

'I'm here to ask you about Lee Melis.'

The man grimaced, fear taking centre stage and something else that Joe couldn't put his finger on. He lifted the mobile phone to his ear.

'I'll call you back.'

He hung up without saying goodbye, just like in the movies.

'Are you a policeman?'

Joe was old hat at this question and answered without having to think.

'No, but I am investigating the disappearance of a man called Lee Melis. I have reason to believe he visited this property shortly before his disappearance. Could I come in ask and you some questions?'

'What if I say no?'

Joe had rehearsed this too.

'I will leave, and if and when, I submit my report to the police, I'll let them know of your refusal to co-operate and advise them accordingly. I may suggest they might want to pay you a visit, perhaps with a warrant to search your property.'

The man glanced over Joe's shoulder as though his neighbours could already see the swarm of police cars blue lighting it up the road. He opened the door wider.

'You'd better come in then.'

Joe stepped inside and the man closed the door behind him. Joe took in the opulent and slightly ostentatious hallway decorated in whites, golds and browns. It wasn't to his taste and looked like it had been picked out of a magazine with instructions to *just get it done*. Joe wanted to ask the man if he was divorced.

'Do you mind taking your shoes off?'

Joe nodded and slipped off his Adidas Original Samoa Vintage and left them on the tiled floor by the front door as the man led Joe into a lounge. A sixty-inch LCD hung on the wall above a white fireplace. Sky News played on silent to an empty leather sofa and chairs with French double-glazed doors leading off into a large garden. In the corner was a desk covered in paper with two computer monitors taking up the rest of the space. Joe couldn't see if the computer was on but guessed it was.

'May I have your name?' asked Joe, taking out his notebook and pen.

'You don't know it?'

He said it like he was regretting letting him in.

'All I know is Lee Melis came here. I can find your name if you don't want to give it to me.'

'I didn't mean that. My name is Bernard Harrison.'

He said Bernard like it was a foreign name. Ber*nard* of Scotland *Yard*.

'And you are?'

'Joe Zuccu.'

'Joe what?'

'Zuccu. It's Italian. Well, Sardinian actually.'

'Sardinian? I've been to Sardinia. I stayed in Costa Smeralda.'

That figured, Joe thought. He nodded like he was impressed. Now they had a connection.

'Lovely island.'

Joe nodded. Maybe he wasn't so bad.

'Please, take a seat.'

Joe went and sat on the sofa. Bernard took a seat, perched on the edge of one of the armchairs. He put his hands together like he was about to give Joe some bad news.

'So, you're a private investigator?'

'Of sorts. I'm working for Lee's sister.'

Bernard nodded, still uneasy about the confession Joe felt was about to come his way.

'So, what can you tell me about Lee?' asked Joe.

Bernard nodded some more but kept his eyes on the cream carpet. He shifted in his seat like the truth wanted to escape from his body but couldn't find a way out.

'I had nothing to do with his disappearance. When I found out he was missing I just knew it was only a matter of time before I got that knock on my door.'

'Why?'

'Lee was here. Before he disappeared. You know that. I know how this works, Mr Zuccu. You know more than you're letting on. I know you know more. You just want me to tell you what you already know and then more. Am I right?'

'You're very warm is all I'll say,' said Joe, not really having a clue what he was going on about.

Bernard smiled, pleased with himself for being so clever.

'So tell me what I know. And then some more.'

'Lee was set up. They got him here. I think they told him it was a party or something. But it wasn't. Not really.'

Joe nodded, wanting to write this down.

'Yeah. Go on.' He said it like it was old news.

'They didn't tell me they were setting him up. I was just having a get together and Bobby asked if he could bring some people over. I couldn't really refuse.'

'Who's Bobby?'

Bernard squirmed.

'A man I bought coke off.'

'Know his surname?'

'No. Just as Bobby.'

Joe nodded for him to go on. He'd come back to Bobby.

'So I had a few of my friends round and Bobby was supposed to be bringing the charlie and a couple of friends I'd thought, but a few of them turned up along with Lee. At first it was all cool. Lee seemed very polite and unconcerned. But I noticed an edge. I got a bad vibe you know but I couldn't work out what it was and I just thought I was paranoid.

'I get like that you know when I've had too much. Paranoid. I used to, I should say. I haven't done charlie since. Anyway, I swear I didn't know what they were going to do.'

'What happened?'

'After about half an hour they all went into my bedroom. Bobby said they needed to talk about something and I wasn't going to say no. So they all go in and next thing I hear is shouting and all sorts of commotion like they're having an argument, then I hear these shouts and bangs. It sounded like they're smashing my bedroom up, and then after a bit, they all march out and leave. They didn't say a word. They just left.

'So I'm like, what the fuck is going on and my friends, who quite frankly aren't used to any of this sort of stuff, are terrified. Bobby and his gang have gone so I go into my bedroom and the first thing I see is the blood over my bedroom carpet, which cost rather a ticket to get that properly cleaned I can tell you, and then I see Lee on the floor. They'd beaten him up. He had blood all over his face. I think his nose was broken. His eyes were bruised and he looked half-conscious. It was awful.'

'What did you do?'

'Well I got him up of course. Onto the bed and I was going to call an ambulance but he begged me not to. He came round a bit, went into the bathroom and cleaned himself up. Then he asked me to drive him to a pub which I did. It was the Six Bells. And that was that. That was the last time I saw Lee.'

'What about Bobby?'

'He called me the next day. After the party. He said I should forget about what I saw. He offered me a few grams of coke as an apology. Said it all got out of hand and he didn't mean for it to happen.'

'Did you accept the coke?'

Bernard pondered the question.

'I, well, I had no choice. I didn't want to take it.'

'But you felt you just had to. Did you ask why they beat Lee up?'

Bernard shook his head.

'And you didn't call the police?'

Bernard shook his head again, ashamed.

'So you scored off Bobby and Lee was a friend of Bobby's?'

'Sort of.'

'Sort of?'

'Bobby got his coke off Lee.'

Joe let this sink in.

'Bobby got his coke off Lee? So Lee was Bobby's dealer? Is that what you're saying? But Bobby and the others all beat Lee up?'

'Bonkers I know,' said Bernard.

'Who were the others?'

'I didn't know them. There were three of them. I only knew Bobby and Lee sort of but that was only because I went to meet Bobby once and Lee was there. The other guys I did not know at all.'

'How do you know Lee was selling drugs to Bobby?'

'He told me. He said Lee was the one who sorted him out. He was polite to him too. Deferential. Until the party and then he turned on him that is.'

'So maybe they robbed Lee?'

'Maybe.'

Joe was silent for a moment as he worked through various scenarios. None of them made sense. He was missing a piece of the jigsaw.

'You know where Bobby lives?'

Bernard shook his head.

'You know where he hangs out?'

Bernard shrugged.

'All over.'

'How did you meet him?'

'In a bar. I was drunk and he offered me some coke. And then I started buying off him.'

'Which bar?' asked Joe.

'It was downtown. The Slug and Lettuce.'

'How did you know Lee was missing?'

'Bobby told me.'

'I need you to call Bobby.'

'What? Why?'

'I want you to arrange to buy some more coke off him.'

'But I don't want to buy any coke off Bobby.'

'I know you don't. But I want to talk to him. I want to meet him.'

'But… But then he'll know I gave you his number.'

'Yeah, true. But I'll have a word with him and make sure there are no comebacks.'

'I don't think so. I don't want to get involved in any of this.'

'But you are involved. A missing person was beaten up by potential suspects in your home. How do you think that will play out as you're waiting to see if you can get bail?'

'Bail?'

'Bail.'

'This is ridiculous.'

'I'm not the one scoring cocaine off these guys. Look at it this way, would you rather I try and sort this whole mess out or the police?'

Bernard stared at the carpet like he wanted to be sick.

Bernard got his phone out.

Joe felt things were finally starting to come together. He was on the trail and getting closer although he was still bugged by the feeling that he was missing something crucial. Maybe it was just the sad thought that Lee ended up like this.

But people change, he told himself. He may have remembered Lee as some mellow stone head from way back but that didn't mean he wouldn't become a drug dealer hanging out with lowlifes. Everyone seemed to agree he had issues whether it be with alcohol or drugs or just his mind. Joe knew plenty of people who had fallen by the wayside.

He came out of Bernard's and sat in his car, figuring out his next move. He had some time to kill and there was one loose end he had not yet looked into. He drove away and was soon on the dual carriageway heading to Ringwood. He put the DMAs on the stereo and turned the volume up. On his sat-nav he had the address he had found in Lee's notebook, Charlie Chan style.

For a place so near Bournemouth Joe hardly knew Ringwood. It had the famous brewery and he thought back to the tour he had taken some years before which had been followed by an hour in the brewery bar sampling of all their wares for free. It had been a good afternoon. But besides that, he knew next to nothing about the place besides it was sleepy and old.

The sat-nav led him through the town centre. He was pleased to see it had a Koh Thai restaurant there at least. Soon he was away from the shops and amongst houses until he reached his destination.

He parked up and surveyed the house he had come to visit. It was older than the rest of the houses on the street, built around the turn of the last century. He got out of the car and made his way up the small, neat front garden to the front door and rang the doorbell. The door was opened by a tallish, middle-aged man wearing a striped shirt.

'Hi, I'm looking for a friend of mine called Lee Melis. I don't suppose you know him do you?'

The man let this information sink in and there was a very slight pause as he gathered his thoughts and spoke carefully.

'I know Lee Melis.'

Joe heard plates clattering behind him and glanced over his shoulder. He could just see a figure in the kitchen washing up.

'Do you know where I could find him?'

The man hesitated. He turned behind him and called out.

'I won't be a minute darling.'

A middle-aged woman glanced back from the kitchen. She wore washing up gloves and had dark, greying hair.

'Okay dear.'

She sounded American.

The man went outside and pulled the door. He led Joe up to the garden gate and checked the house before speaking as though he didn't want to be heard.

'Who are you exactly and how did you get my address?'

'My name is Joe Zuccu. I'm a friend of Lee's. I found your address amongst his things. He's gone missing and his sister has asked me to find him.'

'Zuccu? That Sardinian by any chance?'

Joe was impressed.

'Yeah. My dad is Sardinian.'

'I've been there many times. I haven't seen Lee I'm afraid. Have you called the police?'

'His sister is looking after that side of things. I'm just trying to help. How do you know Lee?'

Joe sensed something out of the corner of his eye. He turned to see the woman in the house peeking out from behind net curtains.

'AA. Alcoholics Anonymous. Lee was there. Did you know?'

'I did.'

The man turned to see what Joe was looking at and spotted the woman.

'My girlfriend doesn't know about any of that and she's probably wondering what this is all about.'

The man motioned to his girlfriend with his head to leave them alone. She moved away from the window.

'And I don't want her to find out.'

'Fair enough. Could I just ask for your name?'

'Simon Ashton.'

'Okay, so did Lee come out here then?'

'That was ages ago. He came over a couple of times. But that was it. I haven't seen him since.'

'Any idea where he might have gone?'

'Abroad I would guess. I know he wanted to travel.'

'His sister has his passport. He hasn't gone abroad. How was Lee when you saw him?'

'We were both in AA. It was early days for both of us so on edge would be a good description. I really can't tell you much else about him.'

Joe realised it had been a wasted journey and the guy sounded weary like he wanted to finish up.

'If you do see him could you ask him to contact his sister. She's very worried.'

'Of course. I wish I could help. Good luck.'

They shook hands and Joe left. The man watched him get back in his car before walking back into his house.

Joe started his car up and drove away.

CHAPTER THIRTY-THREE

1986

DOCTOR WALKER

Doctor Walker walked along the corridor with his head down and files under his arm. It had been an uneventful morning and he was already looking forward to a drink later when he got home. His pace slowed when he turned the corner and approached his destination. He stopped outside the room and lifted up the bunch of keys on his belt and soon located the master key that let him enter any room in the hospital. He nodded at the Orderly who sat outside the room and put the key in the lock then turned it, hearing the familiar clunk of possibility. He opened the door and peered in.

Rhona O'Shea lay handcuffed to her bed. She was on her back and was staring up at the ceiling. If you looked closely you could see the marks around her neck where she had tied the sheet and had tried to kill herself. But she had failed.

Doctor Walker watched her.

Rhona turned her head and stared at the doctor. Her face was passive but her eyes were alive and glowed. She smiled a small smile and the doctor felt a chill pass over him. He closed and locked the door quickly then hurried on to his office.

For the rest of the day he couldn't shake off the feeling that Rhona knew something that he didn't know, and whatever it was, it was bad.

CHAPTER THIRTY-FOUR

1996

LEE

I visit Mandy in London. She's just moved up. I get a coach to Victoria, then take the tube down to Stockwell, change to the Northern Line and head down to Tooting Broadway. Even the journey feels like an adventure. I've never taken the coach up before. The National Express is cheap and not too bad.

I read on the way up. It's *The Thought Gang* by Tibor Fischer, which is a book Mandy lent me before she left which I'm going to give back. It's a decent book and I'm really into my reading now. The tube is noisy and packed. I take my time making sure I go down the right tunnels and head in the right direction. I know I must stand out as a tourist, but looking round, a lot of other people are in the same boat and stand out a lot more.

At Tooting Broadway Mandy meets me. She's looking cool as usual and I give her a big hug. We've got closer over the last year or so and she's really one of my best mates. She moved up a few months ago and I waited a while for her to get settled before suggesting I pay a visit. A few other people have come up to London now. It makes sense if you're bored of Bournemouth as there isn't much going on. I've done all the clubs, bars, and sights. It only comes alive in the summer.

We walk down the high street and I notice the area is mainly Asian. Bournemouth is full of white people so it's kind of strange for the first five minutes and then it just feels normal.

Back in Bournemouth we had a mate called Saj who was Asian. He got so much racist abuse it was unbelievable but it's that small-town mentality, where people hate their own shadows because they're black, that has driven people like Mandy away, and made Bournemouth even more boring. Saj left as well, a year or so back, and I heard he's in New York now working as a professional dancer which makes sense since he's an amazing break dancer.

Mandy lives on Kellino Street just off the high street and I dump my bag there to meet her two housemates. Ben is about our age and is from Switzerland. He's just finished Uni down at Kent and speaks with an American accent since he went to an international school over there. Mandy says he's amazing on the guitar and he seems friendly. And there's also Kate who is thin and wears tons of make-up and has just got a job at MTV. She comes across as a bit of a space cadet but I feel she's not as daft as she looks.

Mandy shows me her room and it's a bit like her old flat but cooler. From the window you can see and hear the high street. I wonder where I'll be sleeping later on. Me and Mandy have never been like that and I wouldn't even try anything. We're mates and she's helped me a lot since I told her about my psychosis with weed and that. She's made some rolls for lunch so we eat them in the extension at the back of the kitchen and smoke cigarettes. They're vegetarian rolls since Mandy no longer eats meat.

'How's Bournemouth then?' she asks.

'Still the same. I'm temping in an office which beats factory work. I have to wear a suit every day.'

'Oh no.'

'Yeah. But better than a boiler suit,' I say.

When I first got to wear a suit I felt like what you did when you first start shaving, all grown up and important. I got it from Burtons and even though it was just off the peg it felt like it fitted me beautifully. And then, just like shaving, it becomes a drag when you realise that this is it, potentially for life. But although I seem to mainly be filing all day it was better than working in that pie factory in Poole I was in for ages. I'm still not sure how I made the jump.

I'd like to think it was my C.V. which, since I've started reading, has gotten more articulate as I put in more adjectives about what a great worker I am. That or I was just in the right place at the right time when a position came up.

'I'm temping too. Down in Wimbledon,' says Mandy.

'Near the tennis courts?'

'No, it's on the high street and Wimbledon Village is up the road which is well posh.'

'We're missing you back home. It's not been the same since you left.'

'The offer is still there to come up.'

There's a spare room in the house which Mandy offered me. It's tempting but I'm nervous about making the jump. The thing is I feel safe in Bournemouth. I know where I am. I know I'm in my comfort zone but it's how I feel.

'You know what I heard the other day? If you only go where you've already gone you can only get what you've already got,' says Mandy.

'Who said that?'

'I can't remember. Someone said it when I was pissed.'

It's a cool phrase and I nod like I'm considering it. Mandy has a habit of coming out with things like that.

'I'm thinking about the offer,' I say.

'Well don't think too long as we need to fill it soon.'

'So what's the plan then?'

We head back to the tube and up to Clapham to a bar called The Frog which is opposite the Common. Ben and Kate come too and over a few drinks I relax and start enjoying myself. It's lovely weather and things do feel different and cool.

Oasis blares out from the stereo behind the bar which I don't mind even though Liam Gallagher nicked his attitude from Ian Brown. I look around me and everyone is young and enjoying themselves. It's just so different to what I'm used to.

Mandy calls Bournemouth *The Wasteland* which she says she got from David Bowie who used the same word to describe where he came from and I'm getting it now. London feels like the kind of place where no one cares what you wear or do. Mandy was called Mad Mandy back in Bournemouth because she was unusual. She wore different clothes to everyone else who wore shirts to clubs and were happy with their lot. But up here she's just Mandy.

'I like being anonymous now. No one judges you or knows your history or who you shagged,' she says when I tell her what I'm thinking. I nod in agreement but know there wouldn't be much to discuss if people were gossiping about who I've shagged.

By the time we leave The Frog I'm feeling tipsy but I'm buzzing. The plan is to head down to Balham and go somewhere called The Bedford for more drinks and food. After that we'll head upstairs for some comedy night where Mark Thomas is performing. I've seen him on the telly so I'm looking forward to it. We hit the high street, and as we pass a bookmakers, Ben suddenly pipes up.

'It's Grand National day.'

I look over and William Hill have made an effort to bring in punters by putting bunting up around their betting shop. There's a couple of women in William Hill T-shirts on the door trying to persuade people to come in and put some money down.

'Horse racing is cruel,' says Mandy, but Ben looks like a child who's spotted a sweet shop. A child who's also a bit drunk.

'But the Grand National is famous. Come on, let's win some money.'

So we all troop into the bookmakers giving the two women smiles as we pass them. Inside there's information up on the wall telling you how to make a bet. Ben and Kate start examining who the horses are that are racing. I stay back next to Mandy.

I would put a bet on but I haven't got much cash. I know Mandy doesn't really like it either. I watch Ben and Kate laugh at the names of the horses as they try and fill out betting slips. I love the spontaneity of things like this even though Mandy disapproves. She's cool with it though and I look around the place.

Everyone looks busy as if they know what they're doing. And then I spot a woman standing next to man in the corner. She has some kind of hat on like she has cancer and is about forty or so but she seems to be staring at me. I glance back to see if she's looking at someone behind me but there's just a wall with some televisions above me. Maybe she's looking at the television, but it feels like she's looking at me.

Ben and Kate come back clutching slips, having put their bets down, and we leave to continue our adventure. I look back at the woman as we leave and she's still watching me. London is weird I tell myself and put her out of my mind.

CHAPTER THIRTY-FIVE

2001

AMY

The television in Clive's office showed images of the remains of the Twin Towers smouldering amongst an emotionally devastated city. Amy watched the screen, still transfixed weeks later on the attack in New York City as Clive, her editor, read through her article *Books that Predicted the Future.*

'The background stuff is good but the graphic novel still doesn't stand up. You're making this the centrepiece, Amy, but you haven't got enough to go on.'

'What about the report?'

'But Rhona O'Shea is dead so she couldn't have written the graphic novel?'

Amy inwardly flinched. Her scoop wasn't working out.

It had been Steve who had made the first comparison. He was an avid and life-long comic reader who had alerted her to the graphic novel's existence. *The Warning* by Trey Griffin written in 1999. He was a friend of a friend and had phoned her out of the blue, excited at what he held in his hands. When she had sat across from him, staring in disbelief at the images of destruction that matched those of the World Trade Centre, he had casually offered his opinion.

'You know the writing reminds me a lot of this other writer called Rhona O'Shea.'

'Who's she?'

Amy had taken her time. She read Rhona's books and noted the similarities. Agreed it could be possible. But she wanted proof. She went in search of Rhona and commissioned a report. A report from a forensic text analyst, an overweight man in a stained white shirt who dropped words like *idiolect* and *linguistic uniqueness* along with *authorship* and *consistency* in his monotone voice that went up in pitch at the end of each sentence.

But all the same, he was extremely convincing. He said that the language people used was just like a fingerprint. Unique to each individual. She gave him the graphic novel, *E.T.* and *The Return*, and according to him, the author of all three books was the same person. The same analysis that had identified Ted Kaczynski as the Unabomber back in 1996 now seemed to identify Rhona O'Shea as the author of *The Warning*.

'And don't forget the plot similarities too. The quest to find and save someone in each book. Not as definitive as the linguistic matches but it should also be considered.'

The only stumbling block of course was that although the book came out in 1999, Amy had discovered Rhona had died eight years before.

After Shirley Verne revealed Rhona's death, Amy had dug deeper for more detail. Rhona had gone trekking in the Alps with a boyfriend back in 1991. There had been some kind of storm. They got separated. The boyfriend managed to get down the mountain, but Rhona hadn't. The body was never found.

The boyfriend was Andrew Hunter, which may explain why he had not returned her emails. Perhaps he was still too distraught after all this time to talk about her work. Or maybe he was just hiding something. Amy eventually found an everything-but-in-name obituary in the *London Irish Daily*, a newspaper Rhona had once worked as a journalist. Considering Rhona O'Shea had been an author of some note this was all the coverage there seemed to be on her death as though the world really had truly forgotten about her.

It wasn't an official obituary because Rhona would not be declared officially dead, or presumed dead to use the actual official wording, until seven years later. The article talked about her literary career and her cult following amongst avid science-fiction fans. The details on anything else were sketchy. Rhona retained her mystery in death it seemed.

All this left Amy with was a standard article which may have been interesting and raised some tantalising questions about precognition but it failed to land the sucker punch and produce a living author who predicted the Twin Towers attack. Without Trey Griffin or Rhona O'Shea her scoop of revealing that a cult writer had re-emerged to make the prediction of the century had come to nothing.

'I don't care what the analysis says. She died before it was bloody written, Amy. You need to be careful making claims like that. Especially at the minute. It devalues the whole notion of textual analysis and would come across as sensationalist.'

'So what do you want me to do?'

'Change it. Make it broader and just comment on the alleged similarities. People don't want to be freaked out any further right now.'

Amy got the lift down to her office and buried her frustrations. On the way she thought about Rhona O'Shea. She knew she didn't have the story she wanted but she had become intrigued by the author and how she was said to have dreamt of the future.

Soon after the publication of her first novel *E.T.* Rhona had been interviewed by a journalist called Sandy Savage, which Amy was sure was a made-up name, for the magazine called *Fantasy Fiction* that has been around from the 1950s until the late 1970s.

'Where do you get your plots from?'

'I dream them.'

Three words was all Amy had to go on that might have revealed how Rhona did it. But it fitted with what she had read about other people who claimed to have seen future events in their dreams. The interview had been the only time she made any kind of revelation. Old copies of these types of publications could only be found now in second-hand books and comic stores which Amy had become increasingly familiar with as she trekked to and phoned places in search of any reference to the elusive author. Apart from the interview in *Fantasy Fiction* Rhona O'Shea always maintained she just made up her stories and events that oddly came true and never discussed or revealed her creative process.

Science fiction, by its very nature, could arguably be relied upon to correctly predict technology to some extent. Arthur C. Clarke had predicted satellite communications after all. But Rhona's predictions were something else. Specific, odd even, and in relation to the World Trade Centre, terrifying. The whole thing with the report and authorship of the graphic novel made it all the more mysterious.

Amy was annoyed. The truth seemed just out of her grasp. She only had half the story. The truth would have to wait.

CHAPTER THIRTY-SIX

2019

JOE

Joe sat in his car behind the Sainsbury's store in Boscombe and waited for Bobby to turn up at three o'clock. Bernard had described Bobby as a bearded white man in his thirties who looked *a bit fucked up* and wore a short black leather bomber jacket. So far Joe had seen a few men and women who fitted that description, but they didn't have the leather jacket or the body language.

At ten past three Joe got out of his car to stretch his legs. There was a chance Bernard had cancelled the pick up after he had left but Joe would put money on it that Bobby, following the tradition of every drug dealer worldwide, was just late. The car park was small and relatively easy to track people as they came and went. He was careful to appear relaxed and also scope out the road behind in case Bobby himself was using any security precautions and observing the area before getting closer.

By half three Joe was beginning to think he had misjudged the situation and wished he'd brought Bernard along in case Bobby himself had tried to reschedule or cancel by texting or phoning Bernard. Just as Joe was considering giving up and going into Boscombe, and to Boscanova for a coffee then maybe popping to Gallagher's shop to check out the threads, he spotted someone coming out of the alleyway between Boscombe High Street and the car park.

The man was thin, bearded and wore an angry expression like someone had just given him a parking ticket. He wasn't wearing a leather jacket but a red hoodie with frayed edging. Joe watched as the man scanned the car park for someone. And then his eyes came to rest on Joe and he did something unexpected.

His eyes widened in genuine shock and he momentarily froze like a rabbit in a head light. Joe stayed still himself and met the man's look, trying to appear as non-threatening as he could, like they'd just looked at each other accidently. The man took two steps back, turned and ran. Joe opened his mouth, as though to speak or shout for him to wait, and then his brain caught up with him and he gave chase.

Joe ran after the man through the alleyway and onto Boscombe High Street, pausing only to see which direction he had gone, and spotted him running towards McDonalds. Joe followed. No one seemed to be too concerned by two men sprinting down the pedestrianised high street and people moved out of the way as Joe got into his stride.

The man, who he assumed was Bobby, was still sprinting. Joe hoped it was adrenaline that was pushing him and that it would soon ebb. Bobby got to the McDonalds and carried on, going past the Cellar Bar and on towards Boscombe Gardens. Much to Joe's relief, Bobby started to slow as his legs tired. He glanced back and saw Joe coming up fast behind him.

Joe caught up with him just as they passed the Koh Thai restaurant and he managed to push the man to the ground. Bobby went tumbling over onto the pavement and rolled over hard. Joe stopped, out of breath and for a few seconds, considered the CCTV cameras potentially trained on him. For their benefit he raised his arms as though trying to defuse some kind of confrontation as he walked toward the man and pretended to help him up. Joe yanked him to his feet and kept a firm grip on him as he led him around the corner, off the high street, and into a small alleyway where some restaurant bins sat.

'What the fuck,' said the man, spitting his words out, still shaky on his legs.

Joe got up close to his face.

'You're Bobby aren't you?'

'I don't know what you're talking about.'

'I think you do.'

'Why'd you chase me?'

'I didn't chase you. You ran and I followed.'

With his free hand Joe pinched the man on the upper arm. The man yelped. It was a small but simple technique that Joe had learnt when he had gone through his martial arts phase and had been taught how a simple, small, but hard pinch was an effective way to release chokes or holds in training. It also confuses people as it's an unexpected move.

'What the fuck you doing? You just fucking pinched me?'

'Yeah and I'll pinch you again if you don't tell me the truth. You're Bobby right? You might as well admit it. I've seen your picture anyway.'

'Alright I'm Bobby. So fucking what?'

Joe was surprised how even people you'd think would be a bit more savvy could be just as gullible as the next man. Now he had the confirmation of who he was Joe asked the question that had been teasing him since Bobby spotted him in the car park.

'So Bobby, why did you run when you saw me?'

Bobby glanced away.

'I thought you were the police.'

It was a plausible explanation from someone like Bobby but Joe wasn't convinced.

'No, I don't believe that. You see, I think you know who I am.'

'I don't.'

'I think you and a friend of yours jumped me in Charminster the other night.'

'Not me.'

Joe pinched him again. Bobby yelped in pain.

'Stop fucking pinching me.'

'That's for the other night. You're lucky it's just that. Where's Lee Melis?'

'I don't know.'

Too quick. He had expected the question.

'I think you know who I am and I think you know where Lee is.'

'No I don't.'

'You're a shit liar, Bobby.'

Bobby actually looked gutted, like lying was all he ever wanted to do in life and Joe was ruining his dreams.

'You got your drugs off Lee and then you beat him up. Why?'

'I didn't beat him up.'

'Yes you did or at least the people you were with did. Why? Come on. Just tell me you twat.'

Bobby tried to pull away. Joe gripped him tightly and drew him closer. At the same time he raised his knee fast which connected with Bobby's genitals which sent Bobby bending over in pain.

'Why did you beat Lee up?'

Joe kneed him again. Bobby coughed as though he wanted to vomit. This wasn't going to look good on CCTV if there was any, but Joe had come this far and didn't want to stop now.

'I'm going to ask you one last time.'

'This is fucking police brutality.'

'I'm not the police. You know that.'

'Okay, okay. He's a grass. That's why he got battered.' Bobby said it like he just wanted to curl up in a ball and be left alone.

Joe stepped back. *He's a grass.* Joe noted he used the present tense. But the content of the statement was a surprise.

'Lee? Lee's a grass you're saying?'

'Yes.'

'Who'd he grass?'

'I don't know. Some mushes.'

'You're not making much sense now, Bobby.'

'We got told he was a grass and to give him a slap.'

'Who told you to do this?'

Bobby sighed.

'Lee's dealer.'

'And his name?'

'I'm not telling you.'

'You think I've come this far not to have it?'

'I can't give you his name,' said Bobby.

'Tell me, do you know where Lee is?'

Bobby looked him in the eye.

'No.'

'But you know I'm looking for him don't you? And if it gets to the point where I have good evidence that I think he may have been hurt further after his run in with you and your mates then I'm going to the police and if I go the police they're going to come to you. They probably know you already right? So if you haven't hurt him and you're telling me the truth, then give me the guy's name so I can ask him if he knows where Lee is.'

Bobby weighed up Joe's words.

'I swear I don't know where he went. He's probably just legged it or something.'

'Then give me the name of Lee's dealer.'

'Tom. Tom Martin.'

Joe recognised the name. Tom Martin was the man who had told Joe he had met Lee at an AA meeting. He had given Joe his name and hadn't tried to lie. The man who had been polite and forthcoming but had failed to mention he was a drug dealer who supplied Lee Melis and had then come to suspect him of being an informer. Joe pulled his phone out. It was important to contact Tom now before Bobby had a chance to get his word in and possibly compromise anything.

'Stay there,' he instructed Bobby as he went through his phone history and searched for Tom Martin's number. He found it and pressed the dial button. The phone rang and Tom answered.

'Hello?'

'Tom? It's Joe Zuccu. We spoke before. I'm looking for Lee Melis and I contacted you. Do you remember?'

'Of course. I do.'

'I'm currently here with your friend, Bobby.'

Joe waited for Tom to respond.

'Maybe we should talk,' came Tom's reply. It was measured and calm.

'That's what I thought.'

'How about the end of Boscombe Pier tomorrow morning at ten o'clock?'

'I'll be there.'

Tom hung up without saying goodbye. Joe put his phone away and looked at Bobby.

'You can go.'

'Why did you tell him I gave you his name?'

'Sorry.'

'That wasn't fair.'

'Get over it.'

Joe walked out of the alleyway.

Joe had dinner at his mother's that evening. She made sausages, boiled potatoes and peas with a bottle of white wine to go with it. Joe felt tired and still ached from the attack. He considered phoning Valentina but decided to hold off until he had met Tom Martin the next morning.

'You're quiet,' his mum said.

'I'm tired.'

'You should take some time off.'

Joe thought about this. He hadn't really had a holiday since returning from London. He had found the job in the bar three days after coming back and had been there ever since. Joe thought about his prospects. The big question of what he was doing with his life still hung over him and he knew his mum still wondered if he'll ever answer it.

What was he doing with his life? He was a forty-four-year-old single man with no career to speak of. He had accomplished nothing of note so far with his life and time was running out. He worked as a barman. He didn't know anyone else who did that at his age and knew his old friends must be curious as to what he was up to and probably gossiped behind his back.

Joe had done a lot of jobs in his life, but none were career worthy. Maybe that was his problem. Maybe everyone hated working in offices and doing what they did but they just put up with it for the holidays, security, their kids, pensions, and the nice house if they could get it. Or maybe they just planned better and were happy with what they had and actually enjoyed all of what Joe found numbing.

He shook his head. He was getting melancholy again and didn't want to spend time with these kinds of thoughts. Be thankful he had a job and somewhere to live. He was far better off than a lot of people in the world. He still had choices he could make. He could make some changes. He just had to make sure they were the right ones.

Joe stayed a little longer and helped his mum install the latest version of Whatsapp on her phone. He was proud of his mum at how she had embraced new technology and used it often. She had even started using the shortened style of texting that was popular with teenagers. Like when you're going to be *late* you text *L8*.

When Joe awoke the next morning he lay in bed savouring an unusual rush of excitement and anticipation to be meeting Tom Martin. He realised he had enjoyed the previous few days searching for Lee Melis. Maybe he was being flippant. This was a man's wellbeing on the line. His family were concerned, and a crime may have been committed. But there was a part of Joe that enjoyed the chase.

Joe realised he wanted to find Lee. He really wanted to find him and shake his hand then take him back to his sister to see her smile and cry with happiness because she loved him, whatever his faults. Joe wanted to succeed because then that would be an achievement and he didn't have many of them. In fact, he had none.

CHAPTER THIRTY-SEVEN

1998

LEE

We've had a good day. Lucy and I had come up to London and now we're on the train back to Bournemouth. She sits opposite me and looks beautiful. She stares out the window as we pull out of Waterloo and gather speed, the city racing past us.

I've been going out with Lucy for four months and it's been magic. We met at work. It's an insurance firm. The work is boring but it's no stress. I read books, go to the cinema, and go out with Lucy. She still likes to go to clubs but I try and keep away from them. I hardly drink and I don't do drugs. I'm clean and love it. I'm no longer alone.

We came up to Waterloo this morning and walked over to the South Bank for a mooch. I spent a lot of time looking at the books by the National Film Theatre whilst Lucy stared out at the Thames and smoked. We went across the bridge further down to look at the Houses of Parliament and walked back up to Covent

Garden where Lucy dragged me round a load of clothes shops. I didn't mind that.

We then headed up to Chinatown after stopping off at Foyles Bookshop in Charing Cross Road where I bought some books. After lunch we went through Soho to Oxford Street and to Carnaby Street, Bond Street and then back to Waterloo. We should have come for longer as we're both knackered now, and I would have loved to have met up with Mandy, but that might have been weird. I'm not sure Mandy and Lucy would get on.

Now we're on the train. Lucy has her Walkman in, listening to Techno. That's not my style. I'm more into Drum n Bass at the minute. LTJ Bukem and his *Logical Progression* album is my go to at the minute, and I can't stop listening to it.

We only had one small upset today and it niggles me. We stopped at the corner of Chinatown for an all-you-can-eat Chinese buffet for £5. It was packed with tourists. We loaded our plates up and I ordered some wine. I don't usually drink wine but it's a special occasion and I felt it was expected.

The waiter brought it over and poured us glasses and went off. I think they're usually supposed to hang around for you to check it, but this guy didn't. I suppose if you're eating a £5 buffet he doesn't have to. So we taste the wine and it tastes rank. Lucy makes a face like she wants to spit it out. I'm all for staying with the water but she wants me to call the waiter over and complain. I start to feel uncomfortable. I don't usually go to restaurants.

If we went to a Harvester as a kid, that was something special, and the whole etiquette thing confuses me. I usually stick to McDonalds which I know is bad. Mad Mandy used to say if they have to literally get a clown to come on TV to persuade you to buy their burgers then that says something about the quality of the food. But people buy it.

Anyway, I try and blag it and say the wine isn't all that bad but she's not having it and eventually she complains herself. They swap the wine with no questions asked like they know they've got a dodgy batch and saw us coming. So I feel a bit of a mug as she chugs the wine back. But I can't do anything about it now but I could feel her looking at me as though she's clocked who I really am, like I'm some sort of coward for not sticking my hand up.

Sat opposite her now on the train I get my books out of my bag and start flicking through one. No point dwelling on the meal.

We're soon out of central London and head through the suburbs toward home. Lucy takes her earphones out. Tinny Techno echoes around the almost empty carriage.

'What's that about then?' she asks looking at my book.

'It's a history of people who have had premonitions.'

I hold the book up. It's called *Seeing the Future* and I got it from Foyles from the Mind, Body and Spirit section.

'Premonitions? Like they know what will happen?'

'Yeah. Exactly.'

'Sounds like bollocks.'

'It's not. There's loads of cases where it's happened.'

'Like when?'

I'm not sure where to start. I know my shit as they say. I'm into this. I have been ever since reading that Rhona O'Shea book. In some ways I didn't really need to buy the book I have in my hands although there may be stuff in there I don't know yet.

'Okay, well there was a guy in America back in 1979 who had a dream about a plane crashing and it happened. His name was David Booth. He had the dream for ten nights in a row. He knew what type of plane it was as well and how it would crash. He told the authorities, but because he didn't know the date the plane crashed, loads of people died.'

I carry on.

'Have you heard of Aberfan?'

I'm on a roll now so don't even wait for an answer.

'It was a mining disaster in Wales back in the sixties. Loads of children died. Twenty-four people had a premonition it would happen. Afterwards some guy even set up this thing called the

British Premonitions Bureau and they had something similar in America.

'The Americans even had a government program called Stargate run by the CIA where they investigated premonitions. It only came out a couple of years ago. There was even this author, Rhona O'Shea, who predicted Elvis Presley dying and the Iranian revolution. And that's just some of the things that have happened.'

I sit back. I've made my case but Lucy is just looking at me with her mouth hanging open.

'What?' I ask.

'And you believe all that?'

'Yes.'

Lucy shakes her head like I'm a mug. It winds me up. I want her to understand. We go through a tunnel. As we enter the darkness I make up my mind. We come out of the tunnel and everything is light. I can see.

'I have premonitions, Lucy.'

'You have premonitions?'

'I've had them since I can remember. They do my head in.'

She says nothing but just looks at me. I don't know if she's waiting for me to go on.

'I dreamt of the Challenger Air Disaster and the Berlin Wall coming down. I dreamt of Princess Diana dying in a car crash back in 1994.'

She interrupts me.

'That's sick.'

'What's sick?'

'Don't fucking make shit up about Princess Diana.'

'It's true,' I say.

'You're not funny.'

'I'm not trying to be. I'm telling you the truth.'

'I wanted to go to her funeral.'

'Lucy, I've never told anyone this.'

But I've lost her. She looks out the window, angry, jaw clenched.

'I can't believe you make a sick fucking joke up about that,' she says.

It suddenly feels like she's sitting a lot further away than what she was five minutes ago. Maybe this has to do with the wine. She's been bubbling about it and now she's having a go. I don't like confrontations, so I go silent and we don't talk for the rest of the journey home.

She gets off at Springbourne, a stop early. She says nothing as she picks up her bags and leaves.

I go home feeling shit. My mum's out so I'm alone.

The next day I go to work. I can't see her at her desk but I see Dave who works opposite her. He smirks at me.

'Lee, what's the weather going to be like tomorrow, mate? I want to paint my outside wall. Any dreams on it?'

He calls this out so everyone can hear.

I head to the smoking shed outside. It's an old prefab building they use since they stopped people smoking inside a few years back. Lucy is there with two girls who work on the Assurance section. I ignore them.

'What have you said?'

'I don't know what you're talking about.'

Her tone screams attitude. The two girls stare at the floor.

'You've told people haven't you?'

'Might have done. I was just chatting.'

'That's out of order,' I say.

'I'm sorry.'

'You don't sound like you mean it.'

'Well you should know shouldn't you?'

They all giggle now. Lucy is enjoying this.

'So what you seen lately then?' she asks with mock curiosity.

I could tell her. I could tell them all but then what? They wouldn't believe me. No one would. So I stay silent. She shakes her head and stubs her fag out, exaggerating the action like it's me she's stubbing out. She gets up.

'Maybe we should have some time apart,' she says.

'You're splitting up with me?'

'Yeah, you got that right.'

And she walks out followed by her mates and I'm just left there.

PART THREE

CHAPTER THIRTY-EIGHT

1986

RHONA

The night had progressed like any other. Rhona had got into bed and stared up at the ceiling, the dim moonlight illuminating her room. She had lost weight these last two weeks and looked pale. Around her neck the bruising from the sheet she had tied around it was still visible. Her only mistake had been not to tie the sheet securely enough.

After pushing the chair away, fighting for breath and eventually giving into what she had hoped would be the inevitable, her own body weight and lack of skills with knots had let her down. Or saved her life depending how you looked at it.

She had eventually slid down to the cold, hard floor where she lay until she came around from unconsciousness. She thought of trying again but by then it was too late as an Orderly, on his round, discovered her and called a Doctor all the while keeping the door closed, deterred from going to her aid in case it was another escape attempt. She had no energy anyway and just waited.

They had kept her on suicide watch from then on with a guard outside at all times with orders to keep checking on her. Tonight was the first night alone with no guard coming in every few minutes and the first where she was not handcuffed to the bed. In those two weeks another vision had come to her. But she did not share this vision and instead harboured it in her mind and found comfort in it like a soft pillow.

When she had first arrived here she hoped that the visions were coming less and less and it seemed that was the case. For whatever reason she did not know and did not care. She welcomed the freedom to dream. At any other time and in any other place the dream she had would have alarmed her but this time it brought her pleasure. It was now a waiting game and she closed her eyes.

Sometime later she heard the shouts and awoke. Rhona was not sure what time it was but it was still dark. She lay listening as the shouts continued. And then she smelled the smoke. She got out of bed, went to the window, and saw an orange glow flickering outside. The waiting game was over. She went to the door but it was still locked so she sat back down on the bed.

The shouts turned to screams as terror overtook anxiety. She heard glass shattering and people outside. Along the corridor she could hear others slamming their fists onto their doors, crying to be let out. It got warmer in her room and the smell of smoke stronger until eventually the smoke began to make its way under her door. She heard fire engines, their sirens getting louder by the second. She drew her legs up to her chest and remained on her bed.

The smoke continued to filter in like a snake. The door creaked and the whole building seemed to cry out. She began to cough. She knew she should lie on the floor. Smoke rises but she was mesmerised by the dark clouds filling her space and fearless for what it would mean. It sounded like the end of her world outside her door. She coughed more and more. Her head began to swim from the toxic fumes. It won't be long now, she told herself. An almighty smash sent the door crashing down onto the floor and a fireman, done up in his uniform and breathing gear, entered the room.

She was led out by the fireman and into a corridor of smoke and flames. Acrid smoke and the strong smell of faeces filled her lungs. The door at the end of the corridor that she had escaped out from months or perhaps even years earlier was no longer visible, hidden by the black smoke and tearful screams. Instead she was led the other way into a vacated room and out a window that had been smashed open.

As she climbed through she noted this room had no bars and speculated who might have stayed here. Outside, people seemed to be running in all directions. There was no order. She was led onto the grass and told to wait with others on a verge a little way from the hospital. At that the fireman turned and returned to the blaze. Other patients and staff huddled in their pyjamas and robes, watching the flames devour the building. She contemplated walking off to once again take on the electric fence but chose to watch the place burn instead.

Fire engines and ambulances filled the grounds. Rhona couldn't take her eyes off the fire. The heat was immense and they had to step back a few times. She was in awe of what she was seeing and wondered how many of the other patients had the same dream as her and foresaw this very sight as they slept.

In the early hours she was moved to a conventional hospital where she stayed for the next few weeks as not only flames but scandal engulfed what was left of the hospital. News crews and journalists had swooped on the hospital and very soon questions were asked about what exactly this hospital was and who it was for. For the first time in years, amid all the confusion surrounding the fire, Rhona had access to newspapers and television.

With the rest of the survivors they watched and read with glee as the government came under pressure to explain what exactly had been going on in this place. Six members of staff had burnt to death and one patient had been injured but recovered. The police soon launched a criminal investigation. Words like *cruelty* and *torture* were often used to describe the *crazy experiments* administered by Dr Walker or *Dr Evil*, as the tabloids had started to call him, in the name of some covert program of mind control.

Two embittered staff members became whistle-blowers and exposed everything that had been going on to one of the Sunday newspapers, almost certainly for a very generous fee.

Patients and their families sought legal advice and lawsuits followed. A Commons Select Committee was set up with Walker first on their list ordered to attend. He would be their scapegoat. Pictures and news footage of him being hounded by photographers and journalists filled the TV screen that Rhona watched as he tried to escape their gaze when he came out of his home. His face showed fear as he jumped into a waiting car with blacked out windows and sped away.

It must have all been too much as just days before the hearing Doctor Walker was found dead in his local wood. He had shot himself with an old World War Two Luger. Apparently, apart from his questionable medical interests, he was also an avid collector of Nazi memorabilia.

Questions of foul play were raised as suspicious and inquisitive MPs felt they would now never learn the full truth.

Rhona was questioned by detectives and she told them what they had done. She said Doctor Walker began to make up results so the program would remain funded. Other patients said the same. She didn't know why she had been taken there. She was just a writer. The whole thing was a big con and they had been its victims.

The government went into damage limitation mode. Rhona guessed they would have found the whole affair far more convenient to explain if all the patients had died, but with a long list of survivors, Walker and his senior staff were soon identified as rogue operatives who had fabricated ludicrous tales for financial gain. There were some other minor resignations and very slowly the newsmen moved on.

Rhona was approached by a government lawyer who assured her the police investigation would probably go nowhere but they were offering generous compensation. They asked her if she would take it and sign a contract with her Majesty's government of non-disclosure. She took the money.

When she was finally released she realised it was now 1986 and she had been in the hospital for five years.

They had given her a flat to stay in. Only temporary whilst *they sorted this whole ghastly mess out.* It was in Wandsworth near the Common, and for the first few days, she didn't go out.

She stayed in and rearranged her bedroom like the one at the hospital.

At first she felt nervous looking out the window but forced herself to do it and see the world. She put the television on and drank tea. She listened to the neighbours arguing and slowly began to feel less fragile. When she stepped outside she walked to the shop and it felt like she could hear every sound there was, from her feet on the pavement to the birds in the sky. She bought a paper and hurried home. Eventually she ventured further and took a bus into central London where she wandered the high street.

Everything seemed both different and the same. She was bewildered at first with the sounds and sights of a city very much alive whereas she felt so very much dead. She sought silence and sanctuary. She sat in a pub until her courage returned. She went home but each day she would do the same thing and go into town on the bus to acclimatise herself once more to city life and began to breathe once again. One good thing was that she didn't seem to dream during this period.

Two weeks in, she bumped into Monty in Leicester Square looking older and smaller but still with the pipe in his mouth. He was shocked to see her and was all hugs and kisses but she froze like a frightened animal and didn't know what to say. Monty led her to a café.

Slowly she gave him brief details as he puffed on his pipe. She had been in the hospital that had burned down. The one in the news. She realised this was the first time she was speaking to another human being for weeks. It actually felt good.

'In the war I met a lot of people like you, Rhona. They called it shell shock back then, but it's called Post Traumatic Stress now, my dear. You need to see someone. I can't imagine what you've been through.'

Rhona gave him her address and he promised to contact her soon. As they parted she hugged him tight and fought back tears as she got on the bus home, even though Monty had offered to pay for a taxi.

Back at her flat Rhona stared in the mirror. She had grown visibly older in the years she had been away. Her black hair had wisps of grey showing. She went to the shop and bought some black hair dye and used it that evening.

The next morning she drank tea and ate toast while writing a list of things to do on a notebook she had bought. At the top of the list were the words 'Live. Live. Live.' As she was clearing her breakfast away the doorbell rang. She went to the door and opened it to find Andrew standing there. He rushed in and swept her off her feet and Rhona thought he would never let her go. He told her Monty had contacted him and he had come straight away.

They sat in her kitchen and she told him everything. Not just about her capture, imprisonment and the experiments but she told him about her past. She described her childhood, the dreams, the guilt, and meeting the man with the Zippo lighter. She told him about her. And she didn't leave anything out.

A great weight seemed to have fallen from her shoulders as she shared all this for the first time with someone she felt cared. That night they slept on top of the covers on her bed and held each other's hands.

When it was light they walked across the Common and stopped for tea at the café.

'I realise I've hardly asked anything about you,' said Rhona.

'There's nothing much to tell. I'm still doing sports reporting. I'm quite a cricket fan now if I'm honest.'

'What about women?'

'You're still blunt and to the point I see.'

'I was just wondering.'

'No. There's no one, Rhona.'

'Did you ever look for me?'

'They told Shirley you had gone away. They sent some legal letter forbidding publication of your new book and said you'd gone abroad. None of us knew what to think or where to start. If I'd known you were only an hour away I would have come. I wish now I'd asked more questions but at the time we weren't together so…'

He let the end of the sentence hang. Rhona took his hand.

'I've missed you and I wish I'd just been honest with you.'

Andrew pulled his hand free and rubbed his forehead.

'Rhona, I need to tell you something.'

'What is it? You're married? I'll understand.'

'Rhona, I contacted MI5 after you told me about your third book. About John Lennon and President Reagan being shot. I told them you had this gift but weren't using it. I was angry. I told them everything.'

Rhona put her hands on her lap.

'And then when you ran away they called me and asked where you might go. I told them about George. You'd talked about him and I guessed you would go to him for help. I know I would. This was all my fault and I'm sorry. I'm so sorry.'

Andrew began to cry. Rhona watched him.

A little boy with his parents at the next table kicked the ball he was playing with under their chairs and came to fetch it. Rhona smiled at the child as he picked it up and walked away. She leant forward and took Andrew's hands.

'I want to go away. I want to go away and I want you to come with me.'

CHAPTER THIRTY-NINE

2004

JOE

It had been tragic. It could almost have been funny. He had taken her out for dinner at a restaurant called Bucci's. It was a southern Italian place in Balham and the food was good. Joe ate there so regularly the guy behind the bar, Vincenzo, would always give him free drinks or desserts. He had eaten there with Mandy before.

The food had been as good as always but the conversation had been bad. But the bad, Joe now realised, had become normal. For some time they had led separate lives. Joe would work shifts and Mandy would head to the gym or see friends when he was home, and even on New Year's Eve, they had spent it apart.

Joe had realised something was wrong but he was fearful of confronting it like he should have done. Instead they bickered, argued, and annoyed with each other so it became part of daily life. Silences and petty arguments filled in where happiness should have been. Joe shuddered as he reflected what he could have done. He could have been so much more mature about it but instead he stuck his head in the sand and made excuses like it was normal to go through such a long rough patch.

They got through the meal making very little small talk. Joe ate his starter and pasta while Mandy had a salad which she pushed around her plate and stared at, just so she didn't have to look up at him.

At the end of the meal he poured them both another glass of red wine and he pulled the small black box from his pocket and placed it on the table in front of her. She looked at it and then looked up at him. Joe had smiled but she didn't smile back. Joe felt hot but carried on regardless.

She was just confused, he had thought. Even at this point he continued to lie to himself.

'What's that?' she asked.

Joe opened the box to reveal an engagement ring he had bought earlier that day. It had only cost sixty pounds. Sixty pounds. He looked around the restaurant thinking he should maybe get on one knee but he wanted to keep this intimate and just between them.

Thank God, he now thought.

'Mandy, will you marry me?'

Mandy stared at him as though he'd just admitted to having carried out a murder. Silence descended, and Joe waited, wishing the ground would swallow him up. He even took a sip of his wine and glanced around nervously hoping no one had seen the ring and was now watching them. The waiter would be round in a minute too and surely he or she would notice the ring and make a comment. Eventually Joe felt he had to say something.

'So?'

'I need to think about it.'

I need to think about it. Joe ran the words through his mind. *I need to think about it.* She could have been the one to finally and painfully end this mockery but like him, she retreated from the truth.

I need to think about it.

Where do you go from there? Well, Joe remembered, they went home. He had swooped up the box and put it back in his pocket before anyone saw it and then hastily ordered the bill. They sat for a few minutes as though nothing had happened.

Looking back, they were just too emotionally immature to deal with it. Too afraid of saying what needed to be said. Which wasn't like Mandy. Joe knew he could be quiet but he often thought about why she hadn't just ended it sooner. She had always been forthright one with her views and opinions so what stopped her here?

He wished he had just asked her. But they went home. When they got in, Joe attempted to bring the subject up but Mandy marched upstairs to the bathroom and then went to bed. Joe sat up for a while and tried to make sense of the evening. He followed her up to bed, got undressed, and laid down beside her. They both lay in the dark, pretending to doze off but both wide awake and knowing something has now fundamentally changed. At last, from the darkness, Mandy spoke.

'I think we should split up.'

Joe lay in the dark and didn't respond. Eventually they both fell asleep.

The next morning they awoke and met in the kitchen for breakfast. Mandy was eating her cereal and Joe made tea.

'Are we still splitting up?' he asked.

'Yes. I think that's a good idea.'

Joe started to cry. He looked back at this moment and cringed. He had felt so vulnerable, so adrift. Mandy stood up and rubbed the back of his neck and they hugged. Joe held her tightly loving her more now than he had ever loved her. Gently she pulled away from him and went to the bedroom where she came back out shortly, dressed and holding a packed suitcase.

'I'm going to stay with Ellie. I'll phone you in a couple of days.'

She left. Joe sat crying alone in the kitchen. The next few weeks were a blur. During that period, they hadn't seen each other and over the phone, Joe sadly agreed he would move out and Mandy stay in the flat until their lease ran out with Joe still paying his half of the rent.

They had met once about a month after their separation at a party. Joe knew she would be there. He was nervous and compensated by drinking too much, then made it obvious he would love to get back with her but she didn't want that.

It was meant to be, she said. It was time to move on.

CHAPTER FORTY

2019

JOE

Clouds hung heavily in the air the next day. Joe parked up in the small car park near the pier and walked down in good time to have a look around before his meeting. The pier was near deserted at that time in the morning in the week. Joe walked up and down the pier once then breathed in the cold air while watching the rowdy waves crash into the shore.

Surfers were already in the sea trying to take advantage of the weather. Joe remembered the failed artificial reef the council had paid millions of pounds to be installed some years before only to discover the designs hadn't been worked out correctly and faulty materials had been used with the result of an artificial reef that didn't work.

As the time neared ten o'clock Joe went down to the end of the pier and stood a little way from two men setting up fishing lines. He leaned on the railings and stared out across the channel towards France. He had missed the sea when he had first moved out of Bournemouth back in the late nineties.

Joe had missed the horizons and the feeling of space. He'd found it disconcerting when he had visited Tooting Lido for the first time and saw people lying on concrete and grass. Joe smiled at the memory and at his own naivety.

'You must be Joe.'

Joe turned around, realising he had been daydreaming and had zoned out. Behind him stood a faintly familiar man of about his age wrapped up in a blue Helly Hanson jacket and hat. He had a smooth beard speckled with white and he seemed to be studying Joe.

'Are you Tom Martin?'

'I am. Pleased to meet you.'

He held out his hand and Joe shook it. Joe recognised the voice from the phone with its soft west country lilt. He glanced behind Tom to see if he was with anyone but saw no obvious back up.

'I'm here alone,' said Tom following his thoughts. 'Like you.'

'Been watching me?'

'For a little bit. You don't recognise me do you?'

Joe stared into Tom's face, trying to picture it without the beard.

'Yeah I do. Sort of.'

'I used to hang around McDonald's back in the day. Galaxy too. I went to Winton Boys.'

Joe nodded, Tom's face coming into sharper focus. Winton Boys was the local secondary school in the neighbourhood where Joe grew up.

'I'm a bit younger that you but I knew all the Winton lot. I remember you. You knew everyone. Very popular. Reputation for being quite hard too. I heard you're still pretty handy.'

Joe's chest tightened as a wave of anger flowed through him which he fought to suppress.

'Did you get me done over outside my work?' Joe asked.

Tom winced melodramatically. He moved alongside Joe, leant on the railing, and put his gloved hands together.

'I'm sorry about that. In hindsight that was a mistake.'

'Why did you do it?'

'Some people I know got nervous you were going round asking questions.'

'What were they hoping to achieve? That I'd just walk away?'

'I suppose,' said Tom.

'So what did you do to Lee? Where is he?'

Tom sighed. 'This has all gotten way out of hand?'

'What?'

'You. This. Lee.'

'You going to tell me then?'

'Are you shagging his sister? This why all the interest? Last I heard you'd fucked off to London.'

'Are you going to tell me or what?' asked Joe.

'I was helping Lee you know. I did him a favour.'

'What favour?'

'I helped him make some money. When he was in AA.'

'Did you set him up drug dealing when you were both there?'

'I wasn't there. A colleague of mine actually met him there.'

'So your colleague was the alcoholic then?'

'He wasn't an alcoholic,' said Tom.

'Now I'm confused.'

'Those places are perfect for selling drugs.'

'You are fucking kidding me?'

'Straight up. Half the people are there to tick a box so they hopefully get community service and not a prison term when their trial comes up for whatever shit they've done. The other half are struggling to stay off the booze so we offer them all something to help.'

Joe looked out to the sea and asked himself at what point a person's morality becomes so corrupted like Tom Martin's had that he would even think to do something like that.

'I know you reckon that's bad,' said Tom.

'I can't think why.'

'If I didn't do it someone else would. Go to any AA meeting in the country and I bet there's someone there doing the exact same thing.'

'So you or your colleague targeted Lee when he was at his most vulnerable?'

'Don't give me that. I remember you. You've done enough naughties not to preach.'

'I know. I actually think they should legalise drugs.'

'I don't. It would screw my business up. Why do you think I vote Tory?'

Joe counted to five.

'So what happened?'

'Lee starts buying and then says he wants to start selling so I let him,' said Tom.

'Coke?'

'You'd better not be a grass, Joe.'

'I just want to know what happened to Lee.'

'Yeah, it was coke. Lee starts selling. He's doing okay and I meet him. He remembers me from way back. But now he thinks he knows me. That we have a connection. That we're mates.'

Joe shook his head.

'I'm not a total cunt, Joe. I'm not some two-dimensional bad guy. I had a building company a few years back. And then the crash happened and it ruined me. I got divorced, lost the house, lost my kids. Lost everything. It got bad. Bloody awful. Life's a fucking struggle in case you haven't noticed. Fuck or get fucked.'

Joe waited.

'I just want to find Lee,' said Joe.

'And I'm telling you and I'll get to that. I got a memory of you from Remix. I think it was a night Carl Cox played. He just worked the decks drinking bottle after bottle of beer and smoking spliff after spliff. I remember you there dancing with your long hair.'

Remix was another old club from the early nineties in Bournemouth.

'I remember that night,' said Joe.

'You ever get nostalgic from those days?'

'Yeah.'

For a few seconds they let the memory linger.

'Lee had mental problems,' said Tom.

Joe waited.

'I mean, he needed help. Serious help. And he thought I was his friend. But I wasn't.'

Joe still said nothing. For the first time he sensed remorse.

'He started drinking again. Being late paying. Not turning up when he should. Just bad at business. Some people thought he was cutting the coke to make more on the side but I don't know.

He was a mess. I told him he should take a rest. Get his head together but he didn't want to know. And then, and then he starts telling me shit that is fucked up.'

'Like what?'

'You ready for this? Like he dreamt of the miscarriages his girlfriend had. Before they happened. Like he knew that she was going to lose the unborn babies. He said he dreamt it. Both times. That it was making him go mad.'

Tom gripped the wooden railing.

Joe's head started swimming.

'I mean, that is fucked up. And he just wouldn't leave me alone. He kept bugging me like I understood him. Did I fuck.'

'And then what?'

Tom shook his head.

'I just wanted rid of him. I even stopped supplying him but he'd still call me or turn up. Like he needed me. So I told the lads I thought he was a grass and to give him a kicking. Tell him to fuck off. I wanted him to just leave me alone. Get the message. He was doing my head in.'

'Round at Bernard's?'

'You've done your homework.'

'So you're responsible for the beating?'

'Yeah. I shouldn't have done it.'

'Why'd you tell people he was a grass?' asked Joe.

'Because I'm not going to start telling people what he told me. I've got kids, mate. That was dark. I just wanted shot of him. For him to piss off and not come back.'

'And then what?'

'Well, he did fuck off. I thought that would be it and he'd be out of my hair but then word was he's gone missing and his sister has got you on the case. Everyone gets a bit nervous. It could look bad. Like we did him in or something.'

'Did you?'

Tom looked Joe in the eyes.

'I swear on my life we never saw him again after that night.'

'What about your boys? Bobby? I mean, they came after me.'

'Bobby is a dick. But he wouldn't do anything like kill someone if that's what you're thinking. Anyway, we thought that was it.'

'So you got what you wanted?'

'In a way. But I feel bad about it. Looking back I should have just pushed him away nicely but you get on the gear and you get all nasty sometimes. I know what I'm like.'

'So where is he then?' asked Joe.

'I have no idea. That's what I'm saying. You're barking up the wrong tree. You have been this whole time. Wherever he went or whatever he's done is nothing, and I mean nothing, to do with me or anyone I know. I swear on my kids' lives. I have no idea what happened to him.'

Joe stood thinking. He had expected some answers. Some bullshit he could see through. But now he wasn't sure what was going on. He didn't know what to say or think anymore.

Tom held out his hand again. Joe took it weakly.

'I've said all I wanted to. And I'm not lying to you. And if you do find him let me know he's okay. I mean it.'

Joe nodded. Tom stuck his hands in his pockets and walked off. Joe turned back to the sea and looked out across the horizon. He couldn't decide whether he had been lied to or been told the truth. He wanted it to be a lie and that Tom was responsible for Lee's disappearance. And that he had turned up to meet Joe and admitted keeping Lee captive somewhere and he was safe.

Or worse, that Tom had even admitted killing Lee. At least it would have been closure. At least they would have found Lee. But that was never going to happen and Joe was angry at his own naivety to even expect any kind of convenient confession. Instead, Joe got the flip side to a coin and another angle to Lee's disappearance. As much as Joe felt that Tom should be lying he felt the opposite. Tom had been telling him the truth or at least part of the truth. He'd freely admitted to having Lee beaten up to get rid of him and told him why. Lee's dreams, his mental health, his obvious breakdown had all been confirmed by everyone Joe had spoken to.

All this time Joe had been a detective on the hunt for the bad guys responsible for a bad deed. He'd been his own hero in some second-rate, pound shop whodunnit whilst all the time ignoring all the clues that the person responsible for Lee's disappearance may have been Lee himself. Lee, lonely, drunk and falling apart with no one to turn to.

Joe didn't like to think what he might have done. He remembered what Tom had said. *He thought I was his friend.* Joe wondered if Lee thought he only had one friend. Until he found out he didn't even have that. He had none.

CHAPTER FORTY-ONE

1986

ANDREW/RHONA

Andrew felt the soft gust of wind and welcomed its cool embrace. He opened his eyes and saw the clear, blue sky smile back at him. He sat up. Rhona was still lying next to him on the towel reading her book. He must have dozed off.

He looked around him. The bushes and trees around the cottage swayed in the gentle breeze. They had been here for four days now after disembarking from the ferry and taking a leisurely drive down from the port, practising their faltering French whenever they stopped for drinks and food at service stations or sleepy villages. And now here they were, in the heart of Burgundy, in exquisite sunshine and never-ending silence.

They had not yet explored any further than the local *supermarché* where they bought ample supplies of food and remarkably cheap and cheerful wine which came in huge plastic bottles that were impossible to buy in England. A ten-minute walk up a windy road led to a sleepy village where nothing ever seemed to open.

Here they were lucky to ever see anyone besides the English family who rented them the cottage they were staying in and who lived in the house next door. In two days' time, Colin, the English owner, was going to take them on a local wine tour where he promised them the best Pinot Noir the region had to offer.

'We should go for a drive,' Andrew suggested.

'Where do you want to go?'

'I don't know. Anywhere.'

He got up and wandered into the cottage and to their bedroom to change. The cottage had three bedrooms and was far too big for them but Rhona had insisted on space. He put it down to her experience at the hospital. She said she wanted to be able to *roam* and not feel constricted. So they paid for a cottage larger than their needs and Rhona seemed happy.

They had done something similar when they went to visit Rhona's parents in Ireland. They had stayed in an expensive hotel with large rooms when he would have been perfectly happy with a bed and breakfast accommodation or to stay with Rhona's parents as they had offered. But their stay in Ireland had made him realise this wouldn't have been a good idea.

They went for just three days and Rhona's interaction with her parents was awkward and uncomfortable. He tried to bond with Rhona's father over rugby and stout which had been successful to a point, but her mother came across as cold and, although he wouldn't say it to Rhona, unloving towards her daughter. Rhona herself seemed distant as well as they all seemed to go through the motions of a family reunion which Andrew felt both parties, besides the father perhaps, did not want.

From Ireland they had travelled back to England and straight to Dover and then across to France. Their adventure so far had been subdued and without incident. It couldn't even really be called an adventure but that is what Andrew had hoped for. He wanted an occasion to enjoy themselves, become intimate after so long and, above all, hope that Rhona had or would forgive him. She never mentioned what he had done but he hoped she understood he had regretted his actions every single day since he had done what he did. Andrew realised he had been lucky up until now. He had few regrets through his life and lived without any real shame for any of his actions. Until now.

In the bedroom Andrew changed his top and glanced out the window. Rhona sat staring off into the distance. He noticed Rhona often sunk into silence these days as though she was daydreaming. She was doing it now as she sat with her legs up to her chest staring toward the direction of the stream that ran alongside both the cottage and house. He tapped the window. She looked up and he waved. She smiled and got up. Andrew went out of the bedroom and met her as she was coming in through the kitchen.

'Are you up for going out?'

'I'll just get ready,' she said.

They drove across the countryside that seemed to stretch for miles. It was either very flat or very hilly. On the hills there tended to be the vineyards. Rhona sat in the passenger seat whilst Andrew drove. They didn't have any goal or intended location but just drove in comfortable silence until they came across a small town with a square and a prominent, well-kept Hotel De Ville.

'Let's stop here,' suggested Rhona.

They parked outside beside a *pharmacie* and took a stroll around the square until they came to a café with outdoor tables and chairs. They each took a seat.

'Maybe we should come back here for dinner one night,' said Andrew noting how lively the place was in comparison to everywhere else they had been to so far.

'Are you getting bored?' asked Rhona, but before Andrew could answer, the waiter came by their table to take their order. They asked for two coffees and Rhona lit a cigarette.

'No, I'm not really bored. Just curious to explore a bit more I suppose.'

'I'm bored,' said Rhona.

'Are you?'

'Yeah. We're like an old married couple aren't we?'

'Not that bad. Are we?'

'We should head up to Paris.'

'I've only taken two weeks off work.'

'We could go on a wine tour and then leave the next day.'

Andrew thought about this.

'I want to get drunk in Paris,' announced Rhona, for the first time in a long time, revealing a glimpse of her old self.

Andrew smiled.

'What?' asked Rhona. 'I'm done with silence. I want to start living again.'

'Where did all this come from?'

'I'm over it. Or at least I want to be.'

She stubbed her cigarette out as the coffees arrived.

'I want to write another book too.'

Andrew stirred sugar carefully into his drink.

'What about?'

'I haven't decided but not science-fiction. I know what you're thinking but I don't have the visions anymore. Or at least they don't come as often. Thank God. I just want to move on.'

Andrew felt relief at this statement and sipped his coffee.

'I wrote another book while you were away,' he said.

'Sci-fi?'

Andrew smiled.

'No, not science fiction. Historical fiction. About a smuggler in eighteenth century England. I'm still tinkering with it.'

'There we go then. Two writers growing old and getting drunk wherever we want because we can. It's decided then. We're going to Paris.'

On the way back to the cottage they passed through a desolate village saved by a small, ancient Romanesque church at its centre.

'Beautiful isn't it?' remarked Andrew and slowed the car.

'Let's go in and have a look around.'

Rhona passed through the small door and into the church. It felt cool inside, the thick walls cutting off the heat and sounds from outside. Andrew followed, stooping slightly to step through. But inside they were not alone.

At the back of the church two elderly women ignored them and chatted in whispers whilst a couple of figures sat on the hard, worn wooden benches facing the front where an ancient statue of Jesus on the cross stood solemnly. Thick columns ran alongside two sides of the church leading to the pulpit and beside the statue of Jesus and the seating, the space felt stark and simple.

Andrew wandered off along the side, taking in the architecture. Rhona watched him. Over the period of their holiday she was reminded of his habits and foibles. The way he held his tea in the mornings, the way he brushed his hair, and the way he made love came back to her as familiar memories that made her happy. The fact he still put his nose to every newly opened pint of milk to check it was fresh still slightly irritated her but also made her feel secure.

He was quieter now and more pensive. Rhona felt like he chose his words carefully each time he spoke for fear of offending. Guilt still hung heavy on his face and Rhona wished things could be different. When he had told her what he done she thought she should feel anger but instead felt resignation.

George Frenton had been right all those years ago. It hadn't been him that had given her up but her ex-lover. She thought their trip would reawaken their spirits, but at times it had instead, dampened them. The trip to Ireland together had been a mistake. She should have gone alone and now France felt like a hangover. Heading to Paris would hopefully change that.

She wandered down the aisle and took a seat near the front and waited. Churches bored her. She had seen enough of them as a child in Ireland. But Andrew seemed genuinely interested so she waited and daydreamed. That had been the hardest thing being in the hospital. The privilege of thinking small thoughts. Having your freedom taken away from you without knowing if and when you might get out robbed you of the mundane rituals of life. Whenever your mind took off it always returned soon to the prison you were in.

Andrew had reached the front of the church and was inspecting the statue of Jesus with thorns around his head and the nails in his feet and hands. Rhona thought how Jesus looked a sorry figure staring up at the heavens, questioning his faith and his father.

She heard a noise and felt someone sit behind her. She continued to watch Andrew but the sound of whoever it was breathing so near to her made her feel uncomfortable and claustrophobic. She was about to get up and wander off when a pair of hands reached over and rested next to her shoulder. Then a face appeared.

She turned to see the man from the coffee shop from all those years ago. The man who had held the Zippo lighter and had told her to write about her visions. The man stared at her for a moment and Rhona couldn't turn away. His face had aged and lined. His eyes were slightly bloodshot and weary. He smelled of cheap aftershave and rotten fruit.

'Hello,' he said. He turned and looked forward as though taking in the architecture. 'It's so calm here isn't it?'

Rhona looked towards Andrew but he had his back to her now as he had stooped to read some Roman inscription on the wall.

'What do you want?' she asked.

'I came to talk to you.'

'I'm not going to write about my visions anymore. I don't even have them.'

'Breathe, Rhona. Don't make a scene.'

Rhona realised she was flushed and sweating. She calmed her breathing.

'I've come to give you a message.'

'Who from?'

'I don't know. How would I know that? Dreams, nightmares, whatever. I don't know where it comes from. But I have a message.'

Rhona waited. The man quickly glanced around him and then leaned in close to her.

'You need to find someone. Not now but in years to come. At least, I think it's in years to come. Things look different. Fashions, hairstyles. You know how it is. When you dream this stuff. Anyway, I think the idea is you find him. And help him.'

'Who is it? How?'

'You'll know who and how in good time.'

'Why should I bother?'

'Because you must. Like I found you. Someone needs to carry on this merry dance.'

Andrew turned around from the inscription and sought out Rhona. She stood up, a little too suddenly and walked towards him.

'Are you okay?' he asked sensing her unease.

'Yes, I was just talking to...' Rhona had turned to point out the man but the man had gone. She searched the church and caught the door at the back closing gently as though someone had just walked through it. 'I was just talking to someone, but it doesn't matter now.'

CHAPTER FORTY-TWO

2019

JOE

'How can you trust the words of a drug dealer?'

Joe sat on Samantha's sofa and he had told her everything he knew. She had sat and listened. He told her about the drugs, about Bernard, Bobby and Tom Martin. He told her about Lee and his dreams. Samantha nodded occasionally but stayed quiet. He laid it all out and then waited for a response. He had expected her reply.

'I can't I suppose,' answered Joe.

'Do you think he was telling the truth? That they had nothing to do with it?'

'I think you need to go back to the police.'

He didn't want to admit he had failed. That much was obvious.

Samantha went silent. Joe's eyes wandered around the lounge. It was nice. It was a newly decorated house in Southbourne where the houses weren't cheap. The kitchen looked like it had just been installed along with the spacious extension and the place had a well-kept, take-your-shoes-off vibe. He was curious as to what she did for a living and where the two children in the photos on the mantelpiece were, but he wouldn't ask. This was all about Lee and asking inquisitive but essentially nosy questions wasn't on the agenda.

'Is that it then?'

'I think I've come as far as I can go.'

Samantha rubbed her forehead and squeezed the bridge of her nose.

'The police won't care if I call them.'

'They have to open an investigation. Surely. He's been missing long enough.'

'What do you think happened to him? You must have an opinion.'

'Everyone I spoke to said Lee had mental health issues. I think that's the key. People who are depressed and have problems like that do irrational things. I really don't know what happened to Lee and I don't want to speculate. I'm sorry. I wish I did know.'

Samantha stared at the carpet.

Joe got up.

'I should go. Why don't we talk tomorrow?'

She got up.

'Thank you for all the help you've been.'

Joe felt bad. 'I'm sorry I didn't find him.'

Samantha nodded. 'You did what you could. Thank you.'

She led him out to the front door and waited for him to put his shoes back on. He'd worn his Firetrap boots this time and he went down on his knees to lace them up.

'I guess you've already spoken to her, but maybe chat to your aunt again. Lee's work mate said they were close. Maybe she has some ideas.'

Samantha frowned. Joe stood up.

'We haven't got an aunt. And nor has Rose.'

CHAPTER FORTY-THREE

1986

RHONA

The storm clouds had already started to hang heavily in the sky when they boarded the overnight ferry back to England. By the time they were out to sea, rain and winds had begun to whip up around them, and the people on board took refuge inside. It wasn't long before people began to be sick, at first in the toilets and then, when the toilets overflowed, in bags and on floors.

It felt to Andrew and Rhona that they were on some kind of hospital ship as they heard the constant moans of the very sick while the ship rocked violently from side to side. They hadn't booked a cabin but instead made do with the seating dotted around the two floors. At first both of them felt fine and were smugly confident they must have the salty sea legs of an experienced sailor. But then Andrew went an odd greenish colour and suddenly lurched off to the overflowing toilets with

Rhona not too far behind as she soon succumbed to the violent crossing.

'This is bloody awful,' said Andrew as they sat with their coats over them after both being sick.

Rhona rested with her eyes tightly shut trying to keep out the misery of mass nausea. She thought back to the man in the church and their subsequent flying visit to Paris when she had attempted to blot out her encounter with the strange man with the Zippo by getting drunk in some small back street Paris bar. The next day she had felt hungover as they had wandered the Left Bank and found the Shakespeare and Company bookstore.

'Surely we should turn back,' Andrew pleaded, bringing Rhona's attention back to the present.

She felt annoyed at his self-pity and wanted to tell him to shut up and get on with it, but she stayed silent and feigned sleep. It was bad enough feeling sick without a boat load of people moaning about it.

After a little while, which felt like hours, she eventually fell into a light sleep.

She dreamt she was on a train. It looked different to any train she had been on. The design was more plastic and futuristic. She looked out the window. The countryside looked like it was England. She heard voices and turned to the carriage up ahead.

Sat facing each other at a table seat were a young man and woman.

The woman had her back to Rhona but she could see the man. He was in his twenties with brown hair and a thin, innocent face. The woman had earphones hanging out of her ears and she could hear the music coming down the carriage. It was hard and fast, a repetitive beat that made her wonder how anyone could put up with it. They seemed to be arguing. She couldn't hear their words, but their body language gave them away.

And then they went through a tunnel. And when they came out it was as though their conversation had been amplified. She now heard every word.

'I have premonitions, Lucy.'

'You have premonitions?'

'I've had them since I can remember. They do my head in.'

Rhona awoke back on the boat. She sat up. Andrew was asleep beside her. The boat was now calm. The storm had passed. Dawn was breaking and out of the window she could see England draw near.

CHAPTER FORTY-FOUR

2019

JOE

Joe and Valentina went to the Koh Thai restaurant in Boscombe, near where he had his run in with Bobby. There was a branch in Bournemouth town centre, but Joe still felt the original restaurant had an edge over the quality of the Thai food and offered a cosier environment. The place was busy. Good restaurants were hard to find in Bournemouth and this was one of them. Joe ordered Boozy Duck whilst Valentina opted for the Phad Thai.

'Have you ever been to Thailand?' she asked.

'No,' he said. 'You?'

'I went with my ex a few years back.'

Joe sipped the chilled beer he had ordered.

'Enjoy it?'

'It was amazing.'

Valentina smiled and looked around the restaurant.

'Didn't we used to go to a club up the road from here when I visited?'

'The Academy. It's called The Opera House now.'

'I had some good weekends down here.'

Joe nodded.

'You're quiet,' she said.

'I don't want to say the wrong thing.'

Joe didn't want to say he'd had a bad day.

Valentina smiled and leaned forward.

'Can I ask you a question?'

'You can but that doesn't mean I'll answer it.'

'Why did you never ask me out?'

Joe looked into her eyes.

'I always thought you'd say no.'

She sighed.

'You put yourself down too much.'

'You lived miles away. Would it have worked? We were teenagers. A holiday romance. Really?'

'I always liked you. You were sweet. Claudio and Matteo always said good things about you.'

'Keep the compliments coming. We're going to be here a while.'

She smiled again.

'Where did all the time go?' she asked.

'Life got in the way. If we had gone out it wouldn't have lasted. I was probably a bit of a dick back then. We would have gone out and it would have ended horribly, and we would never have spoken to each other again.'

'Bloody hell. I might as well go home then.'

'But maybe I'm not so much of a dick now if that can convince you to stay.'

'Well, let's see how it goes then shall we?'

'How has life treated you then?'

'Career wise not bad. Love life shit. You?'

'Shit on both fronts,' said Joe.

'I thought you would be married and have kids by now.'

For a split second an image of Mandy popped into Joe's head. He closed his eyes not wanting to talk about that. Not tonight.

'So did I. But then again, don't most people expect that?' he said.

The food arrived and they ate in silence for a minute or so.

'This is good,' Valentina said.

'I told you it would be.'

'So tell me about what you've been doing then.'

He told her. He gave her his potted history of his life in London and finally coming back to Bournemouth. He skimmed over his relationships, especially with Mandy, and hoped she wouldn't pry further sensing he might be holding back.

'Now it's your turn.'

'Well I went to uni and did the law degree. Then I did law practice for a year in Walthamstow before doing my qualifying training and finally became a solicitor. I moved to Shepherds Bush, moved in with my boyfriend. Years went by. We broke up and I bought a place in Woking. Mum was ill, so it made sense. Breast cancer. She got better. And here I am.'

'When are you going back to Woking?'

'A few days' time.'

'We'd better make the most of it.'

'Woking isn't far.'

Their eyes met and they both smiled.

They ate and talked. Joe talked about Bournemouth, his family, and working in a bar. Valentina talked about her life in Woking and her friends. There were no awkward silences, and as the meal progressed, Joe asked himself if he could make them work. He felt she was doing the same thing. Two people alone facing middle-age and wondering where to go next. They had desserts and Joe paid and they left for a nightcap up the road at a place called The Cellar Bar and watched a live band. By midnight they decided to leave. They walked outside and headed for the taxi rank.

'It's been a lovely evening. Perfect really,' said Valentina.

Joe did what he had wanted to do all night. He kissed her. They stood on the high street and ignored the wolf whistles of a bunch of young men going past them.

'About time, Joe,' she said.

'There was nothing to stop you making the first move.'

'I didn't want to do the wrong thing.'

They got a taxi and gave the driver Valentina's address. They pulled away and sat close together in the back, holding hands.

'You can come back to mine if you like,' said Joe.

'I'm going to go home if that's all the same.'

Joe nodded, crushed as he knew he had said the wrong thing. A perfect night ruined by putting his foot wrong.

'Tomorrow. Let's meet up tomorrow,' she said squeezing his hand. 'I'll call you.'

When they arrived at Valentina's she leaned over and gave him a quick kiss.

'Thank you. And I promise I'll call.'

'Speak tomorrow.'

Joe waited for her to get into the house safely before directing the taxi driver back to his. He spent the rest of the journey metaphorically punching himself in the face.

Arriving home he still felt awake. Mike was out somewhere so he had the place to himself. He got a cold Perroni out of the fridge and slumped on the sofa intending to watch some trash

TV or at least catch up on something he'd recorded on Sky. Instead he spotted Lee's box of papers in the corner and his thoughts turned back to his old acquaintance.

Not being able to locate Lee bothered him. More than bothered him, it made him angry. Angry at himself. He should never have said he'd help. He just got Samantha's hopes up and now, with some mysterious aunt, Samantha still hoped that Lee was safe somewhere.

Joe hoped and prayed she was right. He knew Samantha must be distraught and wondered if she would contact the police. They might call him if she had. On a purely selfish front, trying to find Lee had made life interesting and Joe realised it had given him purpose. He wondered if he'd made the wrong career move early on in life, but back then the police were like the bogeymen of the town, arresting kids for having a good time just because they were high on drugs. He'd seen enough local police brutality to put him off any thoughts of joining them and besides, his caution for possession of pot when he was seventeen probably wouldn't have helped.

His opinions about the police had slowly changed as he got older and one of his mates in London was in the Met who was one the most decent blokes he had ever come across. And it must have been satisfying to feel you did some good sometimes. Arresting people who had done awful things. Finding missing loved ones. Especially finding someone you knew. He hadn't seen Lee for decades and didn't know him as a friend any longer. But through trying to find him, he had gotten to know him once again, more so than before. He was Lee's friend now and he just wanted to find Lee, safe and well, to tell him.

He reached down and lifted the box onto the sofa and emptied its contents out before him. He sat for a moment contemplating the various comics, novels and papers across his sofa.

Lee had kept this box of belongings for a reason, Joe told himself. Maybe there was something here he had missed.

He began by going through all of Lee's artwork. His pencil sketches and the piece *Who Cares Wins*. Joe noticed Lee had tagged one of the pages at the bottom with *Skiver*, his graffiti name. He put the artwork to one side and then picked up an old *Observer Magazine* that had been at the bottom of the box which Joe had originally thought must have been there to start with as Lee didn't strike him as an *Observer* reader.

But now he went through each page and speculated where it might have come from. It might have been Rose's but why keep a magazine from 2001? One story caught his eye. It was a piece by a writer called Amy Greene and was about writers who had predicted the future. There were photos and pictures of various authors and their work.

Joe glanced through it and went on until he got to the end and put the magazine down. He got up and went over to the table, where the notebook he had found in the box, was sitting. He picked it up then sat back down. He flicked carefully through each page again looking for any more notes or indentations he might have missed. The book was empty save for the three numbers and the page of the address in Ringwood.

He put the notebook down and fetched himself another beer. As he opened it he considered going through everything again the next day with a clearer head and decided to check out the comics and then call it a night. He sat back down and looked though each of the comics carefully.

They were all published by a company called Ash Comix and were all from the late nineties and early noughties. One was a thicker novel with a plane crashing into the World Trade Centre by someone called Trey Griffin. It was called *The Warning*. Joe considered it a bit of a sick cash in on such a disaster.

Joe flicked through it and soon put it down and took a long glug of the cooling beer. He sat, waiting for the motivation to get up and go to bed, when something suddenly struck him. He picked up the graphic novel and went back through its pages.

Something had caught his eye and he was now playing catch up. He found what he was looking for on the fifteenth page. The scene was of a child walking past a wall which had been heavily graffitied. And there in the middle of the wall was the unmistakable tag saying *Skiver*. Joe stared at the art work. He turned back to Lee's artwork and compared the tag Lee had drawn to the one in the book. It was the same.

And now Joe looked at the rest of the artwork, comparing the book to more of Lee's work. It was the same artist. Joe nodded in appreciation. Lee had written a book or drawn one at least. No one had mentioned this. He checked the date. August 1999.

Joe stared at the date, rereading it, then rereading it again. He examined the front cover with the plane going into one of the Twin Towers. He flicked to the end of the book. Not just one plane but two planes featured in the climax as they flew into both towers and brought both buildings down.

And then Joe sat up and put his beer down. Something else had come to him.

He grabbed the *Observer Magazine* and went back to the article about writers who predicted the future. One of the pictures was of *The Warning*, the graphic novel he was now looking at. He had gone past it the first time he had looked through the magazine.

Joe scanned through the article and got to the section where the book was discussed. It talked about the shockingly accurate predictions the graphic novel had made and the horrifying images presented two years before the actual attack took place. It went on to discuss the mysterious author who no one seemed to be able to track down and the fact that the real author may not be the unknown Trey Griffin at all, but someone called Rhona O'Shea who had written a couple of other books back in the late seventies and early eighties where she had also made predictions that came true. The writer of the article had deduced this from some kind of language expert. She also suggested the actual book may have been written before 1991 because that was when Rhona O'Shea had died.

Joe got up and paced the room. Thoughts were swirling around his head. He felt overwhelmed. There was something else. Something bubbling in his subconscious that was bothering him and ringing alarm bells. He stopped.

He had it.

That night he had stayed round Lee's house all those years ago. They had sat on the garage roof smoking weed and high on ecstasy. That's what they had been talking about. That's what Lee had told him. That he'd seen the Twin Towers destroyed by two passenger planes. In a dream.

And Joe had put it down to pure drug gibberish and pushed it out of his mind by the next morning. Boxed it up and buried it in the depths of his drug addled brain to be forgotten about as he battled his come down. Had that long-ago conversation been the reason Lee told his sister to find Joe? He was sending Joe a message. *Remember what I said?* Was it all linked?

He sat back down too wired to sleep now as he considered what to do next.

CHAPTER FORTY-FIVE

1989

ANDREW

Andrew got the taxi driver to drop him in the next street at the top of the hill. When he got out and paid the driver he felt the surging heat of the midday sun on the back of his neck. Sweat patches were already spreading under his armpits and he felt dehydrated. He gripped his small rucksack, put it over his shoulder, and checked the directions George Frenton had given him.

Rhona had been particular that he mustn't take a taxi directly to George's doorstep but somewhere nearby. He circled round some houses and found George's eight floor apartment block. He double checked the address as the apartment block didn't look like somewhere George would live. The brickwork was still visible and in need of a white render like all the other properties in the area. Random electric cables stuck out of the walls in search of a home.

This wasn't the image he had of George living it up in Spain as he buzzed number fifteen and was let in through the main doors. Inside, the lifts were not only not working but not actually there, a bare and empty lift shaft boarded up in its place. Andrew had no choice but to take the stairs and was at least glad the interior of the block was far cooler than the exterior.

As he reached the third floor George was waiting for him at his front door. Andrew shook his hand and noted George had visibly aged since he had last seen him some years before and looked far older than his fifty or so years. He was wearing an open white shirt that still showed the dull scar around his neck, with blue shorts and flip-flops. With his dark, tanned skin, Andrew thought he almost looked Spanish.

'You look like you could use a drink,' said George, showing him into the apartment. As Andrew was led through he noticed George was now walking with the aid of a walking stick.

Andrew sat down in a cool living room that led out onto a small balcony with views that stretched out across the Almeria desert-like landscape.

'How was the journey?' asked George as he fetched two chilled bottles of beer from a small fridge in the small kitchen.

'Fine. All on time.'

George opened the bottles, handed Andrew one, and sat down opposite him.

'Well, welcome to my abode.'

'Thank you.' Andrew glanced around the room with its small TV, settee, bookcase and coffee table which he saw had a copy of *Spycatcher* on it.

'You don't look like you're used to this sort of heat,' said George taking in Andrew's fair skin and sweaty complexion.

'My sister lives in Sardinia. So I am but I need to acclimatise.'

George chuckled and took a swig from the bottle.

'I thought you had a place on the Costa Del Sol?' asked Andrew as he sipped from his bottle, appreciating the cooling liquid.

'I did. But things got too hot down there. So hot I got a bullet in my arse for my troubles. So I came here.'

Andrew nodded not wanting to pry further.

'And yes, I agree this place is a bit of a shit hole.'

'I wasn't thinking that.'

'Something close though. I got ripped off. I bought it unseen. The bloke who sold it to me made it out to be some luxury pad, but when I got here, I found out the whole place had been put up illegally. They want to rip it down for breaching God knows what planning laws they got round here and I'm sort of stuck.'

'What happens if they rip it down?'

'They won't. In my opinion someone along the line hasn't got their drink and is kicking up a fuss. Once a bung has gone their way they'll forget all about it and maybe the bloody place will get finished.'

'What are the neighbours like?'

'There aren't any. Well there's Klaus on the top floor who looks like a Nazi war criminal on the run, me and some gay Dutch guy on the ground floor. We're the only mugs who had no choice but to stay here.'

'You don't want to come back to England then?'

George sighed.

'Come back to what, Andrew? People like me in my line of work are like dinosaurs. Most of my generation are either dead, in prison or out here. My pension goes a bit further here, the food is decent if you stop going to the expat places, and the people are nice. I've even learnt Spanish which isn't something the other ninety-nine per cent of Brits out here have bothered to do. You still see Shirley?'

'Not for a while. She's doing okay though.'

'What about you then?'

'Freelance now. It pays the bills.'

'You hungry? We could go down to the village and get some lunch.'

'Yeah, that would be nice.'

'But I can sense you want to talk first?'

'Sort of.'

'And talk about something you had to come all the way out here for?'

Andrew nodded.

'Let's sit outside. Try and get you a tan before you head back.'

They went out onto the balcony and George lit a cigarette. He leant on the hand rail and looked out across the desert.

'How's Monty?' George asked.

'Retired. I heard he's going around to schools now telling them about the war.'

'That figures. Did you know he was in one of the first units to go in and liberate Belsen concentration camp?'

'No, I didn't know that.'

'He was always telling war stories but he hardly ever told that one. Probably still doesn't like talking about it. He's a decent bloke is Monty.'

Andrew wondered when and why Monty told George this.

'Look at this place. The one thing that bothers me about this area is there's nothing here. Mostly sand. Did you know they shot loads of the spaghetti westerns up the road? It was cheaper and easier than filming in America. *The Good, The Bad and The Ugly* was made here.'

'No, I didn't know that.'

George shrugged and sat down on a plastic chair next to a white, garden table. Andrew followed and took the other seat. George tapped ash into a clean ashtray and sat back down.

'Go on then. I'm dying to know what you've got to say.'

Andrew felt suddenly nervous. Perhaps it was the way George was watching him, seemingly able to draw secrets from even the most discreet of people.

'Rhona was wondering if you still had any connections?'

'For what?'

'She came to you before for a passport.'

'She wants another one? What's she done now?'

'Nothing.'

'Nothing yet?'

Andrew didn't answer and sat, trying to remain calm, all the while feeling the sweat gather and drip about his body whilst George watched him, with not a drop of perspiration on him.

'I heard they had her in that hospital that burned down,' said George.

'They did.'

'She's an enigma isn't she?'

'She's willing to pay.'

Andrew pulled the rucksack he was still holding onto his lap and opened it. He took out a thick envelope and placed it on the table, looking around as though afraid they were being watched.

George gazed at the envelope and seemed unfazed by potential witnesses.

'There's two thousand pounds in there. She'd like a passport, birth certificate, and a driving licence.'

'That's a lot of money. And as much as I hate to say it, it's too much.'

'Rhona said you deserved it.'

'I always thought she might have believed it was me that gave her up.'

Andrew winced and hoped George hadn't noticed.

'She knows it wasn't.'

George scrutinised him a beat too long and took a draw on his cigarette.

'Does she know I'm living like this?' he asked.

'I don't think so.'

'Of course I'll help.'

'There's something else.'

Andrew took a folded slip of paper out of his top shirt pocket and placed it on top of the envelope.

'What's that?'

'A little extra. In a week's time there's going to be a horse race. The two thirty at Goodwood. The details and the name of the horse are all on there. I believe the odds for the horse are rather high at the minute, although I'm no expert. Rhona has suggested you might consider placing a small bet on the horse. She feels it might be worth your while.'

Andrew watched George as the words registered and sunk in. He would swear he almost saw a glint of a tear in his eye as he answered.

'That's very kind of her.'

Andrew watched Rhona weeding in the garden as he waited for the kettle to boil. She seemed to enjoy being in the garden these days and their lives together had taken on a kind of gentle, domesticated routine but with a twist since they had moved in together about six months before. Since Andrew's trip to Spain and the slow implementation of the next stage of their plan, their days had been spent mostly together.

Andrew did the occasional bit of writing for various newspapers and publications whilst Rhona tended the garden and decided on unusual dishes to prepare for their dinners. He had finally finished his book on the eighteenth-century smuggler and he was overjoyed that it had been published to above average reviews.

He tinkered with other stories when he could. Occasionally they would go to the cinema or out to eat. Andrew felt like they had become the stereotypical middle-class couple. The twist though was the pile of money currently sitting on the kitchen table.

Andrew poured boiling water into Rhona's cup and let the tea bag sit whilst he only gave his a quick swirl with the spoon. He took it out and added milk, smelling it first to check it was fresh. She had told him about the man in the church in France and the dream she'd had with the young man on the train she had been tasked to find. She had also been having other dreams, she told him, very different to the ones that had tormented her since childhood.

She began to dream of sporting events and more specifically, their outcomes. Horse racing seemed to stick out, and on the first two occasions, Rhona had told him the name of the horse she dreamed had won a race and left it at that. When she had a third dream, and once again saw a horse, this time called Foxtrot, win at Ascot, Andrew returned the following Saturday with two hundred and fifty pounds and placed it on the table in front of her.

He had researched the horse and discovered it was real and racing that very Saturday at odds of 50-1. He had got the bus to the high street and went into the nearest bookmakers he could find to lay a bet of five pounds for the horse to win. He had intended to say nothing if the horse lost but instead he stood in the smoky betting shop surrounded by desperate faces full of fading hope and watched the horse win.

Suppressing his immediate desire to jump up and down in celebration, he quietly collected his winnings and left as quickly as he could as though he had committed an unforgivable crime and needed to get away as soon as possible in case anyone should tap him on the shoulder. He had never gambled before, even during all his sports reporting days, and the euphoric rush of endorphins that was the result of winning suddenly made the attraction of such a pastime make perfect sense, especially if you knew the outcome. When he had returned and placed the money in front of Rhona he was surprised by her reaction.

'I can't believe you did that. And without telling me. I'm not going to tell you about the dreams if that's what you're going to do.'

'Hang on. Now hang on. This is what we're supposed to do. Have you not considered that?'

'No I haven't.'

'Well I have. Your dreams have changed Rhona. Do you realise that? You dream of this guy on a train and it's someone you believe you must find and then you also dream of horses winning races. The two dreams are linked.'

'Really?'

'Yes really. Or at least I think they are. This is an opportunity for you to have a kind of financial independence, so you can find this guy.'

'Is that how you've justified it?'

'Well, why else are you having these dreams?'

Rhona was silent. Andrew went on.

'You want to disappear, don't you? Then ask yourself how you intend to survive if you do?'

'I've got my compensation.'

'That isn't going to last you. You will need some kind of income eventually. This is it.'

Two days later and partially convinced, Rhona gave him the name of another horse she had dreamt about. It also won. A routine began to take shape. She would give Andrew the name of the horse. He would go away and find the horse, and when it was next racing, he'd put a bet on it.

After the third win Andrew started to visit other bookmakers in case his winning streak would arouse suspicion. He was careful to keep the bets small, and after a couple of months and some considerable accumulation of wealth, he laid small bets on other races in the hope they would lose as he was sure by now his face was becoming associated with inexplicable luck. When the horses he had hoped to lose occasionally won as well, Andrew thought he might have missed his vocation in life.

'This is becoming ridiculous,' said Rhona one Saturday afternoon after Andrew had returned from yet another successful betting trip with yet another pile of banknotes. 'We should give some of this money to charity.'

'We can. We will. But remember this money is being saved for a purpose. To help you find this man.'

'But I don't know how to. I've only had the one, same dream. I don't know what to do about it.'

'Then we wait. We wait for more clues.'

'You've got this all worked out. You're like my manager now aren't you? I'm surprised you're not making sure I get off to bed earlier in case this precious golden goose gets tired and doesn't come up with the goods.'

'I'm simply reacting to what has been presented to us.'

'But it might be the wrong reaction.'

'Someone or something has planned it this way. You're having a dream about someone you have been told to find. You're also having dreams about horses that win races. I'll say it again, one way of interpreting this is that you have been presented with a financial opportunity you should not pass up. Don't look a gift horse in the mouth and all that. Excuse the pun.'

'It's planned?'

'Yes. I think so. Take a small leap and look at the bigger picture. Someone or something is directing this whole thing and we are just playing its game.'

'This isn't a game.'

'Okay, okay. That may have been the wrong word to use but surely you've thought about it. Why did you have all those dreams about things that would happen? Why are there other people like you, because you said there were right, with the same talent? What is the purpose of all this and for whom?'

Rhona crossed her arms and leant against the fridge.

'What's your theory then, because I can tell you have one?'

'My theory is still forming. Have you ever wondered if their dreams are like yours though? Or are their dreams vaguer, or more specific?

'What are you getting at?'

'Well, some people probably have dreams about the future and they just ignore them. Others, like you, have tried to warn people that something is going to happen like alerting the authorities or publishing their prediction. Doing something as best they can without...'

'Without being locked up?'

Andrew ignored her and went on.

'But some who have the dreams must try and act themselves to prevent things happening. Wouldn't they? By direct intervention. Actually doing something themselves to stop it. How much of our history has been changed by people like that so you think?'

'I never knew *when* something would happen,' said Rhona.

'Yes you might not have known but that doesn't mean others didn't. They might have a dream that tells them when, where, who, and what they need to do to avert some kind of disaster. I don't know why. But there must be a reason. A plan.'

Rhona went quiet.

'Something is telling them, you, all this by design. Have you ever thought about that?'

'But why?'

'I don't know why. But it's a logical conclusion. A hypothesis at least. Isn't it? If it's not coming from you it's coming from something or someone, and that someone or something has some kind of knowledge of what is to come. And wants you to react to it. Maybe in some preordained way.'

'Aliens? God?'

'I don't know. Perhaps?'

'Maybe Mickey Mouse?'

'I'm trying to be serious, Rhona.'

'You're right. Maybe there is some grand design. But I'll never know so at the end of the day, why ask?'

'You should ask. There are so many questions. Like what if you have a dream of lots of people getting killed and you interpret that as a disaster. But maybe someone else has the same dream and interprets it as a good thing. Like when you dreamed of the revolution in Iran or Reagan getting shot. Someone might have had that dream and thought great, that's a good thing. And then, and then, how do we know that the person who shot Reagan or Lennon was not directed to do it in the first place? Directed in a dream. Directed to kill someone instead of saving them.'

'I think you're thinking about this too much now.'

'I think I am.'

Andrew wished he'd stopped sooner. Rhona could all too easily make fun of him but he knew this small feeling of humiliation was just his own insecurities and confusion. The fundamental problem was neither of them knew why Rhona had these dreams, and whilst Andrew sought some kind of profound explanation, he was irritated by Rhona's apparent lack of self-reflection.

She was more annoyed she had dreams but didn't really question why, or if she did, she kept it to herself. She was an immediate, impulsive and emotional person who responded to the world around her in that way whereas Andrew, by his own admission, sought out truths in the most obscure narratives in the hope of shaping some kind of meaning.

Andrew realised he had been staring at the two cups of tea on the counter as he had become lost in his own thoughts. He went to the back door and called out to Rhona that her tea was ready before taking the pile of money from the table and going upstairs to place it safely in the shoebox underneath the bed.

CHAPTER FORTY-SIX

2006

MANDY

I'm on my way to meet Joe. I haven't seen him for almost two years now. Too long. I emailed him last week and asked if he wanted to meet up. He's living in Islington at the minute, so I suggested somewhere central. He got back to me the next day and said he'd like to meet.

I'm nervous. He's probably wondering what I'm going to say. I still don't know what I am going to say but I know I want to say sorry first of all. It all ended horribly between us and it's been bothering me. I really liked Joe but I'm thinking I just wasn't ready for such an intense relationship.

I'm older now and maybe wiser. I like to think I'm not so judgmental either and I just hope we don't meet and I realise I've made a terrible mistake and got his hopes up or anything. I know I hurt him. I was hurt and I was the one who broke us up.

I've thought about him a lot over the years and I want to tell him that, as he is sensitive as much as he pretends not to be and Ben, who stayed friends with him, says he was in pieces when we split up. It's like a loose end that I still feel needs closure... but there is also a part of me who wonders if closure is what I actually want.

I am happy. Well, I think I'm happy. I enjoy my job. I enjoy life. I've been out with a few guys but nothing serious and maybe I just miss being with someone. Someone like Joe.

Is that bad? Everyone gets lonely right? But am I just being selfish? I don't know. I just wish someone could tell me. But I'm going to meet him and if things are okay and not too tense and we get on and if he still likes me, then why can't we see each other more? And maybe, just maybe, we'll see what happens?

I cross the road to turn down the street towards the tube station. It's dark now and I hear footsteps behind me. Someone calls my name. My full name which is weird and I turn and

CHAPTER FORTY-SEVEN

1996

RHONA

Rhona walked across the Common and stopped by the small, man-made pond where middle aged men and small boys were sailing miniature yachts. She watched them for a minute or so, drawn in by their enthusiasm, concentration and enjoyment. She wished she had a hobby such as this that would fill her time.

Since her faked death she had preferred to be behind closed doors which she knew was unhealthy and felt the risk of being recognised was small now. She always wore a hat or hair cover of some kind though, and made sure to be the quiet, unassuming and friendly neighbour.

She spent her days mostly gardening and reading now. She considered writing another novel and had made various false starts, but nothing seemed to grab her. She now realised she'd entered another stage in her life where being a novelist was perhaps behind her. Even if she did write again she would have to publish under a pseudonym which would be complicated and fraught with her real identity being discovered.

Her actual death and reinvention had been somewhat stressful as she had to make her way back to England alone, in disguise, and hadn't met up with Andrew for some time. He had taken on the majority of the planning and execution but had to act like the concerned and ultimately grieving boyfriend.

The thought of all those poor people who went to look for her up that mountain made her feel enormously guilty. At the time she and Andrew had convinced themselves that disappearing like that, by such extreme means, was the best and the only thing to do to avoid any future possibility of being spied on and imprisoned in some way.

But over time, and with little to go on except for the same dream about the couple on the train, she now found herself questioning that decision. She could have just lived an ordinary life as Rhona O'Shea but now she was Barbara Rose who had a fake passport and criminal charges hanging over her if she was ever found out.

Occasionally she had nightmares where she found herself back at the hospital, oddly tormented by her past now rather than the future. The nightmares were generally the same with the doctors around her in her white room with tubes being put down her throat and electrodes around her head until it got so intense she awoke in the darkness of her bedroom. But she had coping strategies in place and would just turn the lights on and force herself to think rationally.

One thing she didn't seem to suffer from now were her funks that had troubled her since childhood. That was one blessing at least. She still had the occasional dream of some horse race which Andrew was still convinced were meant to finance whatever search she would undertake for 'the man on the train' but there had been no search unless it meant she should perhaps be getting on trains every day in the hope of bumping into this young man. Perhaps the man with the Zippo lighter had been wrong. Perhaps she wasn't meant to find him, but wait for him to come to her, which seemed somewhat unlikely.

She walked on to Clapham high street where she was meeting Andrew. He still lived in Hampstead and they met regularly and were talking now of the possibility of moving in together. Rhona was sure she had been forgotten so maybe it was safe. She liked this area, so if they were to live together, she hoped it would be around here.

Andrew was already seated at a table in the small French restaurant they liked to dine in. The restaurant was cosy and intimate, and the food was always good. He got up to kiss her when she arrived. He smiled and still looked youthful whereas

Rhona felt middle-age creep up on her features like an unwanted guest.

As she sat she suddenly remembered a conversation they had a few months previously. Andrew had raised the issue of children. Rhona had immediately made her views quite clear.

'I never want to have children.'

Andrew had left it at that. He had not asked her why and if he had, she would have told him. *In case our child is like me*. But she had seen that her position had understandably stung him and now, as she sat opposite him, she realised that he could still be a father, just not with her. It would be quite reasonable if he chose to leave but he had stayed, living their lie, out of love. Rhona felt guilty.

'It's a lovely day out. Why don't we walk over the Common afterwards?' said Andrew.

'I've just walked across there.'

'Okay, well how about the cinema? *Secrets and Lies* is playing.'

Rhona picked up the menu and smiled, knowing full well the cinema was his ultimate plan. Andrew was still predictable. To get here he knew she would have walked across the Common and his cinema-going and love of films was still as undiminished as when they had first met. She watched him choose from the menu and knew he would pick frogs legs for starters with a steak for main as he always did when they came here, washed down with a Pinot Noir which would show its effect later when he would nod off in the cinema.

She realised how predictability had become her life now. When you are young, she thought, you are not ruled by routine or bored of its familiarity as everything seems new and undiscovered. New experiences are savoured and not truly appreciated until you get to an older age when nostalgia can take root and unfulfilled dreams and ambitions take their bite.

'Do you know what day it is?' he asked.

For a few seconds Rona thought she had missed some kind of anniversary or something similar but nothing came to mind.

'It's Grand National day.'

'Really? How interesting,' she said sarcastically. Since placing bets on a regular basis Andrew had taken a keen but tiresome interest in horse racing, which was inevitable she realised.

'Why don't we put a bet on after this and watch the race before we go to the cinema?'

'How romantic. What next? A boxing match with front row seats so I can try and catch some flying blood.'

'You still haven't been into a bookmakers. After all this time. Grand National day is exciting. Even my dad always used to put a bet on when the National was on.'

'When are you going to start writing again so we can talk about books for a change?'

'You know, I'm thinking that writing about all this would make a great book one day.'

'You'll have to change the names or wait till I'm dead.'

'I was going to wait till you were dead anyway.'

Rhona laughed.

'You'll just get carried away and make it a story about bloody horse racing,' she said.

'People would buy it. I could sell it down the race track.'

'I don't have any winners for this race if that's what you're hoping.'

'Doesn't matter. It'll just be a bit of fun.'

'Is that so?'

'Come on. There's one on the way to the Picturehouse. You never know what will happen with this race.'

Rhona shrugged, wondering what could possibly happen that was so exciting. She went back to the menu and the waitress came over to take their order. Andrew had closed his menu, having already decided what he was having.

CHAPTER FORTY-EIGHT

2006

JOE

The Beatles second *Anthology Album* played on the stereo behind the bar. It was Joe's own copy and he had brought it in from home that morning. Greg, the Australian manager, had been playing a lot of Mammas and Papas, and Sonny and Cher lately, and whilst he didn't mind the Mamas and Papas, Sonny and Cher were starting to grate.

The first two Anthology CDs were still his favourites of the three albums of out-takes and different versions of The Beatles recordings. He preferred the mid-sixties Beatles when they were writing songs like "Ticket to Ride", "Rain" and "Paperback Writer" to their later stuff and especially the *White Album* which he thought were too long with too many inferior songs compared to their earlier work.

Saying such things out loud would of course always lead to intense and heated discussions with Sylvester, the Argentinian chef and self-confessed Beatles nut, who could always be relied on to make a loud and passionate stand for the merits of the *White Album*. Joe would just have to say *overrated* and Sylvester would see red.

Joe sat on a stool at the end of the bar reading *The Evening Standard* as "Norwegian Wood" played. Sid sat nearby sipping a pint. He was a regular who still came to The George even though it had transformed from the locals-only spit and sawdust establishment it had been for decades to the gastro/hipster odyssey it now must have seemed to Sid with its craft ales and homemade scotch eggs and sausage rolls.

In the eating area out back were a few people including mums and dads with kids getting an early dinner. He didn't mind working at The George. It had a chilled-out vibe and was relaxed about lock-ins and the staff could eat whatever they wanted from the menu for their dinners.

Soon Greg would be off to Europe and Joe was tipped to take over. He'd been working bars now for years and he'd held positions like assistant manager and caretaker-manager but this would be the first place he would properly and solely run. The best thing about it was that it was already up and running success with a lively local bunch of regulars who, although they all might have looked like they could only afford second hand cast offs, were all well paid young middle-class professionals employed by various hip media companies who ensured that people like Sid were being priced out of the area. The only problem was discouraging the taking of cocaine in the toilets but even that wasn't a big issue.

Joe finished the paper and stood up to pace the bar. At the weekend he was taking a grading in his Krav Maga which would be another five-hour physical and mental ordeal to pass to Grade Four. He had been into Krav Maga since Mandy took him to his first session. He'd attended various clubs for a few years before sticking with one and becoming an avid student.

He had done a bit of boxing and BJJ but he preferred Krav for its emphasis on fitness and variety. Boxing had been useful for learning correct striking technique and footwork, but he hadn't really enjoyed getting punched repeatedly in the face by younger men all out to prove themselves in the ring. Joe realised you needed a killer instinct in boxing and a certain aggressiveness which he no longer had, if he ever had it in the first place.

In boxing you also weren't allowed to use many of the moves Krav trained you to deploy to end a fight quickly, like strikes to the eyes and throat, and was another reason Joe took to Krav. He didn't really want to fight any longer than necessary.

Thinking of Krav also invariably led him to think of Mandy. She hadn't turned up for their meeting two days ago. Joe had waited for two and a half hours in a bar in Covent Garden nursing one pint until he had given up and gone home. He had texted her and had considered phoning but decided against it. She had either forgotten about it or decided not to bother.

She wouldn't want to hear his voice and it would be awkward. Joe would sound desperate and hurt all over again. Even after all this time he still missed her and her email asking to meet up had sent adrenaline and hope racing through his body. He wanted to ask why she wanted to meet up but he didn't wish to come across as needy. She probably just wanted to see how he was or ask some kind of favour.

Maybe she was just bored or perhaps she had emailed him by mistake and she had intended to ask another Joe to meet her. It was possible. Ben said she had moved on and was seeing other guys. Joe had cried when he heard that. He couldn't help it. It hurt. Maybe it was his Italian blood but he wore his heart on his sleeve sometimes and he hated himself for it. He didn't want to feel like this. He wanted to move on and forget all about her, but he couldn't and he felt less of a person for it. Like he was weak and just not strong enough. He breathed out deeply which was more of a sigh and glanced at Sid, wondering whether anyone had ever broken his heart.

As he moved down the bar the front door opened and he was surprised to see Ben walk in. Having just thought about him made it all the more peculiar. He hadn't seen Ben for a while now and they had kept in contact mostly through the odd text, and whilst the wild hair was shorter, he now sported a fat beard he was still the unmistakable Ben of old he had always liked. But Ben had a solemn look on his face as he paused by the door and looked at Joe, a look that immediately shook the welcoming smile from Joe's face.

She was dead. Mandy was dead. Murdered. Stabbed in the street. Two days ago. Near the tube. The killer had not been caught. It was just some random attack.

Near the tube. She may have been coming to meet him.

For a few seconds the words had failed or refused to register. Joe had stood across from Ben, a stupid half smile on his face as though he were expecting and hoping this would be some awful joke. And then Ben began to sob.

At that moment, Joe remembered now, Sid, who was out of earshot of the conversations, had put his hand up to get Joe's attention and pointed to his empty pint. Joe nodded and automatically went over and poured Sid a drink. Ben stood and waited at the end of the bar with his head bowed. Joe served Sid and came back.

Things were hazy after that. Ben had given Joe the few details there were and left, unable and unwilling to talk further. He said he wanted to tell Joe the news to his face and he'd done that now. Joe had finished his shift in a daze.

It wasn't until he got home, went straight to his room, and sat on his bed with the light off that he allowed himself to cry, howl and curl up in a ball. And remember the one woman he had ever loved.

He had never been good enough for Mandy. He was out of her league. She was too sophisticated, too intelligent and too passionate to find him attractive. It took a while to realise all this when you look back on a failed relationship searching for clues for why and when it all went wrong. He was a failure and she was a success. His apparent lack of ambition put her off him. He irritated her. He never read books.

Joe had come to understand that truth is a painful emotion, especially if it's about you. He felt ashamed as he looked back on his time with her. He had been in love with her. He would look at her when they were sat watching television and give himself a pat on the back realising now it should have been a tap on the back with a voice saying *you know this isn't going to last.* And it didn't last because she was not in love with him.

Mandy was the reason he no longer enjoyed this city and moved north of the river where fewer memories of her existed. His heart had been broken and everywhere and everything seemed to remind him of her. Now he would never, ever see her again. He had made a fool of himself and knew deep down that he would eventually leave this city. Because he couldn't stay now.

CHAPTER FORTY-NINE

1998

LEE

I couldn't stay at work after what Lucy has done so I tell my manager I feel sick and leave. Dave and Lucy give me sly looks as I grab my coat and go. I can feel them talking about me so I don't wait for the lift and take the stairs. I don't even want to wait for a bus so I walk back and up past Asda, wishing Mandy was still living in her old flat nearby so I could go round and talk to her.

I walk fast, my hands clenched. I don't even notice the traffic or people or even if the sun's shining or whether it's pouring with rain. I reach Winton at some point. I go into The Pines pub on the high street. It's a crappy bar but I want a drink.

At this time of day there's mostly old men with their single pints, crosswords, and a couple of workmen with paint sprayed clothes who've crept out for a couple of cheeky lunchtime beers. I stand at the bar and order a Stella. I wonder if I should just get straight on the vodkas but I know spirits make me sick, and today and right now, I just want to feel angry and ashamed.

You never really know anyone properly, that's the problem. Everyone has an agenda and everyone's a cunt. I fling a fiver over the bar and take a big gulp down. Stella is properly rough and you can taste the shit chemicals they put in it but right now it's exactly what I want.

I take my tie off and stand with my hands stretched out and resting on the bar like some copper is behind me patting me down for gear. The bargirl gives me a wide berth. She can smell the fuck you attitude I've got raging inside me at the minute. I take another gulp and want to cry when some woman comes and stands next to me, which considering the bar is deserted, makes me turn to her. She's got black hair and is waiting to be served and ignores me. She's probably drunk and soon I'll join her. I go back to my beer as the bar girl serves her a coke. I give her another glance and wonder why she's in this smoke-filled shit hole drinking that and she looks at me.

'Hello Lee,' she says.

I do a double take. She's got an Irish accent and for a second I think she's my old geography teacher who was Irish but it isn't. She does look sort of familiar but my old teacher was about seventy when I was at school and is probably dead now.

'Do I know you?'

'No, but we need to talk.'

Fuck this. Probably a wind up and I'll see Dave and Lucy in a minute pissing themselves in the corner somewhere. I actually look for them wondering if they've followed me here to put the boot in further. But I can't see them and I'm not in the mood for conversation so I pick up my pint intending to walk off but then I realise my pint is half empty now so I'll want to order another soon so I hesitate.

But I also want to get away from this weirdo so I finally decide to get a seat and turn to walk off, hoping she leaves soon. And then she pipes up again.

'It's about your dreams. It's about what you've seen.'

I stop dead in my tracks and turn around.

CHAPTER FIFTY

2019

JOE

Joe sat waiting in the Nero's café in Covent Garden and watched people pass outside the window. He figured that even if nothing came of this meeting he would still have had a free day out in London.

After his discovery, which he still couldn't make any sense of, he had gone to bed and slept badly. The next morning he had emailed Amy Greene, which hadn't been difficult as she still worked for *The Guardian.* She came up top of his Google search of "Amy Green journalist". He had fired off a short email along the lines of 'I'm looking for someone who I think is connected to Rhona O'Shea who you wrote about in 2001 and I know it's a long shot, but I wonder if I could ask you some questions' and left his mobile phone number.

He didn't want to say too much at this stage. His phone rang about half an hour later as he was on his rowing machine and it was Amy. She had a posh voice, and for the first time in ages, it was she who was asking all the questions. She sounded interested and sincere. He explained who he was, who he was looking for, mentioned the comics – especially the one with the World Trade Centre – and his crazy idea that his missing friend had been the artist. Amy went silent and eventually spoke.

'I'd like to meet up. Could you bring along everything you have about this?'

'Okay, sure. Where do you want to meet?'

'London. I'll pay all your travel expenses.'

So that was that and here he was. She didn't want to waste any time and he had gone straight away. The worst thing was Valentina had phoned and he had to explain that he was busy as something important had come up. It was the truth but it still felt like an excuse. He hoped she believed him but he wasn't sure. She had phoned like she said she would. And now Joe was playing it cool. Except he wasn't.

Damn, thought Joe. He promised himself he would call her and arrange to meet up when he got back to explain everything he'd been up to.

On the train to London he read the graphic novel from cover to cover. It was a good read and he studied the artwork carefully, looking for any more clues. He wished he had more examples of Lee's work to go on. He had phoned a couple of old friends who were still graffiti artists. He asked if they knew of any of Lee's work that was still around but they doubted it.

Illegal sprays usually meant the artwork was temporary. Those that had carried on spraying had gone mostly into legal commissions, but as far as he and they knew, Lee hadn't done this. As the train pulled into Waterloo the thought struck him that perhaps Lee had gone onto drawing more graphic novels under different names or even perhaps the same one. He googled Trey Griffin but didn't even come up with the one novel he strongly suspected he had drawn.

It felt odd being back in the capital and decided he'd head up to Soho next, and after a coffee in Bar Italia, make his way along Oxford Street to see what had changed. He even thought of popping down to Tooting and having a drink in his old local, the Antelope pub, but decided against it. There were too many memories there.

His phone buzzed and it was a text message. It read *I'm here* and Joe looked to the door and half rose then waved to the woman who stood scanning the café. She spotted Joe and made her way over and introduced herself. She was probably a little older than him and dressed well. He noticed her sparkling white Superga trainers when she sat down. She put a file on the table and shook his hand, meeting his gaze with focused intent.

'Nice to meet you at last,' she said.

'And you.'

'Thank you for coming up at such short notice.'

'No problem.'

She scanned his face and Joe wondered what she was thinking.

'So remind me again how long your friend has been missing for?'

'About five weeks.'

'And you say he was a graffiti artist?'

'Yeah. He was. His tag was Skiver. It's the same one in the book. The exact same.'

'And he had that tag before 1999?'

'Yeah. Since school probably.'

'You said you'd bring some of his art work?'

Joe reached down and picked up his small rucksack. He got out all of Lee's artwork and the graphic novel. Without asking Amy started going through it, studying Lee's outlines carefully and then comparing them to the book.

'It certainly looks the same. Did he ever draw comics before?'

'Not as far as I know.'

She froze. She had come across Lee's *Who Cares Wins* piece.

'Oh my God.'

Amy opened the file she had in front of her. She searched through various bits of paper until she found what she was looking for and pulled it out. It was section of the graphic novel. She handed Joe the page.

'Take a look.'

Joe took the page. It was a scene in a café with two people talking. It looked like it was set in New York City. Behind them, outside, there was a wall and graffitied on the walls were the words *Who Cares Wins*.

'I didn't see this.'

He wanted to pick up the graphic novel to find the relevant page, annoyed that he had missed it. Amy read his thoughts.

'You won't find it in the book. It had been cut out before publication.'

Joe was confused.

'When it was submitted the publisher thought the page count was too high so wanted to cut it down a bit. This was one of the scenes they cut.'

'How did you get this?'

'From the publisher. I met the guy who ran Ash Comix years ago. He still had everything except any bloody idea who wrote or drew it.'

'Well, that sort of proves it. Doesn't it?'

'There's a good chance he did the artwork I'd say. Unless he copied it. And the style.'

'In your article you said the author was this woman. Some writer.'

'Rhona O'Shea. But she died whilst mountaineering years before this was written. But her body was never found. And yes I do think she was the author. I had someone study her work and the novel. A language expert. That was his conclusion. She had also written two books about a young boy on a quest. The graphic novel follows the same structure. And her books were about predictions. Elvis Presley dying. The Iranian revolution. She could have dreamt about the Twin Towers too.'

'Lee had dreams as well.'

'What?'

'He told me back in the early nineties he had dreamt about the Twin Towers being attacked.'

Amy looked stunned.

Joe smiled.

'Maybe she didn't die. Maybe they worked on it together. He had the ending and she had the story,' he said.

Amy stayed silent as she mentally reconfigured whatever theory she had.

'If Rhona was still alive they may have done. If one person could predict the future then there must be others. And they might know each other.'

Amy drummed her fingers on the table searching for answers.

'It's too big a jump.'

'When I was looking for him someone mentioned he was close to his aunt. But he didn't have an aunt. That could be her couldn't it? Tell me about Rhona. What do you know about? What did she look like?'

'She was Irish. She would be nearly seventy now. Black hair. They might be in Ireland.'

'Lee's sister has his passport. Do you need a passport to go to Ireland?'

'Not officially. They may not even be together. This was written a long time ago. Her ex is English, but he's got family in Italy. They could even be there and Lee in England somewhere. We still hit a brick wall.'

'Italy?'

'Yeah, well Sardinia to be exact.'

Joe tensed up. He suddenly couldn't breathe as the realisation hit him.

'What?' asked Amy.

'I know where she is.'

CHAPTER FIFTY-ONE

1998

LEE/RHONA

It took a long time to convince him. They sat on a table by the window in The Pines pub as Lee drank pints of Stella and Rhona told him stories he couldn't logically explain or clearly comprehend.

She knew about his dreams.

'My real name is Rhona O'Shea.'

'She died.'

'I faked my own death.'

'Why?'

'To hide.'

She told him her story. How she had dreams too. How she wrote about them. How she was imprisoned. *How speaking out can be dangerous.* And then she told him about the man with the Zippo lighter and his instructions to find Lee to help him. And about how she had dreamed of him.

Lee sat leaning over the table as she spoke, his head getting lower and lower as her strange story unfolded until his head ended up almost touching the table. His eyes looked up at her and when she stopped talking, he blinked. He searched her face for lies.

'How did you find me?'

'I'd dreamt about you being on a train and then I saw you in London. Two years ago. In a bookmakers in Clapham. And we followed you back here and watched you ever since. Until you got on the train. And I realised it must be the right time to talk to you.'

Lee twisted in his seat. This kind of thing just didn't happen in Winton, Bournemouth.

'That's bloody creepy.'

'I'm here to help you. Whatever you've seen, you need to warn people.'

He tried to remember the photo of Rhona O'Shea that he had at home on the inside cover of his copy of *The Return*. He knew Rhona had dark hair but he couldn't be sure this was the same woman. Nothing made sense.

'How do I know you're not just winding me up because it sounds like you are?'

'How would I know about your dreams? Have you told people what you've seen?'

'I need another drink.'

He got up and went to the bar. Rhona sat and waited. She could sense his turmoil as he ordered a drink, glancing nervously back to the table as his mind did somersaults at what he was being told. He didn't trust her. Not yet anyway. She remembered her own encounters with the man with the Zippo who had given her vague instructions all those years ago and how she had felt. Confused, bewildered, and unsure.

He came back from the bar.

'I didn't ask if you wanted anything?'

'No, I'm okay.'

Lee wandered back to the bar to pay for his pint. That one small act told Rhona all she needed to know about Lee. He came back with his drink and sat down. He took a gulp of his pint.

'Art is the lie that enables us to realise the truth,' he said eventually. 'You tell a story to hide what you're saying. Is that what you're suggesting then? Do what you did? Write a book or something? I'm not as stupid as I look. I read you know. I've read your books. Do you still have them then? The dreams?'

'Sometimes.'

'But you've just told me you got put in some hospital when you tried to warn people. So, why should I do that?'

'We can hide who you really are. You need to do it anonymously.'

'But why bother? You didn't stop any of the things you said would happen from happening.'

'But you need to tell people.'

'I could just phone the police or the authorities then.'

'And say what exactly? You've had a dream? Do you know when whatever you saw will happen? You might as well just stand in Hyde Park Corner. At least more people will listen.'

'But if people ignore what you tell them then what's the point?'

Rhona stared into space. This was the question she had asked herself time and time again. If anything, Lee was astute enough to comprehend that she essentially seemed to be telling him that his efforts were futile.

'Because we're leaving breadcrumbs through time. Because people will slowly realise that when they look back, the warnings were there all the time, but they had ignored them and persecuted those people who had spoken out. And then things might change.'

'How do you know that?' Lee asked.

'I don't. But staying silent will destroy you. By speaking out, by protecting yourself whilst you do it, you might keep your sanity.'

'You haven't been driven mad yet then?'

'I don't know. I may have.'

Lee gulped his pint down and looked away.

'What is it you've seen?' she asked.

'And there are others? Like you? Like me?'

'Yes, I think so.'

'It's like *Highlander* isn't it? People all around the world who can live forever. But in this case its people who can see the future. Sorry, I'm talking shit. I think I'm drunk.'

Lee eventually accepted a lift home from Rhona. Andrew had parked around the corner in his car, waiting patiently but didn't say anything when Rhona and Lee appeared. Lee practically fell into the back seat filling the car with alcohol fumes. Rhona got into the front.

'I said we could drop him off home.'

Lee shouted out his address and gave vague directions to his house and Andrew pulled away without saying anything. He exchanged looks with Rhona as Lee sat in the back, swaying and talking to himself. Rhona gave him a hopeful smile and turned around to face Lee.

'Call me in the morning. My number is on this.'

She held out a piece of paper. Lee snatched it away and swayed some more.

'Stop the car.'

'Are you sure? We're not there yet.'

'I don't want you to know where I live.'

'But you've just told us and we know where you live anyway,' said Andrew.

Rhona glared at him.

'Stop the car. You're not going to kidnap me,' cried Lee.

Andrew sighed and pulled over. Lee swung the door open and staggered out.

'Call me,' shouted Rhona after him but he had already slammed the door shut and was walking off unsteadily down the street. They watched him lurch down the road.

'Well it seems that went well,' Andrew said.

'Yes.'

'Did he tell you what he'd seen?'

'No.'

'Do you think he'll call.'

'I hope so.'

CHAPTER FIFTY-TWO

JOE/LEE

Joe wanted to get the train back to Bournemouth straight away but Amy insisted they go back to her house and fetch her car to drive down. Joe reluctantly agreed, trying to hide his impatience. They took the tube to Chelsea and picked up Amy's red two-year old Vauxhall Astra. Within an hour they were on the M3.

I call back the next morning. When I wake up I feel hungover but that soon vanishes when everything comes back to me. She's staying at some hotel in town so I get the number five bus in and meet her at the Moon in the Square. She's with the same bloke who gave me half a lift home last night and he looks harmless enough as he sits and says nothing with his Diet Pepsi. She asks if I want a pint but I stick to water. She gets to business.

'I'll write the plot and you just deliver the message.'

The message being my dream which she's itching to know about.

'Why do we have to write a book? Why can't it be something else?' I ask.

'Like what?'

'What about a comic?'

Joe sat as Amy drove and made small talk and told him about her career. It sounded interesting and he hoped she wouldn't ask what he had done with his life.

So we agree, I do the artwork and she makes up some story linked to my dream but now she wants to know what it is. She wants the money shot, the punchline, the what-this-is-all-fucking-about. So I tell her.

'I saw two passenger jets crash into the World Trade Centre. It's a terrorist attack. Both towers will come down and thousands will be killed.'

Rhona gives me the steady eye but Andrew looks like he is shitting it.

Traffic slowed Joe and Amy up and they were reduced to a crawl near Winchester. Joe hoped he could remember the exact address now and he tried to visualise the route to the house as they got closer to Ringwood. Amy became quieter whilst Joe silently questioned himself and hoped he was right.

We get it done. It's mental really but Rhona gives me an outline. I go away and come up with the artwork. It starts off tricky. I draw something and then screw it up and chuck it away because it's not good enough. I start again but slowly I get into the groove and it starts coming together. So much so I forget about Lucy and that twat Dave. I still go into work but I'm focused now and I couldn't care what anyone says. I'm on a mission and it's as though they can tell something has changed because Lucy looks a bit gutted I'm giving her zero attention and just doing my own thing.

And the story is good. It's about a boy who grows up being able to have dreams that predict the future. I added the Challenger Air Disaster and Princess Diana to the mix and Rhona loved it.

'Draw what you know,' she said. So I did. And maybe she did too but with words.

The boy tells a neighbour about his dreams but the neighbour works for some government facility and in no time the boy has a secret government organisation after him as they want to lock him away. They end up catching him and they do loads of tests in some weird hospital but the boy escapes and manages to go to New York where he persuades some down-on-his-luck American lawyer to fight his corner and try to warn everyone the World

Trade Centre is about to be attacked. But he's ignored and then it's my part when the Twin Towers are blown up. The ending had the vibe of Planet of the Apes with Charlton Heston banging his fists into the sand wondering why it all went wrong. I find my artwork improves as I get further into it. I go back and read my old 2000ADs and Frank Millers' The Dark Knight Returns for inspiration. I'm on a roll.

Rhona and Andrew eventually get a place in Ringwood as they reckon with Bournemouth being a tourist town it would be too on top for her to be seen about too much. So we start off meeting in town and then switch to Ringwood. I go round their place for what she calls conferences. I like working with her and in a few weeks the job is done. The ending is easy. I just draw what I'd seen.

The planes, the impact, the clouds of debris and people jumping out of windows as they start burning to death. I draw the people on the ground as the towers come down. The massive wave of toxic smoke that sweeps through the streets I have never been to and never seen in real life.

It's weird seeing it on paper for the first time. It's like I've drawn round my mind in tracing paper and it freaks me out. We tweak it and rewrite bits, and when we're happy, Rhona goes off and does her research.

She comes back with this company called Ash Comix. It's a new outfit and they're keen for content and she had already sent it in without telling me which pisses me off a bit as I wanted to send it to Marvel and DC Comics but I let it slide when they email and say they're keen to publish. So now we have to be a bit sly as she is very keen not be seen or linked to this in any way.

It ends up we communicate through email and they're happy with that. I only ever have to go in one time to get the money that is in cash which is all a bit cowboy and Rhona makes me wear some daft blonde wig as a disguise. I enjoy going in and would have loved to have stayed and checked out their office and found out more stuff but Rhona waits in the car and is insistent that it's got to be an in and out job. I've got to be Trey Griffin which is a cack name but again, I let it slide. We get the cash, which isn't what this is all about but she lets me keep all of it.

'So now what?' I ask wondering what out next adventure is going to be.

'We wait,' she says.

Joe and Amy pulled up outside the house.

'Is this it?'

'It is.'

They got out of the car and made their way slowly up the garden and towards the front door. Joe looked up and down the street and saw no one around. He knocked on the door and they waited. After a moment he knocked again but there was still no answer. Amy shuffled impatiently around on the doorstep and he began to consider he might have made a mistake bringing her all the way down from London and just turning up at someone's house on a hunch.

After all, the dark-haired woman in the kitchen had only said one word. It had sounded American at the time, but it could have been Irish. But it could have been American. Joe started to feel like he had failed yet again. Simon, the boyfriend, had mentioned he had been to Sardinia. But that didn't mean he was Rhona O'Shea's boyfriend. Ber*nard* had been to Sardinia.

Joe, feeling increasingly self-conscious, walked over to the front window and peered in. Inside he saw a tidy lounge with a sofa, television and a bookcase. He tried to make out what books were on the bookcase in the hope of seeing one of Rhona's titles as if that might supply some kind of proof. But he couldn't see that far, and even if he could, for someone who had faked their own death to have one of their own books on their bookshelf didn't seem realistic.

'Now what?' asked Amy. 'We wait?'

'I suppose so,' answered Joe, unsure if he should just apologise right now and admit he might be wrong.

He walked over to the gate by the side of the house leading to the back garden and considered going through it as if it wasn't locked. He could see the well-kept garden from where he stood and the large shed which he decided might have been converted to an office from the double-glazed window on the side. He turned back. Going through could put him into a difficult position if anyone was watching.

They walked slowly back to the car and Amy unlocked the doors. Just as Joe was about to say he may have made a mistake two figures emerged from around the corner up the road. It was a man and a woman holding bags full of shopping. They stopped when they saw Joe and Amy.

Amy stared at them and Joe took a step forward to get a better look. It was Simon and his girlfriend. They were holding hands. After a pause they walked towards them.

'It's her,' said Amy. 'That's Rhona O'Shea.'

CHAPTER FIFTY-THREE

2019

LEE

The crumbs of time bullshit Rhona had waffled on about turned out to be just waffle. Ash Comix were full of it. They said they were going to print up a thousand copies but I reckon there were less than half that. You couldn't even buy it in Bournemouth and I had to order a copy. It turned up weeks later.

So the novel came out and then what? Nothing. Rhona said we did what we could but it didn't feel right. It was like knowing a bomb was going to explode but you just didn't know when. And how the fuck were we warning people? So I waited and Rhona goes back off to Ringwood with Andrew. And then 9/11 actually happened and the world changed.

I watched it on TV at home as I took a sickie that day, and by the afternoon, it's everywhere. At first people couldn't comprehend what they were watching. I went out for a walk and actually overheard someone joke they're going to get *The*

Towering Inferno out from the video library that night. But by the next day it started sinking into the psyche of the nation and everyone starts shitting it. I called Rhona but she was all quiet on the phone like it was bugged.

And I waited. And nothing happened. There's one main article in *The Observer* magazine and I only know that because I went round Rhona's and she had a copy there. And I soon see why.

This journalist who wrote the story, which is all about writers who have predicted the future, has had some study done and has worked out Rhona wrote it. I'm impressed but Rhona was bricking it as she was supposed to be dead.

The article didn't even mention the art work. I did get it. Most of the words were hers but it is a graphic novel after all. I even left my tag in there on the sly thinking any graff artist worth their salt would clock it but guess what. No graff artist even read it because no one read it.

I felt let down. Like I wasted an opportunity by listening to this person. Rhona tried to sweet talk me and I know she knew she screwed up. We argued. She tried to blame it on me as I wanted to do a comic, as she called it, but I told her she was the one who found Ash Comix and agreed to whatever Mickey Mouse deal they offered. We were both steaming and I left. I do like Rhona but not at that moment as we both knew we'd made a monumental fuck up.

I didn't know what to do. I could have come out and said I did it but I never wanted that. I just wanted people to notice. But no one did so I got on with life. And life carried on for me as though nothing happened although wars were kicking off everywhere. I was still the big fucking loser I'd always been. Years trundled on and I kept this big secret inside me. I felt guilty. Like I killed these people. Like I caused all this. I could have stopped it if I'd thought about it properly.

And you know what Joe, I think this all went to shit, really went to shit when Mandy died. Yeah, Mandy mate. I know you went out with her. I know you loved her. She told me about you and what had happened. And I knew you must have suffered like me when you found out she had been killed. It bugs me they never caught her killer.

I spoke to her the day she died. I don't know if you know that. She was about to go out and meet you. I was actually going to tell her everything and unload all my shit but she was so excited to be seeing you so I thought I'd leave it for another time.

She still loved you. That's what I think anyway. She still loved you and wanted to get back together with you. That's what I reckon. Her death destroyed me. She had always been the one I had turned to. The one person that had always been there to talk me round or hold my hand. I wish now I'd talked to her earlier about my dreams. Before it was too late.

I talked round it but never opened up properly. I don't know what she would have done but she would never have got me to write a bloody graphic novel. I never told anyone about what I'd seen with the Towers. It was too much. Except you but you probably don't remember.

If she hadn't died I would have talked to Mandy when the miscarriages came too and she would have had an answer. Advice and kind words. But she wasn't there. When she went I was all alone with just my thoughts and my dreams to drive me into the ground. And you know what? I never dreamed about what would happen to her. If I had I would have saved her.

And I was still having the dreams. And it's all very well saying you need to warn people about such a big event. But what if the big event is only big to you? What if you finally think you've found the person you love, you plan to start a family, your girlfriend gets pregnant, and it's the best day of your life, but then, you dream she miscarries.

Do you tell her? I went to pieces. I prayed I was wrong. I insisted she rests, visits the doctor, eats the right food and I hoped. And I hoped and I hoped and I hoped. But it still happened. She gets pregnant again. And I have the dream again but this time I tell her. I tell her everything. I tell her about 9/11 and all the rest.

She freaks out and tells me I'm sick and I shouldn't say things like that. And then she miscarries again. Again mate. She hates me now. Fucking despises me. Somehow it's my fault. I had good as killed my own children according to her. I agree with her and add it to my body count. Life is fucked.

Don't remember me as a drug dealing. That was a means to an end. It was my escape plan. Make enough cash and leg it to Rio. Start again and forget about it all. But I couldn't forget and I fucked that up too until a bunch of losers didn't even want me till I'm so far down the food chain I'm starving.

And I have another dream. This one is worse than 9/11 and it is going to happen. Brexit and Trump and all that shit is nothing compared to what it leads to. And now I know how this will end. What I have to do. What my part is. I have found my meaning. I left you the clues Joe to find me and now, I leave this to you.

CHAPTER FIFTY-FOUR

2019

JOE

Amy stares at Rhona like she has seen a ghost but all I want to do is find out where Lee is. Rhona and Simon, who I later discover is called Andrew, come up to us. Amy starts asking if Rhona is actually Rhona like she's found a treasure chest and Rhona nods. Amy looks like she's going to explode and I cut in.

'Is Lee here?'

Rhona nods.

'He's asleep. He's not well.'

'I want to see him,' I say.

We go up to the house and Andrew is sheepish but Rhona is all matter of fact. She opens the door and we follow her in. She leads us up the stairs to a bedroom door that is closed and knocks gently. I just want to shove the door open but I wait patiently.

There's no answer so she opens the door and the bedroom is empty. The bed is made up neatly and there are some freshly ironed clothes on a chair. I recognise a Superdry shirt and know it's not Andrew's.

'Where is he?'

'I don't know. Maybe he went out.'

We fan out across the two floors calling Lee's name but the house is silent. We congregate in the kitchen and I can tell Amy doesn't really care about Lee. She's just desperate to interview Rhona but Rhona is like me, she's concerned. She might be stony faced but I can see the fear in her eyes. I look out into the garden. Rhona does the same and we both see the converted shed and we think the same thing.

We move out to the garden. There's an air of panic now and Rhona moves fast. She marches up to the shed with me right behind her. The door opens. She looks at me like it should be locked. She knows. She bloody knows.

We enter.

Lee is hanging from a cross beam.

A knocked over chair lies on the floor under his legs.

He is still, and he is dead.

I rushed up to Lee anyway and lift his legs up to support his body. I don't recall what is said but Andrew and Amy come in. Amy screams and stood frozen to the spot whilst Andrew cut Lee down with a pair of scissors.

Rhona sobs and sunk to the floor as Andrew calls for an ambulance. Amy kicked into action and got a sheet to put over Lee. Before she does I notice the T-Shirt Lee is wearing. It's a white Pan Am Orion T-shirt sold by Last Exit to Nowhere. I know it's a sign.

I sit down on the floor too but I don't know what to do. I notice a big neat pile of paper sitting on a chair next to me. It has my name on the top sheet. *For Joe*. I feel like I'm in a trance. It's a letter from Lee. To me. I start to read it. And he tells me what he has dreamt.

The End

Author Biog

Carlo Ortu is a film director, author and musician who lives in the seaside town of Bournemouth, England with his wife, their two children and two cats.

27321630R00260

Printed in Great Britain
by Amazon